Blue reminded himself that Everly had careened over the long unmarked road that was officially called Hardy's Pass. It was the only road on the island during the roughly seven days a year it was not actively treacherous. It led directly to the sprawling lodge here in the cove, ramshackle wood cabins connected by wooden stairs and boardwalks, where Blue had been living since the night Isaac had turned out to be a whole lot more than a legend. With a handful of other brothers-in-arms who'd gotten out of the special forces just like he had and shared not just his desire for a mission but a great many of his own very specialized skills.

At least three of them had weapons trained on her right now.

Not because they thought she was a threat, of course. No one who intended to do harm out here—a good thousand miles west of the middle of nowhere—would roar up blaring classic Bruce Springsteen and then jump out the way she had, calling his name like they had been tight once upon a time. Alaska Force wasn't just a home for wayward veterans who hadn't quite adjusted to civilian life. Isaac hadn't set it all up in the fishing lodge his family had once operated as a summer tourist trap out of the goodness of his heart.

Alaska Force was a last resort for people who needed very serious solutions to very complicated problems.

SEAL's
Honor

AN ALASKA FORCE NOVEL

MEGAN CRANE

JOVE
New York

A JOVE BOOK
Published by Berkley
An imprint of Penguin Random House LLC
375 Hudson Street, New York, New York 10014

ISBN: 9780451491497

First Edition: November 2018

Printed in the United States of America
1 3 5 7 9 10 8 6 4 2

Cover photos: Couple © Claudio Marinesco / Ninestock;
Alaska background © dagsjo Zel / Getty Images
Cover design by Sarah Oberrender

For all our heroes.

Acknowledgments

Thanks to Kerry Donovan and everyone at Berkley for believing in this book!

And to Holly Root for always believing in me.

Special thanks to Maisey Yates and Nicole Helm for all their encouragement and enthusiasm while I was writing this book. Not to mention convincing me I could write it in the first place! And to Lisa Hendrix for reading the draft and correcting my many Alaska errors. Any remaining mistakes are mine.

I'm eternally grateful to my Thursday afternoon writers' group, who give me support and belly laughs, complete with strong coffee and delicious pastries. What more could any writer need?

Above all, my thanks and love to Jeff, who isn't only my hero but is truly heroic in every sense of the word. I'm so lucky we get to do this life together.

One

You go to the edge of nowhere in a little fishing town in Alaska called Grizzly Harbor. Then you sit in a dive bar called the Fairweather until they find you.

Blue Hendricks must have heard it a hundred times from his brothers in special operations during the usual discussions about what they'd do with their lives if they survived whatever hell they'd found themselves in that day. It was everybody's favorite legend during a long night in a foxhole.

He threw some cash on the scarred, chipped bar counter that hadn't seen a polish in a lifetime or three, and faced the fact that he shouldn't have listened to all those stories. He certainly shouldn't have believed them. The Fairweather was just another dive bar, if farther away from everything than others, and no one was coming to save him from facing his uncertain future without the navy.

He really should have known better.

Blue didn't understand what had driven him to come all the way to this nowhere town next door to a frigid glacier or two. It was barely on a map and sat practically crushed beneath a snowcapped mountain.

Not that he was in a place to judge, as he was barely a man.

Now that he was no longer a SEAL, a reality he hadn't had enough time to digest yet, he wasn't even the well-tuned machine he'd prided himself on being all these years.

But he wasn't nearly drunk enough to engage with the mess he carried around and had been pretending wasn't there for years now. Not drunk enough and definitely not dumb enough to start that game of internal sudden death when he'd been a civilian for less than seventy-two hours, and most of that time he'd spent hauling his ass to the middle of nowhere in search of a stupid legend.

The trouble with that was obvious on numerous levels. The first and foremost being that he was now stuck in the middle of nowhere like a complete dumbass, because the ferry from Juneau stopped here only twice a week in the endless winter months, and that was weather dependent.

The shady, ramshackle Fairweather called itself a bar and grill and seemed to lean more to the bar side of that equation, propped up on stilts above the dark water of the sound that brooded out there in the late February gloom. Blue had seen a decent-looking burger or two and some fries that looked like a heart attack on a plate—

his favorite—but he'd decided to drink his dinner instead. It looked like most of the people in here had done the same. The bar itself wasn't much more than a collection of ratty pool tables, woebegone locals in varying shades of camo-colored clothes, as if a moose hunt might break out at any moment, and what had to be the most extensive collection of off-color bumper stickers ever assembled. As wallpaper.

There wasn't a single legendary thing about this place.

Which meant Blue was going to have to figure out his life all on his own.

He ran through his options as if he were prepping for a mission. His hometown, outside Chicago, was out. Blue had left that place in a hurry when he was seventeen and had never looked back. Or gone back. At all. He had a Harley stashed in storage in another part of what the folks here in Alaska called the Lower 48, but he would never call himself a biker. And he didn't want to change that, unlike some of the men he knew who had left the service and gone deep into that life. The same way he didn't see something like the CrossFit Games in his future. Much as he enjoyed keeping his body in what passed for top physical condition, he didn't want to make it his whole life. He liked riding his motorcycle and he liked working out, but not enough to lose himself in either one of those things like it was a new religion.

The truth was, he was still hung up on the old one.

Which was why he was here, staring down at a long pour of whiskey and wondering why the hell he hadn't taken one of the security jobs he'd been offered. They were everywhere. Los Angeles. Chicago. New York. Slick corporate outfits looking for men with Blue's set of skills and experience. Some were even run by former SEALs, just like him. SEALs took care of their own, which meant Blue knew he could find a place if he needed one, but he wasn't ready to be taken care of just yet. He might have retired, and Lord knew he had aches and pains and scars, inside and out, that his seventeen-year-old, newly enlisted self couldn't possibly have imagined. And it made him feel a hell of a lot older than he was, because he knew what he'd been capable of at his peak—but none of that mattered.

He wasn't done.

The kind of work he'd done as a SEAL required a pinpoint accuracy he didn't quite have anymore. He'd accepted that. Part of training to be consistently excellent meant always knowing his limitations. And with young guys coming up all the time, there was no sense holding on when he knew he couldn't deliver the way he wanted to. He refused to let his teammates and his country down, and Blue might have been carrying a mess or two around inside him, but he wasn't that narcissistic. If he wasn't giving two hundred percent at the highest level of peak physical performance, he was holding his teammates back. That was unacceptable.

He was done with his beloved SEALs. But he wasn't ready to resign himself to a life of playing bodyguard for rich old men and their snot-nosed kids. And he'd believed in what he'd done for the last twenty years, so mercenary work held about as much appeal to him as rolling up to the bikers he'd seen at bars all over these United States and pretending he respected men who brayed about freedom while spitting on everything he'd put his life on the line to defend.

Pass.

The good news was, Blue's version of a scaled-back level of physical performance, not good enough for the kind of SEAL missions he'd been a part of, made him look like a god in comparison with a regular person. He could still meet all the BUD/S training standards at competitive levels, thank you. He could still kick just about any ass he encountered, for that matter, and could probably defuse the situation before it got there—even out here in an Alaskan bar that seemed chock-full of the kind of men who wrestled bears for fun on a slow winter's night. He might have been walking among regular people again, but he wasn't quite a civilian.

The truth was, Blue didn't have the slightest idea how to be a civilian and didn't really want to learn.

Which was why he was here, running down legends he should have known better than to imagine could be real.

When he was done with this wild-goose chase into the snowy Alaskan wilderness and had finished surrendering his dignity and self-respect to an urban legend, Blue thought now, he could always kick it up a notch and go deep into the *X-Files* thing. Head down to the misty forests in Washington and Oregon and look for a Sasquatch, maybe. Go look for UFOs in Roswell. Hunt down the goddamned tooth fairy, while he was at it. All sounded far more likely to be real than a mysterious special ops unit operating out of a fishing village stuck up on stilts in the Alaskan Panhandle, accessible only by boat or plane or summertime cruise ship.

Maybe he'd even chant names into a mirror at midnight with a candle, like in that old ghost story, to see if something appeared. At least that would provide him with some entertainment.

Blue knocked back what was left of his whiskey and turned to go, figuring he'd find a room in one of the handful of lodges and inns on this mountainous little island and maybe rethink those bodyguard offers after all. Why not trail around after doughy businessmen and self-obsessed celebrities? A lot of guys did it. He was sure he'd adapt eventually.

He'd been a SEAL for twenty years. He was good at adapting. It had been his job. His calling. His entire life.

But when he slid off the barstool and turned to go, automatically checking the exits and any potential problems with a single swift glance, a man walked in.

And Blue froze, because he recognized him.

Not the man himself. He was a total stranger. But Blue still knew him.

He was lethal. A harsh reckoning on two feet, and it was always funny to Blue that men like this—men like him—didn't set off alarms when they walked into places where normal people went about their lives, never knowing how quick and easy it could all be taken away. And would have been about a hundred times already if it weren't for all the men like the one who walked toward him.

Like the one Blue saw in the mirror when he could stand to look.

The stranger walked like a marine, and Blue pegged him as Force Recon in two steps. It was something about the grim, ready set to his shoulders and the way he commanded the space around him as he moved, as if he'd already plotted out contingency plans for every possible outcome. He threw an assessing glance around the room, and that confirmed it. More than Force Recon, Blue thought as the man drew closer, moving like a threat. He'd swear this guy was Delta Force, despite or possibly because of the battered jeans he wore, the snow-packed boots like all the locals, and the dark beard on his face that made him look like maybe he was trying to blend into this frontier town the way Delta Force did in all the worst places in the world.

But he blended about as much as Blue did with all these relatively soft, safe people, for all that they were Alaskan and hardier than the average American.

Meaning: not at all.

The man walked directly to Blue and stopped, then lifted his chin by way of a greeting. He didn't check out Blue's whiskey shot glass or the money on the bar, but Blue had no doubt that the man in front of him knew exactly how much he'd had to drink, what he'd tipped, and how long he'd been here. All in a single glance Blue hadn't caught.

He stood straighter, squaring off his shoulders almost unconsciously.

"You look like a SEAL," the man said, and he sounded like every arrogant SOB marine Blue had ever encountered. Which was to say, all of them.

"You sound like a marine," he replied. The eye roll was implied.

The other man studied him a moment.

"You feeling a little antsy?" he asked gruffly. There was a hint of a smile on the other man's hard face, but it didn't take. "I get it. You're not underwater, which means there's no place for a SEAL to hide while the serious shit goes down."

Blue eyed him like he was thinking about taking offense, when instead the traditional obnoxious greeting between different branches of the military made him feel more relaxed than he had in a long time. As if he might just make it on the other side of active duty after all.

"Nice town." He offered a bland grin. "Until you and your marine buddies roll in and start blowing it all up, that is."

The other man didn't grin in return, but his eyes crinkled slightly in the corners, which was as good as a belly laugh from an individual carved out of pure steel and trouble like this one. He nodded at the stool Blue had vacated, waited for him to slide back onto it, then claimed the one next to him. He lifted a couple of fingers in the bartender's direction.

Blue knew three things then. That this was a man used to leading other men. That the places he led them were likely versions of hell, but he brought them back out again, one way or another. And that he led by example. Which was all Blue needed to know.

They sat there in comfortable silence. Chris Stapleton rasped his version of quiet southern despair on the jukebox. It seemed fitting even this far north and west. There was the clink of pool balls and the rise and fall of various alcohol-infused conversations in the background, here in a place that hadn't seen much sun in a while.

Blue studied the whiskey in front of him and used the

mirror behind the bar to stay alert to the man who exuded so much menace and calm beside him.

"Just out?" the man asked after some time had passed.

"Less than seventy-two hours ago."

"No wonder you have that new-car smell. Don't worry. It wears off."

Blue grinned at that, and raised his whiskey glass in a salute that was only half-mocking. He took a pull, then returned his attention to the bar mirror. There was a pack of four outdoorsy-looking men in the corner getting rowdy with a busty waitress who didn't seem at all fazed—or impressed—by their attention. There were more men at the pool tables, telling one another fishing stories Blue didn't have to hear any details of to know were exaggerated, if not outright lies.

And he figured it was the bartender who'd recognized what Blue was and called the man beside him. Unless this place was wired, but Blue had done his usual surveillance when he'd come in, and he hadn't seen any cameras. His money was on the old man behind the bar, with a mouth that looked as droopy as his mustache and a map of questionable decisions all over his face.

"It's hard to find a way home," the marine said quietly. Almost offhandedly, but nothing about the man sitting next to him was anything but ruthlessly deliberate. "Takes a while."

Blue met his gaze in the mirror. The other man's was hard like flint, gray and sure. Steady.

"I don't know what home is," Blue said. If his voice was rough, he blamed it on the whiskey. Not stray memories of his tense childhood in that house outside Chicago he never wanted to see again, because he'd never considered it his home. Not the friends he'd lost on too many missions to count, who would never make it home at all. "I stopped looking for one a long time ago. What I want is a mission."

And that was when the man beside him smiled.

"You can call me Isaac, brother," he told Blue, like everything was settled. Then he lifted his own glass. "Welcome to Alaska Force."

Two

"You must remember me," said the woman who'd just screeched to a noisy halt in the dirt that passed for a driveway out behind the rickety old lodge. Blue was standing guard in the endless Alaskan summer sunshine, pretending he wasn't doing just that. As if someone would just be standing around aimlessly at the end of a road only fools ever tried to drive, but the woman didn't look like the sort who would make that distinction.

Much too soft, even with that haunted look on her face.

She threw herself out of the car as if she had someone on her tail. Blue knew she didn't, because they'd been monitoring her approach since she'd turned onto the only road—such as it was—that eventually led from Grizzly Harbor and over the usually impassable mountain to the back side of this remote Alaskan island. Where the deliberately hard-to-reach headquarters of Alaska Force was spread over what had once been a summer fishing retreat for the very hardy and very, very rugged.

Neither was a term Blue would use to describe this woman. She was delicate. Above his pay grade, if he had to guess from the quality of her clothes. And as weak and insubstantial as the jacket she wore against the ever-changeable and usually cold Alaskan summer weather.

But she surprised him by taking a few steps in his direction until something, maybe a belated sense of self-preservation, made her stop and sway on her feet.

"We grew up on the same street," she insisted. "I'm Everly Campbell."

And Blue didn't want to remember her. He opened his mouth to claim he didn't.

But he did.

The last time he'd laid eyes on little Everly Campbell, she'd been a pudgy, solid thing with pigtails and a too-solemn expression, waving at him from the back of her ridiculously girlie bike on the street where his mom and stepdad still lived.

He doubted he'd waved back.

What he really remembered was the bike, not the girl, he told himself. The bike had been bedecked with too much pink and actual streamers that flapped around when she rode it in those irritating, incessant circles in the street between their houses. Some mornings he'd heard the snapping sound they made from his bedroom up under the eaves in his stepdad's harsh, bitter house, long before his lazy teenage butt had wanted to be awake. If he'd thought about the girl across the street at all, it had been because little Everly lived exactly the kind of charmed American Dream life—two doting parents, a popular jock brother, a set of golden retrievers, even a freaking white picket fence—that Blue thought everybody deserved and, more, had joined the navy to protect.

He'd enlisted the day after his high school graduation, left behind the commuter town outside Chicago where they'd grown up, and gone out of his way not to think about either it or her since.

Until today.

Blue liked his past where it was. Buried and forgotten. Not up in his face on a southeastern Alaskan island so difficult to reach it operated as a kind of natural fortress.

"Come on, you must remember me," said the woman who was definitely Everly Campbell, all grown up and not the least bit pudgy any longer. She sounded far more confident about his memory than she should have, to Blue's mind, given it had been so many years. A lifetime. He crossed his arms over his chest and eyed her where she stood in the overgrown yard next to her haphazardly parked car, which he could tell at a glance was a rental. With Chicago plates. Which suggested she'd actually driven the three thousand or so miles to get here, give or take a ferry or two. "You and my older brother, Jason, are friends."

"I don't have friends."

That was strictly the truth. Blue had brothers-in-arms or acquaintances, nothing in between. He liked it that way.

"Fine." Everly sounded more strung out and desperate than simply impatient, which rubbed at his hero complex like an itch he couldn't scratch. But he was trying to get over his hero complex. Mostly. "You did in high school."

His memories of high school were dim and blurry,

focused more on his stepdad's temper than whatever weak teenage nonsense had cluttered up his days. And he didn't really want any clarity on lost and happily forgotten yearbook crap, especially since he'd never bothered to pick his up, much less collect signatures from people he didn't want to remember.

Everly took another ill-advised step toward him. "Jason played football."

"Good for Jason. I didn't."

"I know that. But the two of you hung out. He knows what you've been up to all these years." Something about Blue's expression must have penetrated, because she swallowed. Hard. "I think he kept in touch with one of your stepsisters?"

More crap Blue didn't want to think about.

"High school was a long time ago, little girl."

But that only made her face light up, which was the exact opposite of what he'd intended.

And to add insult to injury, she was pretty. Very pretty.

Damn it.

"See? You remember me. No one calls a grown woman *little girl* like that, all raspy and dark and menacing, unless they're trying to make a point."

Good thing she was irritating. " 'Raspy and dark and menacing'? Really?"

Everly waved a hand, and though something about the gesture struck him as frantic rather than dismissive, he ignored it and kept his gaze trained on her face.

"I'm descriptive. It's part of my job. Now it's second nature, basically."

All of this sounded like trouble, but not the kind Blue

liked to handle and was trained to solve. This sounded instead like the kind of trouble he'd been avoiding for the past twenty years. The kind of trouble that came with his mother's bad choices and his stepdad's late-night rants and all those choking, suffocating ties of stepsisters he'd never wanted and neighbors he'd never chosen and people who wanted something from him when he didn't respect them. When he couldn't and wouldn't respect them.

Pass.

There was a reason he never went home. And never would. The last thing he needed was a specter from that time, right here in front of him, like his past had a rental car and an evident death wish.

"I don't care," Blue said, his voice hard. "About your brother or your job."

He didn't say *or you*. He figured that was implied.

Everly sighed at that, but she didn't deflate. She also didn't slink back to her car and leave, the way she should have if she'd possessed even the barest hint of self-preservation. And for a moment there was nothing but the sound of the tide coming in, the summer breeze hinting at the coming fall weather, although the air was still warm enough in the afternoon sun. Not that cold bothered Blue much. He'd spent so much of his life uncomfortable, courtesy of the United States military, that the alternative made him edgy.

The woman standing there in front of him was just a new form of discomfort.

Everly Campbell should not have been anywhere near him. She shouldn't have been able to find him in the first place, much less remind him of the life he'd led before he'd become a SEAL. She should not have been within a

ten-mile radius of him, because the kind of blood Blue
had on his hands never washed off, and he'd stopped trying, and she was still made of picket fences and cute
little dolls and happy golden retrievers who rolled around
in leaf piles. All that sweet suburban happiness hung
around her like a kind of mist.

He wanted no part of it. Or her.

But it didn't keep him from noticing that she was
definitely not a little girl anymore. Blue bet she despaired
over the curves she'd packed into skinny jeans, a T-shirt
with something cute on it, and a sleek blazer in a too-
bright shade of blue. *Despair* was not the word Blue
would use to describe those curves, however. Not when
his mouth was watering.

She'd lost the pigtails. Her hair was strawberry blond,
hanging in long layers around a face that begged for a
man's hands. Her face was a problem. Straight up. Sweet
and smart at once, with a wide mouth that invited all
kinds of deeply impure thoughts.

Blue had spent years filled with only impure thoughts,
happily, but he refused to entertain such notions about
Everly Campbell.

For more than a perfectly understandable moment or
two, that was, because he wasn't dead.

He reminded himself that she'd careened over the
long unmarked road that was officially called Hardy's
Pass but was colloquially known as Hard-Ass Pass. It
was the only road on the island during the roughly seven
days a year it was not actively treacherous. It led directly
to the sprawling lodge here in the cove, ramshackle
wood cabins connected by wooden stairs and boardwalks, where Blue had been living since the night Isaac

had turned out to be a whole lot more than a legend. With a handful of other brothers-in-arms who'd gotten out of the special forces just like he had and shared not just his desire for a mission but a great many of his own very specialized skills.

At least three of them had weapons trained on her right now.

Not because they thought she was a threat, of course. No one who intended to do harm out here—a good thousand miles west of the middle of nowhere—would roar up blaring classic Bruce Springsteen and then jump out the way she had, calling his name like they had been tight once upon a time. Alaska Force wasn't just a home for wayward veterans who hadn't quite adjusted to civilian life. Isaac hadn't set it all up in the fishing lodge his family had once operated as a summer tourist trap out of the goodness of his heart.

Alaska Force was a last resort for people who needed very serious solutions to very complicated problems.

No one came here for fun. Mostly, no one dared come here at all. Especially without an invitation.

Blue refused to accept that Everly had the kind of problem she'd need a man like him to solve.

No matter how pretty she was.

"Great to catch up on old times," he said while she was still frowning at him, likely considering another run at him with more memories he didn't want to entertain. "Really. If you survive another pass over that road, which I have to tell you is unlikely, make sure you tell your mom I loved her oatmeal cookies."

Everly's frown deepened, and that was a head trip. He remembered the little girl on her nauseating pink bike, and yet the woman in front of him made him . . . greedy. Restless in ways he understood perfectly and refused to indulge. No matter how much he wanted to strip off her funky blazer and help himself to—

Stand down, he ordered himself. Especially that part of himself that wasn't listening to anything but the surprising need pounding through him.

"My mother is a thoracic surgeon," Everly replied after a moment. "She's never baked an oatmeal cookie in her life."

Blue didn't give an inch. "You need to go home, Everly. Wherever that is."

"Chicago. And I can't."

"You can. If you don't feel like suicide by mountain pass, take a seaplane somewhere a whole lot safer than Alaska, which is pretty much anywhere else. You don't belong here."

"I can't."

She took a step closer to him, and this time she didn't seem to think better of it. Blue was giving her a look he knew from experience made grown men back off and fall all over themselves to apologize, but Everly took another step toward him instead, which put her in arm's reach.

A very bad call on her part.

"That wasn't a suggestion so much as an order, sweetheart," he growled at her. "I don't know what you think you're doing here. I don't have any interest in running down memory lane. High school sucked. I don't talk to my stepsisters and I don't care if your brother does, because I don't talk to him, either. I guarantee you that whatever you want, I can't help you."

"If you can't, no one can," she said, and there was that strung-out, desperate thing in her voice again. He could see it all over her. It made her distractingly pretty green eyes in that problematic face of hers shine too bright, as if she were fighting back tears, and that was it. He was boned.

Blue wasn't built to ignore a cry for help.

Especially not from a pretty woman who'd known him when he couldn't help anyone, not even himself.

Behind her, he saw one of his Alaska Force brothers drop soundlessly from the tree where he'd hidden himself like the terrifyingly accurate marine sniper he was, because threat or no threat, anyone who rolled up on the lodge here in Fool's Cove was an opportunity to practice for the inevitable day when it really was an adversary. Griffin Cisneros nodded coolly at Blue, then melted off around the far side of the lodge like the six-foot-two ghost he was, all glacial focus and ice straight through, so quietly that Everly never knew he'd been there. It was one of his specialties.

But Templeton Cross—ex–Army Ranger, ex–Delta Force, and always happy to play the jackass—took a different approach. He strolled on down from the command station in the trees, where he'd been the one to clock Everly's rental car roaring down the winding, dizzyingly steep mountain road in the first place, a huge smile on his face, like this was a party.

"You didn't tell us you had friends," he said, aiming that giant grin of his right at Blue. "I had money riding on you being born mean and alone."

"I don't have friends," Blue said. Again. He scowled at Everly as she gazed up at Templeton, who was six feet and four inches of a beautifully mixed DNA cocktail that made the average female walk into things when she saw him. Blue reminded himself that he had no reason to care that Everly appeared to be maintaining that average. "Everly isn't a friend. And she's leaving."

"I apologize for his manners," Templeton told her, with exaggerated courtesy, probably because he knew exactly how much that made Blue want to take a swing at him. "Sometimes I think he was raised in a sewer."

"A four-bedroom suburban Colonial, actually," Everly replied. She shrugged when both men stared at her, her gaze shifting back and forth between them like she didn't know which one of them she found more intimidating. "I grew up across the street."

"A figurative sewer." Templeton stuck out his hand. "Templeton Cross, ma'am. It's a pleasure to meet anyone who can get under my man Blue's skin, a feat I personally would have told you could not be accomplished without a bullet, some luck, and very good aim."

Blue shoved Templeton's outstretched hand away from Everly before she could take it, and opted not to question that move. Or the way the other man grinned wider, as if he didn't need to question it because he already knew the answer.

"I will never understand why Isaac doesn't keep you on a leash," Blue muttered.

"Isaac would never put me on a leash," Templeton explained to Everly, who hadn't asked. As if he didn't see Blue slowly losing his cool right there next to him, when Blue was quite certain he did. "That would be a deep violation of the bonds of brotherhood, obviously, but would also hurt my feelings."

As if anything could hurt him. The man was as bullet-proof as he was deceptively talkative. All that chatter lulled the enemy into a false sense of security, because Templeton was one of the deadliest men Blue had ever met. And Blue pretty much knew only the most lethal individuals alive.

He didn't bother telling Templeton to STFU again. It would only delight him.

"Get in your car," Blue ordered Everly. "And go before the next rain, which will probably be tonight, when half of that pass will wash out again and you really will die up there."

"They think I murdered her," Everly said instead, looking startled, as if she hadn't expected to speak. But the words kept coming. "They can't decide if I'm a cold-blooded killer taunting them with my crimes or a very sick woman who doesn't know she's committed them in the first place."

Templeton went still and intent, while Blue studied the paleness in her cheeks and the lack of any mascara, which he should have paid attention to earlier. It was unusual for a pale redhead with copper lashes like Everly to go without, and slightly jarring when he really looked at the preciseness of her haircut and how it was clearly meant to showcase her face in a very specific manner. Her haircut and the clothes he'd already identified as high quality told him she was a woman who probably wore makeup, but wasn't today.

If she hadn't been Everly freaking Campbell, shouting out his name in the middle of Alaska like a blast from the entirely unwanted past, he would have already noticed that.

And then there was the fact the jeans she wore were faintly baggy in the knees, which suggested normal wear, but also at the waist, which hinted that she'd lost a few pounds—maybe too quickly to get a belt or a smaller pair. Her fingernails were short—too short for a woman who wore jeans so obviously expensive and a pair of flats in a complicated metallic color with teal soles that he knew at a glance cost as much as or more than the jeans and certainly had no business in a glacial wilderness. The way the blazer fit her told the same story, and made her ragged nails that much more of a tell.

And he felt like a dick. Because he'd been so busy fighting with ghosts in his head that he'd deliberately missed the fact that Little Miss American Pie was actually here because she was in trouble, just like all the other lost and tortured souls who found their way to Isaac's remote hill and the deadly little army he'd assembled here.

"Who did you kill?" he asked casually, and she flinched.

"Rebecca. My roommate. But I didn't kill her. I saw her get killed." She swallowed, hard. "I think I did. I mean, I know I did, but there's no proof, because when I got back with the police, there was nothing there." She looked too vulnerable, suddenly. "Or maybe the police are right and I'm a complete psycho. Either way, I need help."

Blue exchanged a swift look with Templeton. His brother nodded, then headed toward the lodge to gather the team in the big room, once a lobby, they used as the official Alaska Force office when there was a client around. Blue waited until he heard the door swing shut behind Templeton and then he moved closer to her. Too close, if he was honest. Because now he could see the way her pulse throbbed in her neck, and that wasn't going to help anyone. It only made him feel more greedy.

The kind of greedy that was a hell of a lot more trouble than he planned to get into, no matter what she had or hadn't done.

Maybe if he kept telling himself that, he'd keep his hands to himself.

He tilted his head to one side. "Do you think you're a psycho?"

"If I thought I was a psycho, I wouldn't have driven twelve hours a day for almost five days straight to find you when the police told me to stay put," she threw at him, in a tone that told him she was barely holding on to her own composure.

On some level he was glad. It meant it wasn't just him losing it today.

"Why did you? What made you think that hunting me down was a good idea?"

For a moment she looked more lost, and Blue had no idea why he had the urge to reach out to her then. He repressed it. Hard.

"Because," she said.

"That's not an answer."

"Because you're . . . you."

Blue sighed. "Let me guess. Your brother lives some soft, sad life somewhere, and he likes to get off thinking back on his glory days in high school like every other douchebag with a soft, sad life. And he thinks I owe him something because back when we were teenagers, he wasn't a complete dick to me. Is that why you're here? Your brother thinks that all these years later I'm his pet commando because we were lab partners for five minutes one time?"

Everly rocked back on her heels then, and suddenly she didn't seem quite as lost. But the strangest thing was that he did, with the way her green gaze met his and held, as direct as a touch, when he had no intention of letting her touch him. That way lay nothing but madness, he could tell. She had that look.

To say nothing of her connection to all that unfortunate history he wanted to forget.

"Jason is a pediatric surgeon who does Ironman Triathlons in his spare time," she said after a slight pause. She didn't bring up the oatmeal cookies her mother didn't bake. Or the fact that Blue kept reading her wrong, because he wanted her to be dismissible. He really, really wanted it. "I don't think he's sad, but what would I know? I'm his sister, and he lives across the country. He doesn't tell me all his stuff."

"I'm sure he's a terrific guy." Blue glared at her, and she still didn't crumple, and that meant either she really was a suicidal psycho—though, as much as he wanted to, he didn't get that vibe from her—or she was an even bigger problem than he wanted to face. "Maybe if I'd thrown a few footballs around on summer evenings, I'd be a terrific guy, too, but that ship sailed a long time ago. And I mean that literally. I was in the navy."

This time when Everly frowned at him, it was more than a head trip. The breeze picked up her hair, and he could feel it brush against his arm below the sleeve of his

T-shirt. And the way she looked at him made something inside him kick, hard.

It wasn't pity. He wouldn't have taken that well.

But he thought maybe this was worse. It looked a whole lot like compassion.

"You're a hero, Blue," she said quietly, but with conviction. As if that were an undisputed fact instead of a complex he was working to eradicate. And more to the point, a lie. "That was why Jason told me to find you."

Then she reached over and made everything much, much worse by putting her hand on Blue's arm.

He didn't want this. The shock of connection that slammed through him, like he'd never had a woman before. That sympathetic gleam in her eyes. The fact that she didn't just *need* him but *knew* him—or some old version of him he hadn't considered *him* in years.

He didn't want any of this.

Blue didn't know why the fact that she'd known him when he was scrawny and weak was so powerful. She should have been nothing to him except the memory of a pink bike outside a dismal house he'd never considered his home in the first place. He didn't know why she got to him at all. Or why her hand on his arm seemed to burn its way through him, like she was leaving new scars on his battered skin. And then lighting him up, deeper still.

He didn't like it. Any part of it.

"Please, Blue," Everly said softly, as if she trusted him on a personal level. Not just for his skills and abilities. When she had no reason whatsoever to do something so foolish. "Will you help me?"

He knew he was a goner when he didn't fight it. When he only looked down at her as if he really was the hero her brother imagined he was. Blue knew better. If he was any kind of hero, he wouldn't be here. He'd be done. He'd be kicked back somewhere, trailing movie stars and collecting cash, instead of paying more penance in Alaska Force.

Heroes didn't need another mission. Heroes had nothing to prove.

But that didn't mean he couldn't play the part for a little girl who'd gone and grown up pretty, and looked at him as if he could move the whole mountain that loomed behind them if he chose.

He'd never so badly wanted to be someone he wasn't. Not even when he was seventeen and still believed he could live up to the legend of his long-lost father. Not even when he'd been that deluded.

"I'll help you," he told her, just to see her green eyes light up.

And regretted it the minute he said it, because Templeton was right. Everly Campbell got under his skin.

The smart move would be to send this woman back into whatever mess she'd made to handle it on her own, because no matter what it was, it couldn't possibly be as bad as the things he'd done.

But while Blue might not have been a hero, he was a man who kept his promises.

If she could be saved, he told himself, he'd save her. For that scrawny kid she remembered who'd never managed to save himself or anyone else. Blue, on the other hand, was a lost cause. Some men had been born damned, and he was one of them, no matter how many Everly Campbells he tried to save.

And no matter how distractingly pretty she was.

So Blue sucked it up, promised himself he'd never give in to that greedy hunger within him, and led her inside to meet the rest of the reprobates who made up Alaska Force, before he thought better of it.

Before he came to his senses and sent her home.

Three

Everly woke up startled, her heart trying to claw its way out of her chest, the way she'd done every morning since the night Rebecca had died. She was almost used to the kick of it. The panic as she looked around to make sure she was safe. The dawning realization that maybe she never would be again.

Time was running out. She felt that deep inside, like her own breath.

But this morning was different.

It took her a minute to realize what the problem was as she looked around the small log cabin, her ability to see helped considerably by the deep blue light leaking in around the sides of the curtains pulled haphazardly across the windows on the far wall.

Her gut told her it wasn't morning at all. Her watch told her it was 1:03. And this was Alaska, land of the midnight sun farther north, so Everly guessed that 1:03

was unlikely to be the following afternoon no matter how tired she'd been. She eased herself up on the bed and looked around the small room she found herself in, trying to piece together what had happened.

And where the hell she was. Specifically.

She knew she was in Alaska, of course. It was the details beyond Alaska itself, the biggest state in the Union and the last, best frontier, that escaped her.

She'd been in that rental car forever. Hour after hour, day after day, fueled by panic and adrenaline. She'd kept pushing herself to drive farther and faster because she'd been so certain—or had wanted to be certain with every part of her that dared imagine she might get out of this mess—that the legend of Blue Hendricks her brother had shared with her over the phone one night would save her.

That he had to—*he had to*—because no one else could.

The ferry from Skagway had dropped her off in the colorful, quaint village of Grizzly Harbor after it had whisked her across glacier-studded seas she'd hardly believed were real even as she'd gaped at them. Mountains draped in clouds and fog, still capped with snow though it was summer. Sparkling blue skies everywhere else, arched over the mysterious northern Pacific Ocean. And evergreen trees on every surface, sturdy and windblown and a deep, rugged green. The town itself seemed torn from the pages of a picture book, atmospheric and pretty despite, or maybe because of, the weather-beaten, jagged coast where it sprawled just above the waterline, as if it were fighting to stay afloat. The buildings were painted bright colors that should have been jarring, bold and evocative against the gray sea despite their peeling paint, and

Everly knew that only a short month ago she wouldn't have been able to walk three feet without snapping a few thousand pictures.

A month ago, when she'd still been the person she used to be. A month ago, when she'd still had a normal life and the projected life span to go along with it.

But she hadn't come to Alaska to sightsee. Or to mourn the slow-motion loss of her entire life, likely quite literally if she couldn't find Blue Hendricks and beg him to help her. She was on a mission—though it hadn't taken long on the walkways that passed for the streets in tiny Grizzly Harbor to figure out that no one in the whole town wanted to tell her where Blue actually lived.

"Oh, around," the man in the general store had said with a shrug. He'd nodded in the vague direction of the dive bar Everly had walked by on her first pass through the little fishing village that clung to the base of the mountain, barely above the high-tide line and scattered up into the trees along the steep incline. "You'll run into him sooner or later."

But *sooner or later* was time Everly didn't have.

It took her a while longer to figure out that the tiny, remote cove where Blue and his equally intimidating buddies were holed up might as well have been on a separate, possibly armored island; it was so inaccessible. Instead of right here on the same rather small island in the Alexander Archipelago, the range of submerged coastal mountains that made up the bulk of Southeast Alaska and created the many sharp, hilly coasts and deep fjords that Everly had seen from the ferry.

But even when she'd realized how much farther she

still had to go, after she'd foolishly thought she'd finally reached safety in Grizzly Harbor itself, she hadn't stopped to have a long sob about the extreme unfairness of all this the way she'd wanted to.

Life is unfair, she'd told herself harshly instead, because harsh was all she had left these days, and it was better than the alternative. *Better to know it than be surprised by it.*

She had to keep moving forward, as fast as she could, or she would collapse. And Everly knew that if she allowed herself to collapse, if she fell down on the ground the way she wanted to with every last, protesting cell in her body, she would never get up again.

She'd felt the same thing that night in her Chicago apartment, almost a full month ago now. She'd stood there in her usual nighttime outfit of a tank top and pajama pants, barefoot and half-asleep in her own bedroom doorway. Everly had looked at the horror unfolding before her, right there across her living room, and she'd frozen. Her heart had beat once, a stunningly violent kick that had made her feel dizzy. Sick.

And she'd known that she had one split second to act or there would be no action. One split second to move or she would never move again.

Everly had been moving ever since.

It had taken one pointed conversation with the unfriendly owner of the Water's Edge Café, the first and only café Everly had found in Grizzly Harbor, to learn the name of the place where Blue lived. Supposedly.

"You don't want to go to Fool's Cove," the woman had told Everly, eyeing her as if taking her coffee order had been offensive enough, but asking questions was up there with a personal attack. She'd slid her hands in the back pockets of her jeans and shaken her head like Everly was an idiot. "It's for fools. It's right there in the name."

But getting to Fool's Cove had seemed relatively straightforward, the café owner's attitude and its name notwithstanding. Everly had pulled up the map on her mobile phone with what iffy cell service she had, and sure, the road over the big mountain had looked squiggly— but after almost a week of driving across the greater Yukon and Alaskan wilderness all by herself, sleeping in her rental car when necessary, she wasn't afraid of a little squiggle.

Until she understood that what she drove over that mountain wasn't so much a road as it was the suggestion of a road, and not much of a suggestion at that.

She'd gotten through it in white-knuckled, ear-popping, potential-heart-attack-at-any-second silence. She hadn't looked down at the steep drop-off that had sometimes seemed to be all of a crumbling inch away from her tires. She'd kept moving forward, because that was what she did now.

Or she'd inched forward, to be more precise. Whatever worked.

And then, sometime later, as she sat in a room crowded with very big and obviously dangerous men who looked as lethal as Blue did all these years later, and sounded three times as scary, it had all caught up to her. All the weeks of terror. The panic and fear. All the running and hiding and locking herself in the bathroom to sleep fitfully in the apartment only she seemed to believe had been the scene of so much horror. The vats of coffee she'd chugged to keep herself functional. The sugar she'd inhaled in case the coffee didn't quite work. It had all rolled over her and knocked her out.

Or so she assumed.

She didn't remember falling asleep. But the fact that she was sitting in an unfamiliar bed suggested that she had, and heavily enough that she had no recollection of being moved from the lobby of the lodge to . . . wherever she was now.

Everly rolled off the bed, checking her watch for the fifteenth time, as if that would make it say something that made more sense than 1:07 a.m. with all that weird light outside. Her jacket had twisted around as she'd slept, so she tried to tug it back into place as she stood. She looked around, taking in the dim, quiet interior of the cabin. It didn't look like anyone lived here or ever had. There wasn't much more than the bed she was lying on, a scarred dresser in one corner, and the battered wooden floor beneath her feet, all looking wholly unused and untouched, as if this were a hotel room no one had occupied recently.

She saw her foldable, metallic flats on the floor next to the bed, curling up where they lay like pill bugs with cheerful teal soles. Usually the sight of them made her happy, but not today. *Tonight,* she corrected herself. She didn't slip her feet into them, padding over instead toward the windows that flanked the front door, the unearthly light glowing around the edges of the curtains.

She eased the front door open, surprised when it didn't creak the way she'd expected it to, since it looked so rough and felt so heavy. Something about that seemed to shudder through her, as if the door were a clue to a mystery she hadn't realized she needed to solve.

But then it didn't matter, because she was easing her way out onto the wide porch that jutted out over the cove below. And that should have been arresting enough. The Alaskan mountains were bold and high, capped with snow though it was high summer, and they loomed everywhere she looked. The sea was a dark, murmuring presence all around, in case she was tempted to forget she was standing on an island in the Gulf of Alaska, thousands and thousands of miles from anywhere. The strange, far northern light in the middle of the night was a kind of blue predawn and stirred her up inside in ways she didn't quite understand. It felt magical. Otherworldly.

Yet what she noticed far more than the landscape was the man sitting out on one of the benches on the porch in the light of a lantern she wasn't sure he needed, as if he'd been there a long while. As if he were standing guard, whether to keep her in or others out, she didn't know.

And he was far more magical than the sky.

Blue.

His name moved through her like the tide against the shore below. An insistent, irrevocable clamor.

And it was worse now. Much worse than it had been when she'd thrown herself out of her rental car and staggered toward him, hoping like hell he remembered her.

That had all seemed so desperate, a part of all the panic and horror that had taken her over. She'd noticed how he looked. Of course she'd noticed. He was big and hard and scowling, and had added about a hundred pounds of sleek, lean muscle to the wiry teenage form she remembered. All of it in places she was entirely too female—even if she'd been scared so long she hardly remembered that she'd ever felt something, anything else—*not* to notice.

But this was worse.

He was just *sitting there*, for one thing. Not pacing around behind the lodge, in and out of the watchful trees. He had his feet kicked up on the bench and was looking down at a tablet in his hands, his head propped up behind him as if he'd never been more comfortable in all his life than he was then, lounging on a wooden bench after one in the oddly deep blue morning.

And maybe it was because she'd just slept—and hard—but Everly didn't have it in her to deny what washed over her at the sight of him. It wasn't just that he was beautiful, though he was. God help her, he was.

Blue Hendricks was what people dreamed about when they conjured up the word *hero*. Tough. Strong. His dark hair was cut short as if he were still in the military, but the starkness of it only called more attention to the undeniable masculine beauty of his face. His mouth . . . got to her. It made her insides quiver, funny and low. His tough jaw saved him from prettiness, and the lines that fanned out from his dark eyes suggested that he was capable of acting a lot happier and friendlier than he had around her so far. He hadn't shaved recently, but what might have looked scraggly on someone else looked nothing short of perfect on him. He was out there exposed to the Alaskan elements in cargo trousers, boots, and a T-shirt that did things that should have been preposterous to his hard, wide chest and impossibly sculpted biceps.

Everly told herself that the fact that this man happened

to be stupidly hot had nothing to do with . . . anything. But her breath seemed to tangle there in her throat regardless. And she knew the reality that he was *that attractive* was something she was going to have to get over. Or find a way to ignore, anyway.

Because what mattered far more than how ridiculously good-looking her once-upon-a-time neighbor had become was the unmistakable fact that the man was a loaded gun. A deadly weapon in male form. And she'd never been happier in all her heretofore pacifist life to see that much artillery packed solid and lethal into one obviously capable man.

Blue didn't move a single astonishingly hard muscle when she came through the door. But Everly had no illusions that she was sneaking up on him. It was possible he'd known the very moment she'd woken up inside, well before her feet touched the floor. She doubted she'd have managed to sneak up on him if it had been pitch-dark out here, much less when he was as bathed in the strange indigo light as she was.

She didn't think he was the kind of man people snuck up on.

"What happened?" she asked, her voice husky.

She told herself it was from the unexpected nap. Because that had to be sleep in her throat, not the odd reaction she was having to Blue himself, like something almost uncomfortably fizzy was working its way over her skin and sinking deep beneath it, down into her bones.

Because her life was already complicated enough.

He didn't look up. "You fell asleep. Hard. In a room full of people."

There was no reason that should have made her feel so . . . fragile. "Where am I?"

"If you don't know where you are, Everly," Blue said in that gruff voice of his that rolled over her and then shook through her like some kind of thunder, setting off competing storms inside her whether she liked it or not, "then you're in more trouble than I thought."

"I know I'm in Alaska," she said, as if she expected him to start handing out prizes for the right answers. Like the people-pleasing Miss Goody Two-shoes she'd been her entire life, until a month ago when she'd been recast as a lunatic Girl Who Cried Wolf who was maybe also a psychopathic killer. Or something. Maybe her parents' disappointment in their less accomplished child wasn't misplaced. "In a very hard-to-reach place a million miles from anything resembling a city, called Grizzly Harbor. Well. This is Fool's Cove, technically. A . . . suburb of Grizzly Harbor?"

"Congratulations. You looked at a map."

"A lot of maps, actually. My GPS doesn't always work out here."

Blue set his tablet aside then and fixed that dark, assessing gaze of his on her.

But this time, Everly was prepared. She still felt as if she were falling, the same way she'd felt when she'd rolled out of that car and staggered toward him across the dirt and weeds and roots in the cleared bit of woods behind the lodge. She'd felt as if she were toppling from a great height, like the mountain itself, then hit the ground hard, flat on her back so that she lost her breath.

That was what it was like when Blue Hendricks looked at her.

It was how she'd known it was him. Oh, sure, if she looked closely, she could see the hint of the skinny, feral boy she remembered—but he'd always had this effect on her. When she'd been a little girl, she hadn't known what it was—she'd just known that he was her favorite. Her hero.

She knew what it was now. It was just . . . him. He was electric.

And he was the only one who could help her.

"You nodded off in the middle of a meeting you apparently drove three thousand miles to make happen." Blue's gaze was steady. Discerning. As if he were trying to see right through her. Or, worse, already did. "Who does that? Is this a drug thing?"

Maybe it wasn't surprising that Everly felt transparent. Pale, really, all the way through. Or maybe that was the odd summer light, making a new set of accusations about her character and choices and entire freaking life punch through her like bullets. Making her wonder how much more she could take.

As much as you have to, she told herself.

She made herself stand taller when she wanted to droop. Or maybe curl into the fetal position and sob. "I guess I was tired."

"Because you drove here from Chicago."

"I was afraid they would stop me at the airport if I tried to fly."

"But you figured the border would be a piece of cake."

"I guess I didn't think about the border. But they didn't stop me."

"What was your plan if you couldn't find me?" he asked, in that quiet, considered way he had, which only made him sound more menacing. "You were just going to turn around and drive back? And then hand-wave away the two-week absence to any interested parties?"

"That, or I figured someone would just kill me already, and end the discussion right there," Everly retorted. Her teeth hurt, so she unclenched them. "At least this way I got to see some really pretty scenery first."

"I like the attitude," Blue said, though his tone suggested otherwise. His tone plus the hard way he was studying her. "Who knows? It might save you."

"And here I was hoping that you would."

Blue laughed at that. And maybe it was the strange light all around him that made this seem like some kind of dream—though definitely not a good one.

Everly had always prided herself on her ability to read people and situations. It was what made her good at her advertising job, dealing with clients who never, ever said what they wanted, and would then get furious if the agency failed to deliver what was in their heads. But she'd been reading this situation wrong from the start, and Blue was probably one more thing she wasn't seeing as she should.

It didn't take a psychic to understand that Blue Hendricks was not a man to be trifled with. A wise woman would have maintained a healthy distance and a matching level of scrupulous courtesy so as not to set him off.

Too bad Everly couldn't remember the last time she'd felt anything resembling healthy.

"Even if I was the hero you're dumb enough to think I am?" Blue laughed again, with even less humor than before, and Everly had to fight to breathe through it, because it was yet another weapon, and he wielded it too well. "What makes you so sure that I would want to save you? Some girl I barely remember?"

"You remember me. I get the feeling you remember everything. In minute detail."

"I remember things that matter."

That stung. She knew it was meant to, so she only raised her brows in a kind of challenge rather than let the deliberate slap drag her under. "Your friends said they would help me. If you don't want to, you don't have to."

"My friends don't get to make this decision, little girl. I do." His mouth—God, she had to stop staring at his mouth and imagining . . . *things*—curved. It didn't make him seem any more approachable. "You're a ghost from my past, not theirs. That makes you my problem. That's how it works here."

"Then I guess this is my lucky day." She folded her arms in front of her, and blinked as she took in the strange twilight that made the water look like wine and the pine trees seem like intent, hovering spirits. "Or my lucky night, whatever. Because I feel pretty certain that if you weren't going to help me, you wouldn't have tucked me in for a nice nap in your cabin."

His mouth curved again, but this time, it made an echoing heat curl through her. She could feel it all the way down in her toes.

"This isn't my cabin. If you were in my cabin, you'd know. You'd get a very specific invitation, and you'd have no doubt what your role was once you got there. And here's a hint, Everly. I don't like damsels in distress in my bed."

She pressed her toes hard against the wooden deck

beneath her, happy it was cold enough to clear her head. Because under no circumstances could she permit herself to think about his *bed*. Much less herself in it. With him.

In a specific *role*.

"Are you going to help me, Blue?" she asked, and she didn't mean for her voice to go so soft halfway through the question. Almost plaintive.

She sounded almost exactly as scared as she'd been every moment since that terrible night back in Chicago. She hadn't given in to the fear, not in all the awful, confusing weeks since. She hadn't let her own panic sweep her under, drag her down.

And she didn't know why—standing here on a remote porch in the middle of the Alaskan summer night with a man she found as overwhelming as the impossible light at this hour—she felt so shaken. As if Blue were the thing that might break her, after all.

Or maybe that was just any normal woman's reaction to imagining herself in Blue's bed—but Everly shoved that thought aside.

Blue didn't reply. He let one moment drag by, then another. His dark gaze never left her face, and Everly felt herself redden. She told herself it was nothing but leftover emotion, secondhand sensation, from everything she had been through. Nothing to do with imagining invitations to Blue's actual cabin, she assured herself.

Of course not.

But she realized she was clenching her arms tight against her body, as if she were bracing herself for a blow.

"Tell me what happened back in Chicago," Blue said, long after she'd decided he might never speak again. "Exactly what happened."

"I thought I already did."

"You gave me an overview. Maybe you thought you'd tell us all the details in the office? But you fell asleep."

All Everly could remember from that office was the men. A lot of men. It had seemed like a crowd of them, a battalion, each one bigger and more intimidating and gruffer than the next. She'd curled up in an oversized armchair in one corner, tucked her legs beneath her, and tried to calm her roaring pulse. She couldn't remember the names, tossed out too quickly. Or maybe she hadn't tried to hear them because she could barely take it all in.

That she'd found Blue. And that he came with big, strapping friends who were just as overwhelming, clearly ex-military, and obviously lethal as he was.

"I'm not on drugs, by the way," she told him. Awkwardly. "To clarify."

He nodded, as if he'd already come to that conclusion himself. "You don't have that flat, dull thing going on in your eyes. But you wouldn't be the first pretty woman to pop prescription pills and pretend she didn't have a problem."

"I drink coffee like it's my job. So depending on your view of caffeine, I guess I have a problem. But only that problem. No narcotics as a chaser to my skinny mocha latte."

"I looked you up." Blue tapped the tablet next to him, though the screen was dark. "You work at an ad agency. My impression of ad agencies is that they run on cocaine."

"Why is it important to you that I be a drug addict?" She frowned at him. "Do I look like a drug addict?"

"You look skinny, weak, and frazzled," Blue said, and it was the unvarnished way he said it that got to her. That made her feel shaky on her feet. As if he wasn't offering an opinion but reciting facts. Obvious, inarguable facts. "Much skinnier, weaker, and more frazzled than any of the pictures posted on your social media accounts."

"One minute I'm pretty but possibly a pill-popper, and the next I look like crap. Got it."

"I'm real sorry I'm not as cuddly and sweet and cordial as you expected your fantasy hero to be, Everly. That must suck for you. Captain America isn't real, but I am, and like hell am I getting caught up in a mess if it's all in your head."

"It's not in my head." Blue's eyes narrowed, which was how Everly realized she'd pretty much shouted that at him. That and the echo from the trees standing sentry behind them. "I've had entirely too many people tell me I'm making things up lately. I'm pretty creative, but even in my wildest imaginings, I couldn't kill off my roommate in my dreams and have her actually go missing the next day."

"Unless you killed her in a drug-fueled rage and were so out of it you imagined the rest of it."

"I've heard of drug-fueled rages, but not drug-fueled cleaning frenzies that erased all traces of the damage."

"Depends on the drug."

"I'm not on drugs," she told him, and even she could hear how frayed her own temper was getting with each word. "Just like I'm not making things up to get attention, or such a drama queen that I *want* to imagine people are following me. I didn't have a bad dream or a psychotic break. I'm not crazy, and I'm not lying. But you don't have to take my word for it." She thrust out her arms, which would have been more effective if she hadn't been wearing a jacket, concealing her veins. "I'll take a blood test right now."

Blue swung his legs down from the bench and then sat there, facing her. He didn't say he believed her. He didn't assure her she was sane. And still, she felt calmer, as if his full attention was the same thing.

"I don't want your blood," he said quietly. "I want your story. The whole story, nothing left out. Do you understand?"

"I understand," Everly replied, as if it were a vow.

And maybe it made sense that she was barefoot now, standing here on the edge of the world in front of Blue, because it brought her back to that night a few weeks ago when she'd also been terrified. Barefoot and outside herself. She pressed her feet harder into the wooden planks beneath her, again, and told herself she felt steadier when she did.

But the truth was, the only thing that really made her feel steady was the way Blue regarded her. Intent and serious. Unflinching.

Some kind of alarm rang in her head, but she ignored it. She hadn't felt steady in so long that it felt like a gift, here in the middle of this strange, bright night. In this odd place so far away from everything she knew and anyone who knew her. With a man who was nothing like the comic book hero she'd conjured up in her head during her endless drive, but seemed instead like something she'd dreamed up just to fit the rugged backdrop of this isolated place, so still at this hour except for the lapping of the water against the rocky shore that it seemed to quiet her, too.

Or maybe that was just Blue.

"Every single detail, Everly," he said again, and this time it was more like an order than a request, but she liked that, too. "Breath by breath."

Four

Everly told herself that all she had to do was tell her story. There was no reason to feel as if this were a confession, no matter how Blue was watching her, his big arms crossed over his chest and that stoic expression on his face.

This was what she wanted, she reminded herself. This was why she'd come here.

"That night I went to bed early because I had a big presentation the next day," she told him, letting the memories wash over her. Not holding them at bay the way she normally did. "But I woke up again sometime after midnight."

"What time is 'sometime'?"

"I don't know. I couldn't figure out why I was awake, and I lay there for a while, trying to figure out why my heart was beating so fast. I don't know how long I did that, but when I looked at the clock, it was one fifty-two."

"That's very specific."

"It's burned into my head."

Branded, more like. Everly almost reached up to rub her fingers over the welt she was sure must be there on her forehead, broadcasting the last moment her life was anything like normal to anyone who cared to look, but stopped herself. Barely.

"You often wake up in the middle of the night?"

"No. I usually sleep like the dead." That struck her as unfortunate phrasing, and she cleared her throat, but Blue's gaze remained impassive. She found that encouraging, somehow. "The minute my head hits the pillow, I'm out until my alarm goes off the next morning."

She didn't tell him how strange it had been this last month to personally witness all those dark, narrow hours she usually slept through. She didn't try to explain what it was like to sit up, hollow-eyed and half-panicked, staring at her roommate's empty bed at three forty-five in the morning, willing it to be full again.

Things were different in the middle of the night. Time was too round, too broad. The clock was her enemy, slow and sluggish. Every hour seemed soft and insubstantial, and still the minutes barely inched by. Shadows seemed more real and far more threatening. Dreams and waking tangled in on themselves.

And all the insomnia in the world hadn't brought Rebecca back.

"That something your roommate would have known? That you sleep easy and don't wake up?"

Everly considered that. "Rebecca and I were friendly, sure. We weren't, you know, best friends or anything. I don't know if we discussed sleep patterns."

"It was a yes or no question."

"Yes, then." Everly tried not to glare at him. She thought he could save her, it was true. Or help her, anyway. But that didn't mean he was required to be overly nice while he did it. It was ridiculous that she should feel that caving sensation in her belly. As if he was hurting her feelings. As if her feelings had anything to do with this in the first place. "Rebecca and I had been roommates for a year. More than a year. It's safe to say she knows my sleeping habits, yes."

"Do you know hers?"

Everly hated that he made her feel like a liar. It was that steady, unemotional way he was studying her. As if she was as crazy as the Chicago detectives had told her she was, and he was waiting for her to show it.

But whether or not she was crazy, and whether or not he thought so, she still had to answer his question. "Rebecca's more erratic. Sometimes she stays up really late binge-watching entire series on Netflix. It wasn't unusual to find her on the couch in the morning, still watching something she'd started the night before. But it was just as normal for her to go to bed at a relatively decent hour. And then sometimes she would stay out all night. At a friend's or a boyfriend's. You know."

"So we can probably assume that she knew what was normal for you, too."

"I'm not lying," Everly gritted out.

For a moment, that hard gaze of his softened. Even his mouth looked like something other than granite. And Everly had to blink back the excess moisture that flooded the backs of her eyes. She told herself it was the crisp breeze off the ocean, salty and cool.

"I don't think you're a liar, Everly," Blue said quietly, as if he knew exactly how important it was that he tell her that. That she hear it—for the first time since that night. "But you know things you aren't aware that you know. This is just an example."

Her throat was too tight. She managed a stiff, jerky sort of nod, and that only made it worse.

Because that steady gaze of his turned kind and almost took her knees out from under her. "Go on."

She blew out a breath, trying to fight back all the messy things inside of her. Trying to keep herself calm. "At some point after I looked at the time, I heard a noise from outside. Outside my bedroom, I mean. In the living room."

"What kind of noise?" Everly started to answer, but Blue shook his head. "Don't tell me the retrofitted answer. What you decided the noise must have been afterward, when you knew what was happening. What did you think it was when you heard it? Before you went and looked?"

Everly took a moment to think about it. She could remember it all too clearly, and yet somehow not clearly at all. As if it were part and parcel of that same dream. *This* dream. The sickening and seemingly endless dream, edged with fear and panic, that had taken over her life.

She remembered how hard her heart had been beating. That strange scratchiness in her throat. The way she'd sat bolt upright in her bed, listening for the next sound. Some part of her convinced that she'd only imagined the first one, whatever it was.

But every cell in her body had been screaming otherwise.

"I don't know what I heard. It was . . . wrong."

"If you know it was wrong, you know what you heard."

Blue's expression was implacable. And Everly couldn't have said why it made her feel safe. Safe enough to keep talking, anyway. Safe enough to stand there in the eerie Alaskan intense blue, not-dark night and look inside herself more deeply for the answer he clearly thought was in there.

And because he believed it, she did, too.

"It was a soft sort of thud," she said after a moment, as if she were testing out the truth of her words by tasting them, one at a time. "It sounded as if she was moving furniture. Like maybe she'd dropped something behind the couch."

"So that's why you got up? Because you thought maybe your roommate needed some help moving the couch around?"

"Rebecca is built like a ballerina. Willowy and fragile. She can do yoga for days, but I've never known her to move heavy things by herself. And certainly not in the middle of the night."

Blue thrust his legs out before him, his boots making a faint scraping sound against the deck. And calling more attention than was necessary to the length of them, in case Everly might have forgotten how *big* he was.

She hadn't.

"So you get up," Blue said. "You're thinking to yourself . . . what?"

"I don't know what I was thinking. I just wanted to see what was going on."

"Then that's probably what you were thinking."

"You really want this to be cut-and-dried, but it wasn't." Another wave of emotion crashed through her, and she tried to shrug it away. "It didn't even take this long. I woke up. I lay awake for a while. Eventually I looked at the time. Then I heard another sound and I got up. It could have been fifteen minutes. It could have been fifteen seconds. I don't know."

"Sounds like you do know."

Everly sighed. "If you say so."

Blue laughed again, and she wondered, fleetingly, what it would be like to hear this man laugh when he really, truly found something funny. *Precarious,* something inside her whispered. *Much too precarious for you to handle.*

Because one thing she'd learned over the course of this last month was that she wanted no part of anything hazardous to her health, ever again. She hadn't appreciated how pleasant her safe, predictable, mostly quiet life was. She hadn't understood how lucky she was until she'd lost it all.

That wasn't a mistake she planned to make again, assuming she ever made it out of this nightmare.

"So you open your door . . . ?"

Everly stopped thinking about Blue's laugh. It didn't matter. Just as it didn't matter that he was so beautiful, in the way finely honed weapons were beautiful—lethal and gleaming and obviously sharp to the touch. What mattered was what he could *do.* What he and his friends were capable of.

"I opened my door. I remember feeling that I needed

to be quiet, so maybe I did think that something bad was happening out there. Before you ask."

"You don't spend a lot of time listening to your body, do you?" Blue asked.

It was ridiculous that she should react the way she did. Flushed hot and red like a teenager. And then hotter still, because she was embarrassed by her own reaction. For a moment she thought she'd be caught in an endless too-red feedback loop until she exploded—which would at least solve her problems.

But she didn't explode. And Blue didn't stop watching her in that same expectant way, as if he thought they could stay out on this deck forever until he pulled every memory she had straight out of her and slapped them all down between them.

She wanted his help. But she hadn't really bargained on another interrogation. She could still remember the way her stomach had plummeted when she'd realized that the detectives were questioning her, not simply gathering facts—

"I don't know how to answer that," she said here. Now. To Blue, who'd told her she didn't listen to her body, which meant *her body* was suddenly the only thing she could think about. "I don't know what that means."

"Fear is a gift," Blue said gruffly, a different sort of glitter in his dark gaze. "It's your body telling your mind things it doesn't want to know in terms it can't ignore."

"Yes," she made herself say. Aware that she didn't want to admit it out loud, for some reason—as if the admission would make this mess *more real* than it already was. "I was afraid."

"So you opened your door. Quietly."

"Rebecca's door is directly across from mine. Across the living room. The landlord claimed it was two separate master bedrooms, but that's a stretch." Her arms ached when she uncrossed them, which was how she knew that she'd been holding herself too tightly. She ignored it. She cupped her hands together, then tried to sketch the layout of her apartment in the air in front of her. "Bedrooms on either side, living room in the middle, kitchen on one end and bathroom on the other. Home sweet home."

"Take me through it. You open your door. You're already scared, but you don't know why. You're telling yourself she's moving furniture, but somewhere inside of you, you know it's something else."

It wasn't until then, until he said those things so matter-of-factly in that gruff, unfaltering voice, that Everly truly understood how desperate she'd been for someone to believe her. It wasn't until then she realized how worried she had been, all this time, that she really was as unhinged as the police had begun to suggest she was.

That he seemed to believe what she was telling him made her believe *herself* again.

Blue didn't look at her as if she was a lunatic. He didn't look at her with that flat suspicion all over his face. On the contrary, Blue looked at her as if he wanted nothing more than to dig out each and every detail of what she was telling him and look at it in this strange Alaskan light, which might have been uncomfortable but suggested that he really, truly believed what she was telling him.

Everly felt a hard, stiff knot inside her release. It was some kind of relief, she thought. Some brush of hope when she'd almost given up on it.

She knew not to get ahead of herself. Blue believing her wasn't the same as Blue helping her through this or Blue saving her—but God knew, it felt the same tonight.

It wasn't hope that had spurred her on across all those lonely, chilly miles. It wasn't hope that had gotten her over the one-lane dirt track that was barely a road and barely big enough to fit the compact wagon she'd rented. That had been fueled by sheer desperation.

Desperation, acrid and thick.

Hope was smoother. Lighter. An intense relief pooled behind her eyes, like the tears she refused to cry. She blinked the moisture away as best she could, but she held on tight to the relief.

"I could see into Rebecca's room," she told him. "I could see her. She was lying on the floor, except she wasn't. . . . Her body was crumpled. . . ." She shook her head, those same hideous images tumbling through her all over again. As if they were new and just as impossible, just as horrifying. "She was bent in ways she shouldn't have been able to bend. I don't know if I actually saw blood or just think I did."

"Whatever happened to her had already happened, then."

She remembered Rebecca's leg. It had taken her too long to understand what she was seeing. Why everything was wrong, as if she'd been looking through a kaleidoscope and everything was fractured and fused back into the wrong shapes. Her stomach twisted, sharp and hard.

"Or it was still happening—I don't know." She forced herself to breathe. "There were two men inside her room with her. One was squatted down beside her. But I had the impression it was the other one who had done . . . whatever it is he did."

"They didn't see you."

"In my mind I stood there for a very long time. But I couldn't have. I wanted to scream, but I didn't. I don't think I did." She shook her head. "Maybe I just felt like screaming inside. I still do."

"Did they look up?"

"Not for that first moment." He didn't ask another one of his rapid-fire questions, so she kept on, trying to break down a bad memory into its parts. "I just stood there as if I couldn't move, because it didn't make sense. What I was seeing, I mean. I couldn't make it . . . come together." She swallowed, hard, and hated that she was sweating again. Still as afraid and sickened as she'd been then. Maybe she always would be. "I must have made a noise then, because they both looked up as if they heard something."

"There's no doubt in your mind that they saw you?"

"They saw me. Clearly. Just as I saw them."

"Could you identify them?"

"I think so." She shrugged. "I drew them."

Blue frowned. "Drew them? You mean, with a pencil?"

"A ballpoint pen." She stood straighter. "I'm not a great artist or anything, but I can draw a basic likeness."

"Did you tell the police this?"

Everly shrugged again, aware that it was a sharp gesture, her shoulders entirely too defensive. "The police weren't interested."

Blue rubbed a hand over his jaw. "So two goons are staring at you. Your roommate is maybe bloody and probably dead on the floor. What did you do?" He was sitting there so casually, as if it weren't the middle of the night, no matter how deep blue the sky was above them at this hour. As if this were an easy conversation about whatever men like him talked about when they weren't off saving the world. "You walked away unharmed. How did that happen?"

"I didn't walk. I ran." She realized she was trembling. She just hoped that Blue couldn't see it—even though she was sure that those dark, shrewd eyes of his missed nothing, especially with that lantern next to him. "I threw myself back in my room and slammed the door. And I threw the bolt."

"To slow them down?"

"I think I was hiding," she said slowly, trying to parse those tense, terrible seconds that were like a storm in her memory, wild and disjointed. "I don't know that I really thought any of it through. Maybe I figured if I locked the door, that would keep them out?"

"But you didn't stay there."

"They started pounding on the door. And I knew— I just knew—that they would kick it down. And then I would be in that same broken heap on the ground—" Her stomach heaved at that. Everly clamped her lips shut and waited for the sudden spike of nausea to pass. And she thought Blue knew exactly what was happening to her, because he only waited. "So I did the only thing

I could do. I went out on the fire escape, and I climbed down to the street."

"And for some reason they didn't follow you."

"I expected them to shoot me. Or tackle me. Chase me." She shook her head. "I don't know if they did or didn't. I just ran. Until I made it to the police station."

"What were you wearing?"

"Pajama bottoms. Tank top. No shoes." She tried to smile at him, but it hurt her face. "Apparently, that made me seem more insane. Running around Chicago in the middle of the night with no shoes on."

"But they didn't think you were crazy at first. They thought you were a victim."

She nodded, but then considered. "I don't know what they thought. They put me in a room. I sat there for a long time. Hours, maybe. And when they came back in, it wasn't the regular cops I'd spoken to when I'd run into the station. It was two detectives, a man and a woman, and they were not friendly."

"Unfriendly, sure, but they didn't charge you with anything."

"My apartment was empty, apparently. No dead room-mate. Not even any signs of a struggle, they said. They suggested that maybe I suffered from night terrors. They also suggested that I should know better than to waste police time."

"Did you think it was a nightmare?"

"I wanted to," Everly whispered. "I really, really wanted to. But then Rebecca never came home. And a few days later, someone started following me." Blue tilted his head slightly to one side, and she knew what he was going to ask, so she answered it. "It's possible they were already watching me, but it was a few days later that I noticed. Or they let me see them."

"Them?"

"Two men. Different men than the ones who'd been in my apartment."

"Did you draw them, too?"

"Yes." She didn't offer to show him the pad she kept in her bag. She figured he'd ask if he wanted to see her sketches, and anyway, she wasn't sure she knew where her bag was. "Did I pass my latest interrogation?"

Blue's mouth curved again. "An interrogation isn't pass-fail."

"Tell that to the Chicago police."

That curve deepened, and Everly's pulse racketed around inside her veins in a way that spelled nothing but trouble. For a moment she thought it might be visible.

But if it was, he didn't say anything about it. He pushed to his feet and then he was towering over her. And Everly was suddenly starkly aware of the fact that there was nothing and no one around save the towering mountains. The moody sea and the brooding indigo sky above. It was just the two of them here, alone in the summer night.

Blue was huge and obviously lethal. He could do anything he wanted with her and no one would ever know. No one knew she was in the state of Alaska, much less on this little island.

But Blue didn't scare her. Not like that.

"Okay," he said after a while, as if he'd reached a decision.

"Okay?"

"I'll take you back into town," he continued, as if *okay* had been a whole explanation instead of a word. As if he was rendering judgment.

And Everly panicked.

She threw herself forward, hurtling toward the wall of his chest and not really caring when he snagged her in midhurtle, holding her away from him with his impossibly hard hands wrapped tight around her biceps.

"Please," she said urgently. "*Please*, Blue. I don't know what I'm going to do if you don't help me."

"Everly."

She stopped. Her eyes were burning, and she realized the tears she'd been holding back had tipped over at last. And worse, he was staring at the wetness she could feel sliding down her cheeks.

Scowling at it, to be precise.

"*Please*," she begged him. Again.

Because there was pride and there was hope and then there was this. She was all too familiar with this. Sheer desperation.

"First," he said, something dark in his voice that matched the scowl but not that gleam in his eyes, "don't throw yourself at me again unless someone is shooting at you and you need cover."

She sniffled. "Great. Thanks for that addition to my nightmares."

"Second—" And his voice seemed more intense then. Darker. Or maybe that was just the look in his eyes that she couldn't quite read, no matter how it seemed to connect to something low in her belly. "Don't cry."

She let out a breath she hadn't realized she was holding. Then she wiped at her cheeks, and he seemed to take a long, long while to let go of her.

"Sorry," Everly muttered. Though she wasn't. He was lucky she wasn't sobbing herself into a puddle at his feet.

"Third, I already told you I was going to help you, and when I make promises, I keep them."

That felt like a vow and, more, as if he were still holding on to her. When he wasn't. Everly felt something too much like giddy and told herself that it was the brightness all around her when it should have been dark. The road still inside her, messing her up after all those hundreds and thousands of miles.

That it had nothing to do with her pulse. Her heart. Her disbelief that she'd finally found him and that he was *this*. His own personal army. The only person in the world—she was sure of it—who could help her.

"I'm taking you into town because you can't stay here," he was saying. "This isn't a public place."

That was a perfect opportunity to wrench her gaze away from the tractor beam of his. To take a few breaths and try to compose herself. She blinked at the cabin behind them and the lodge farther down, which was really just a sprawling series of interconnected cabins a lot like this one, rambling along the rocky shore. She could see smoke coming from deeper in the forest, higher up the side of the mountain, suggesting there were even more cabins tucked away, out of sight.

As secret bat caves for mysterious superheroes went, she had to admit that Fool's Cove was pretty spectacular. Remote, inaccessible, and stunning all at once.

"Exactly what kind of place is this?"

His mouth curved, and it made her warm. "You don't ask questions. I do." Blue jerked his chin toward the cabin, but he was still giving her that half smile, and Everly had the dazed thought that she would follow him anywhere if he asked. Or even if he didn't. "Get your shoes, Cinderella. It's time to go."

Five

She had cried.

Blue could defend himself against all comers, and had. Often. A knife. A gun. A guerrilla attack. This or that army in any given hellhole, whatever. He'd been there, done that. He had a collection of medals no sane man wanted to earn and a whole lot more scars for his trouble, and he was pretty much fine with that.

He was a hard man to rattle.

But let a few tears roll down Everly Campbell's pretty face in the middle of a dark blue Alaskan summer night and he was at a loss, apparently. Blue did not appreciate uncertainty. That was not how he operated. That was not who he was. *Uncertainty* veered a little too close to *helplessness,* and he didn't tolerate that crap. In the world he'd tried his best to save upon occasion, sure, but not in himself. Not ever.

And yet she'd cried, and worse, it had been obvious it

wasn't any kind of game. It was real. Real emotion. Real panic. Real desperation, written all over her, right there in front of him.

He hadn't known what to do, and he'd *really* hated that. It made him edgy. Restless.

It left him feeling grumpy and out of sorts, which annoyed him even further, since he'd built an entire military career on his composure. His ability to remain calm and unflappable no matter what.

Blue wasn't a big fan of the notion that a ghost from his past could careen over a mountain pass and lodge herself beneath his skin. And yet there was no denying Everly had done exactly that.

To say it bothered the hell out of him was an understatement.

He sprawled at his usual table in the corner of the Water's Edge Café, in the ragtag handful of brightly painted storefronts that constituted downtown Grizzly Harbor, trying to keep his mood off his face, because he didn't want to explain it to the other men at the table.

He trusted his brothers-in-arms with his life, but he also knew them. They would torture him endlessly over any and all perceived weaknesses—a favor he would have happily returned tenfold if the shoe had been on the other foot.

It had already been a long morning. He'd taken Everly into town on one of the skiffs they kept tied up at the docks in Fool's Cove. Isaac had long ago made arrangements with one of the largely seasonal so-called inns here in town for situations just like this one, so it hadn't been any trouble to settle his once-upon-a-time neighbor into one of the rooms, even at such a weird hour. He'd gone back home and grabbed a few hours of sleep himself, then had dragged himself to the 0700 daily community workout in the cabin down on the beach, which Isaac had converted into a stark, unwelcoming, dark box of pain that functioned as Alaska Force's gym.

Pain is growth, Isaac liked to bark out while they were all lifting impossibly heavy things, running like madmen up and down the steepest inclines out back, or doing entirely too many soul-killing burpees at the cold water's edge to allow any complaining. Or much breathing.

Because the truth about Isaac Gentry, Blue had learned over the past six months as much in the gym as in the field, was that the man was, at heart, a sadistic bastard. That was the only possible way an actual human—instead of, say, a cyborg—could stay in such fantastic shape outside active duty.

The daily workout wasn't mandatory. It wasn't boot camp, and there were no drill sergeants roaming around Fool's Cove, for which Blue was eternally grateful. But miss the 0700 sweat and a man could expect the entirety of Alaska Force up in his face.

Hard. Freaking. Pass.

After a typically brutal hour of suffering and struggle, which Isaac cheerfully claimed would make them all better men, because he was one hundred percent the demon from hell Griffin liked to call him in three or four glacially precise languages every morning, Blue and Templeton had transported Everly's rental car back into town. By boat, not that hair-raising suicide-by-mountain road he couldn't believe she'd managed to drive over.

Templeton had loped off to get an extra trail run in,

because he hadn't had enough abuse for the day, apparently. Blue had gone to get food. Now he just needed to drink enough of the rocket fuel masquerading as coffee in the Water's Edge Café to feel like himself again, or so he kept telling himself. He was well into his third cup, and so far, no luck. There was far too much Everly and her tearstained face messing around with his head, not to mention the feel of her arms beneath his hands when she'd catapulted herself at him.

Blue still didn't like the fact he'd *wanted* to let her crash into him. That he almost hadn't caught her, just so he could see how a ghost felt in his arms.

But this was definitely not the time to be thinking about things like that, because two of his Alaska Force brothers sat across from him in the deceptively cheerful restaurant, both as well trained in reading a man's secrets, no matter how hard he tried to keep them hidden, as Blue was himself. If not better.

"You get any more clarity on why your girl passed out like that?" Isaac asked, cupping his palms around the thick, sturdy coffee mug in front of him. It was huge and his fourth, but even the high-octane caffeine served here couldn't make the leader of Alaska Force jittery. As far as anyone knew, nothing could.

"Tired," Blue said with a shrug. "It's a long drive from Chicago."

"Not to mention over Hard-Ass Pass," Isaac agreed, though the look on his face was too studiously blank to be believable. As was his attempt at chitchat.

Still, Blue didn't really want to think about Everly up on that narrow, winding, eroded mountain pass. There was still snow and ice up there, even though it was the height of summer. This was Alaska. The mountains were as crotchety and randomly lethal as the bears. Not to mention all the locals.

And the fact that it bothered him that she'd put herself at risk like that made him even more irritated with himself.

Directly across the table from him, Jonas Crow—special ops designation still too highly classified to mention, though the way he hummed with barely leashed power offered a few clues if a man knew where to look—watched Blue balefully.

That was his usual expression. Today it looked more intense than normal.

"She's trouble," Jonas said, through the beard that made him look particularly ferocious, long and black and as grim as the expression he always wore.

"Because she's a woman or because she's the first person who's ever dared show up at our front door without going through the proper Internet channels to get herself an invitation?" Isaac asked. His mouth twitched behind the beard that, unlike Jonas's, made him seem more approachable and less fierce. Without the beard, he looked too much like what he was. A sharpened blade, ready to strike. With the beard, the unobservant might mistake him for a good ol' boy. "I agree, of course."

Blue glared at Jonas, who blended in maybe too easily with all the rest of the local Alaskan survivalists around here who lived out in the bush and made it into town only when it was necessary and the weather permitted. He was dressed all in camo, his black hair straight and long, and wearing the scowl he preferred during tourist season—on the off chance anyone visiting from the vast and distant south might look at his usual thunderclap expression and imagine he was cuddly. "You think everyone is trouble."

"That's because everyone *is* trouble." That Jonas could talk through a scowl so ferocious remained an enduring mystery, but he was good at defying expectations. "If I liked people, I'd live where they swarmed over everything like ants. Which is everywhere else, as far as I can tell."

"You think Kodiak, population maybe six thousand at a stretch, is clogged and crowded."

Jonas made a low sound that Blue thought was his version of a laugh. "I'm sure it would be a great place to live. If they lost about six thousand people."

Blue switched his glare to Isaac. "And you know better than to encourage his antisocial crap."

Isaac's laugh didn't require interpretation. "The difference between Jonas and me is that I like trouble."

Blue rubbed his hands over his face, feeling the particularly potent mix of tired and amped that he knew from long experience meant that he was bordering on too agitated for his own good. Or anyone else's.

Because he was tired, he told himself. Just tired, and the workout this morning had kicked his butt. It had nothing to do with a woman he barely remembered and the tears she'd wiped away right there in front of him, making him feel like the worst kind of jackass for letting her think he was going to let her wrestle with her situation alone.

Not that he owed her anything. His old life was gone. Until she'd shown up yesterday, he'd have said those days were forgotten, too.

The kid he'd been back then had died a long time ago.

But today that felt hollow.

"Did she tell you her deal?" Jonas asked. He was a ruthless man with a soldier's cool, harsh gaze, and his years out of the service hadn't tempered that at all. Blue doubted he was interested in *tempering*. The story he'd heard was that Isaac had tracked Jonas down out in the vast, impenetrable Alaskan interior and had found the other man living by his wits alone in a hut that had redefined rustic. And isolated. "Or did she sleep through that, too?"

The fact that Blue wanted to punch Jonas and/or demand he alter his tone when he talked about Everly was . . . not good. He did neither.

Instead, Blue relayed Everly's account of what had happened to her that night, point by point. Both Isaac and Jonas listened in intent silence as he talked, letting him get out all the details before they asked any questions.

"Do you believe her?" Jonas asked when he was done.

Blue nodded. "I do."

"You say you don't really know this girl. She could be the psycho the police think she is."

"I knew her when she was a kid." Blue shrugged. "But she doesn't feel crazy to me."

Jonas studied him as if he'd given something away. "Your call, brother," he muttered.

"What's your take on her story?" Isaac asked, cool and easy, like he knew Blue was entirely too tense. Blue ordered himself to relax.

"If it was one asswipe, I'd think it was an accident," Blue said after a moment and another attempt to clear his head with a swig of dark, rich coffee. "The roommate's boyfriend Everly didn't know about and a fight that got out of hand or something. Four separate asswipes sounds too organized to be a domestic squabble or even a visit from the local bookie gone wrong."

Isaac looked intrigued. "I'm not opposed to getting my Eliot Ness on with some gangsters, if that's the kind of 'organized' you mean."

"Because that usually ends well," Jonas said, rolling his eyes. "Most organized-crime idiots are known for making reasonable, rational decisions, like backing down when challenged."

"They don't have to be reasonable," Blue retorted. "They just have to leave Everly alone."

It wasn't until the words were out that he realized there was too much heat in them. Jonas sighed but said nothing. A minute later he pushed back from the table, muttered something about hitting the head, and stalked off toward the back of the café. Other people might throw out a good-bye, but not Jonas, who preferred to simply disappear at will.

Another moment or two chugged by. There was the familiar sound of a screen door opening and closing in the back of the restaurant—which meant Jonas was using his departure as a message, since he made noise only when he felt like it.

Blue met his leader's eyes blandly. "Don't say it."

"What am I going to say?" Isaac asked, sounding wounded and innocent, neither of which Blue thought he'd ever been in his life. "I don't think I've ever seen you play hero before. It's cute."

Blue made an anatomically impossible suggestion, politely enough, and Isaac laughed again. Louder. Longer.

"If you're going to keep disturbing the other customers like this, I'm going to need you to leave."

Blue looked away from Isaac to the woman who stood at their table then, making no attempt to conceal her usual impatient dislike of pretty much everything on earth—but especially of one Isaac Gentry.

Caradine Scott was the owner, only waitress, and head cook at the Water's Edge Café. Her cooking was unpretentious, sized for the appetites of big, tough men who worked with their hands out there in the unforgiving Alaskan climate, and so good that on busy summer afternoons when the ferry came in, there could be a line of tourists out the door and halfway down the street— assuming she didn't get annoyed and close the place down because she didn't feel like cooking that day.

The cheerful decor of the café—bright colors and cute drawings on the walls by local kids, mismatched mugs and plates to create a charmingly eccentric feel—was a lie. Or not necessarily a lie—if Blue was feeling more charitable—but certainly aspirational. Caradine was not in any way cheerful. She was the most prickly female Blue had ever met in his life, which was saying something in a state that celebrated a kind of independent stubbornness that made most Alaskans too much for folks from other, softer, more contained places—the places people here referred to as "outside."

Caradine cooked only what she wanted, when she wanted to cook it. She didn't have a menu, which meant you ate what you were served or she kicked you out. Today she was wearing her usual uniform of battered old jeans, a stained apron wrapped around her narrow hips, and a loose T-shirt that failed entirely to disguise the shape of her body or the fact that she kept herself in excellent shape. Her dark hair was pulled back in a messy ponytail, her fingernails bore chipped black polish, and she had a smudge of flour on one high cheekbone, though no one would dare point that out to her and potentially lose a finger and/or get banned.

"You have one other customer," Blue pointed out. Maybe with a touch of that edginess he was pretending he didn't feel eating at him. "And Ernie's deaf."

Ernie Tatlelik was deaf, half-blind, and of indeterminate age. Weathered enough to be eighty but spry enough to be in his fifties. None of which kept him from being the best fisherman in Grizzly Harbor—or the luckiest, depending on who was telling the story and how jealous they were of his latest catch.

More immediately relevant was the fact that he was sitting in the corner of the restaurant with his gaze trained out the window in front of him while he ate, like he expected the pier to get up and amble off into the wilderness. Blue doubted the old man had the slightest idea anyone else was in the café at all.

"Okay. If you keep disturbing *me*," Caradine amended, smirking the way she liked to do, "I'll ban you."

"You're not going to ban us," Isaac said then, sounding amused though he didn't quite look it. There was something too sharp in his gaze. "You like money too much and we're your best customers."

And then it was Blue's opportunity to read some faces, because everything shifted when Caradine looked at Isaac. The way it always did. Something dark and electric seethed in the air between them, but Isaac only smiled. As if he liked that kind of trouble, too.

Or wanted Caradine to think he did, anyway.

"It's a good thing you have such a high opinion of yourself, Gentry," Caradine said, her voice sweet. Which, given that she was about as sweet as a mouthful of the bitter coffee she brewed, was nothing short of alarming. "Someone should."

Blue could have given his friend and leader some crap about the way he watched Caradine walk away, but he didn't. Because he was just that much of a better person than Isaac was, he told himself piously.

Or, if he was more honest, because he didn't want to hear what Isaac might say in return if Blue jumped in and mentioned the thing no one ever mentioned. That being the mutual dislike that Blue thought Isaac and Caradine needed to work out in a locked room. As long as that locked room contained a very sturdy bed.

"I'm assuming you want to take point on this," Isaac said, as if there had been no interruption. "Since our un-invited guest is all yours."

Blue didn't take the bait and issue denials that would make the leader of Alaska Force howl with laughter. "I don't think we need a full tactical team. Not yet, anyway. No need to pull resources away from other projects. I'll do a little recon first."

"Your call." Isaac leaned back in his chair. "It could still be a domestic situation that got out of hand. Maybe the roommate had that jealous boyfriend after all, and maybe *he* has a few too many idiot frat-boy buddies. You could smack a few heads together and be done with it."

"Possible."

Blue realized he was tapping his fingers against the tabletop, an obvious outward sign of agitation, and not normally the sort of thing he let betray him. He stopped, but he knew it was too late. There was no way Isaac hadn't clocked it. He figured it was his continuing silence on the subject of Caradine that got him a measure of grace in return, because Isaac didn't say anything.

Blue took that as the gift it was. "I'm not sure a bunch of drunk frat boys could engineer a cleanup at all, or in such a short span of time. And even if they tried, I don't think they'd manage to fool the Chicago PD."

Isaac studied him for a minute, and Blue braced himself—while trying to look as if maybe he was actually boneless. In the six months he'd lived here, working with Isaac and the rest, going on their particular missions to solve the kind of problems only Alaska Force could, he'd come to respect Isaac in much the same way he'd respected his commanding officers back in the SEAL teams. But the way Isaac was looking at him now had nothing to do with mission directives. This was personal.

"I thought you barely knew this woman," he said. Mildly enough.

"How well do you know all the kids who grew up with you?" Blue asked. Too defensively. He tried to ratchet that back. "The ones you haven't seen since you were seventeen? That's how well I know her, which is not at all."

"Have you looked around Grizzly Harbor? There are maybe a hundred people here once the weather turns." Isaac shook his head. "I know them all, dumbass. Every last one."

"Everly was a kid when I left. I know who she is— I don't know her. And I'm getting tired of repeating myself."

Blue heard his own voice and barely managed to keep from cringing. That gruff, dismissive tone that he didn't even believe himself. But whatever Isaac might have said to that, and it looked like he had a list or two, he never got the chance. Because the door opened at the front of the café, and Everly herself walked in.

And whatever lies Blue had been telling himself about what had happened on that porch—that a woman who was basically a stranger hadn't gotten to him, that he didn't care what happened to Everly personally, that this was just another mission like all the others he'd run in his career—he couldn't pretend that he didn't feel the kick of attraction when she appeared. As if she'd lobbed a grenade at him and he'd been stupid enough to catch it and hold on tight.

Terrific.

She'd twisted her strawberry blond hair into a knot on the back of her head, messy and haphazard, and it shouldn't have made him want to smile. She was wearing the same skinny jeans that were slightly too baggy and the same completely pointless shoes, but she'd traded the T-shirt and jacket for a long-sleeved top that looked like the kind of performance wool hikers wore, reminding Blue that summer in Alaska did a pretty good impression of a moody fall day down south. Her green eyes were sleepy as she looked around, but they seemed to snap with awareness when she saw him.

Just like he did.

Damn it.

Six

"Oh," Everly said, coming to a stop as the café door slammed shut behind her. Her gaze was on Blue, and it was like he could feel it. Like it was her fingers on him, not her eyes. "Hi."

And then her ears did that thing that had been driving him crazy last night, turning a little red along the tips. Blue didn't understand how he was expected to get any work done under conditions like this. He'd never met a woman who blushed as much as she did. He didn't know anyone *could* blush as much as she did.

It fascinated him.

He knew it should have irritated him. She was like a puppy, wide-eyed and beaming her innocence all over the place. Blue liked dogs, like Isaac's entirely too intelligent dog, Horatio, who was waiting outside for him right now, keeping watch over the sleepy summer streets. Blue also liked women who looked like Everly, for that matter, especially all soft and sleepy, like she wasn't fully out of her bed—an image he didn't need in his head.

But he knew that, sooner or later, she was going to look at him like he'd kicked her.

Sooner rather than later, if he had to guess. That was who he was. Women—and freaking dogs—needed consistency. A man who stuck around and gave them what they wanted.

That had never been and was never going to be Blue. He hadn't gone home since he was seventeen. He wasn't a man who stuck.

Trouble was, at the moment he couldn't seem to care about all the ways he'd inevitably disappoint her. Not when she was still looking at him like she expected him to jump up from the table, climb on up into the sky, and do the sun's job for a while.

Hell, he wanted to. That was the craziest part.

She walked over to stand at the end of their table, glanced at Blue and then away in a dark-lightning sort of way he couldn't read, and aimed a polite smile at Isaac.

"I think I met you yesterday," she said, and maybe only Blue heard that leftover hint of sleep and a few tears in her voice. Or possibly only Blue had such an intense reaction to it. *Settle down,* he growled at himself. She was here for his skills, not his personal entertainment. "But I'm afraid everything was a bit of a blur."

"Isaac Gentry," Isaac said, grinning back at her, looking amiable and charming the way he always did when he turned it on.

He extended his hand. Blue watched as Everly took it,

shook it, and then dropped it. And that tiny bit of contact still wasn't over fast enough for Blue's peace of mind, given the way women usually got silly at the very sight of Isaac and that smile of his.

Everly nodded toward the plate Jonas had cleared and the coffee he'd barely touched. "Is someone sitting with you?"

"Oh, that's just Jonas," Isaac said, still grinning like he was made of nothing more frightening than local honey. "He's like our own personal ghost. He comes. He goes. You never can tell what he'll do or where he'll turn up."

"So more of a friendly ghost, then," Everly said, and her smile warmed a bit, getting less polite and a little more real. "You know what I mean. More charming antics, less blood and fear."

"I wouldn't try to conduct a séance with him," Isaac advised her with a hint of a drawl for good measure. Blue wanted to kick him. And didn't much like himself for the urge. "He probably wouldn't take that well. Also, he's heavily armed."

When she laughed at that, Blue figured he was getting a glimpse of the real Everly. The Everly she'd been before that night in her apartment. The one she'd be again when he did what he did and cleaned up the mess that had dimmed that smile of hers. Made her cry. Made her shake the way she had out on the porch at the cabin when she'd thought he didn't see, and made her come all this way to seek him out in the first place.

Not, of course, that he planned to stick around to see her bloom again. He wasn't that guy. He fixed things, handled the trouble, and then left. That was what he was good at. That was what he knew.

It's all you've ever done, a strange voice deep inside him chimed in. He shoved it aside before he was tempted to imagine it sounded far too much like his stepfather, Ron.

Because like hell was he wasting any brain cells remembering that guy.

Everly sat down at the table, gingerly. She didn't take Jonas's abandoned chair, opting instead for the one next to Blue. He pushed back and told himself it was so he could look at her directly. Not because he could smell the soap she'd used in her morning shower, making her skin smell almost unbearably fresh.

"Are you sore?" he asked her.

When she shot him an odd look, he realized that had come out a little abrupt. And more than a little weird.

"You're holding yourself like you're stiff," he muttered darkly.

He did not look across the table at Isaac.

"I am stiff, actually," Everly said, as if the fact he'd noticed something so obvious surprised her. She tried that smile again, but it didn't look as easy as before. "I guess that happens when you drive for days on end."

"There are hot springs here in town," Blue told her. He contemplated stabbing himself with his own fork to . . . Just. Stop. Talking. But didn't. "A nice bathhouse with women's hours, if you want a soak. It might help."

Everly was much too close to him. She smelled like soap and shampoo, and her eyes were the green of all the pine trees that stood proud on the mountainside and helped him breathe, most days.

"Thank you," she said quietly. As if something was

happening between them and she could sense it as well as he could. "Maybe I will."

"What do you think of Grizzly Harbor so far?" Isaac asked Everly then, dispelling whatever weird hush had taken over the table. Thank God. Blue was sometimes tempted to forget how good Isaac was at this. Exactly this. Putting on this assumed identity he cloaked himself in so well when he moved among regular people.

Affable. Charming. As if he were nothing more than an easygoing, friendly, approachable local tour guide who was lazy and relaxed and usually funny, and who just happened to be among the deadliest men on earth.

"Isaac grew up here," Blue told her.

"So be very careful what you say next," Isaac said with another easy laugh. "I might take it personally. My family's been here since the eighteen hundreds."

"I've never been to Alaska before," Everly said, smiling again. "Is it all like Grizzly Harbor? So . . ." She broke off, as if she couldn't find the right word. "I'll admit I've never seen anything quite like it."

"And you won't," Isaac agreed happily. So happily, like he wanted nothing more than to chitchat about sightseeing and local history forever. "There's a reason people come to Alaska and never leave. That's basically the story of the Gentry family right there."

"When's the last time you ate?" Blue asked Everly. And instantly regretted it.

Isaac gazed at him in a kind of amazement that boded all kinds of ill. Blue could already hear the crap-ton of BS he was going to get about this. In the gym. On missions. For the rest of his time in Alaska Force. It was inevitable. He'd just outed himself as some kind of cozy, protective den mother, for God's sake.

If it had been anyone else, he'd have led the BS brigade himself.

"I . . . I don't know," Everly replied after a moment, blinking as if she were confused.

She couldn't possibly be as confused as Blue, who had until this moment imagined himself about as nurturing as a hungry mountain lion stalking its prey, but that didn't change the fact that Everly looked pale and a few shades too skinny.

"If you don't want to keep passing out," Blue growled, "you'd better eat. Unless you like waking up in strange places with no memory of how you got there."

Everly's delicate brows rose. "Thanks, Dad," she said, with a whole lot more calm than he was currently displaying, and that mildly sarcastic slap besides. But if she thought she could shame him, she was in for a big surprise. "As a matter of fact, I'm starving."

Blue set his jaw, ignored the expression of pure, unadulterated glee on Isaac's face, and lifted his hand to get Caradine scowling in his direction from her usual place on a stool behind the counter, where she liked to hover like a storm cloud when she wasn't cooking.

"Pay no mind to this one's attitude," Isaac drawled as Caradine stomped over. "Her bark is worse than her bite. Loud, sure. But harmless."

Caradine crossed her arms and smirked when she reached the table, but didn't lower herself to snipe back at Isaac. Which Blue thought was a deliberate slap all the same.

But if Everly was wise to the undercurrents zapping back and forth between those two, she didn't show it.

"Can I see a menu?" she asked.

"There are no menus," Caradine replied. Her dark brows rose. "I told you that yesterday."

"Oh. I thought you were just . . . saying that."

"There are two things I never do," Caradine said, sounding almost friendly. For her. "Waste my breath or suffer fools."

Blue didn't know what he'd expected, but it wasn't the grin that spread over Everly's face. She folded her hands on the table and aimed it straight at Caradine.

"I'm not much for fools," she told the other woman. "Or suffering of any kind. I haven't eaten anything in days but stale trail mix from a gas station, entirely too many Skittles, and energy bars that taste like sawdust. I want something—anything—delicious."

"You city girls like all that quinoa and egg whites and whatever else," Caradine replied. "Skinny latte surprise, milk wrenched from poor, unsuspecting nuts, and a side helping of self-hatred, as I recall. I don't serve that."

"I like food," Everly told her solemnly. "A lot of it. Preferably with a whole lot of butter."

Caradine didn't blink. Her smirk reappeared—except Blue thought that maybe it was an actual smile. As impossible as that seemed.

"Food I can do," she said.

"Is it that hard to be nice?" Isaac asked her, and he still sounded lazy, though Blue thought even Everly could hear the sharper edge beneath it.

"I don't respond well to demands," Caradine replied sweetly. "You of all people should know that, Isaac."

And then she sauntered away, leaving Blue no choice but to pretend he hadn't heard a thing, because he valued his own neck, thank you.

Later, when Everly had eaten her fill of the meal Caradine had prepared for her and Isaac had taken off, possibly because his easygoing act was beginning to chafe, Blue threw some money on the table and ushered Everly into the newly bright morning.

The streets in Grizzly Harbor were different from streets in other places, and not only because they weren't really streets so much as dirt paths here and boardwalks there, with a fishing village jumbled all around. Everything was built right on top of each other, because no one wanted a long walk from the general store to the bar once winter hit. Blue remembered his first take of this town. How small it had seemed to him. How alien.

And in six short months it had come to feel more like home than any other place he'd lived, including that house across the street from Everly way back when.

"It's different here," he said. "From Chicago."

He felt stilted. Awkward, almost, which was enough to horrify him down into his bones. Blue did not do *awkward*. He did not do *stilted*. That was the kind of thing that could get a man killed. The only form of social anxiety Blue tolerated in himself was the occasional need for particularly strong whiskey to deal with the inevitable nonsense some people liked to spew. Particularly if the people in question were . . . him. It didn't change the nonsense into anything palatable, of course. Whiskey just made it go down easier.

It was barely eleven a.m. and he was already jonesing for a drink. Because Everly Campbell made him feel what he imagined shy felt like. Something like . . . silly.

He was going to have to excise that, with his own fingers if necessary, because it was unacceptable.

Luckily, Everly really didn't seem to notice that he'd appalled himself into a shocked silence. She was too busy looking around at the village, down the narrow streets that all led to the docks, one way or another. At the last of the morning fog that still clung to the mountains across the sound but had already eased its grip on the harbor. At the bright blue of the inn where he'd stashed her last night and the peeling yellow of the post office across the way.

Grizzly Harbor had been considered a sacred site by native Alaskans thousands of years before the Russians had turned up. Then the American prospectors had come, like Isaac's ancestors, swarming up from Seattle and San Francisco to see if they could claim their share of gold from the Yukon—and when they couldn't, because most of them never found much of anything except hardship and endless winter, they'd settled in out-of-the-way, relatively safe places like this one. The village was a jumble of color, bright against the habitually gray Alaskan skies. A red house here, a shocking coral or green one there, and it all gleamed in the bit of midday sunshine that lit up the protected cove.

"It looks like a postcard." Everly tucked a loose strand of her strawberry blond hair back behind her ear, to keep the wind from playing with it, though it wasn't only the wind that wanted to. "I can't tell you how nice it is to walk around a postcard for a change. For one thing, no-body's lurking behind every tree. Watching me."

"I know every single person on the street right now," Blue told her. He held her gaze, and willed her to trust him. He didn't ask himself why he needed that. He told himself he wanted it, that it would make the job he was about to do a lot easier, but it didn't feel like *want*. It felt a whole lot more raw. A lot more like *need*. "The next ferry won't show up until Friday. Most of the tourists who came in with you yesterday are out whale watching or fishing or hiking along the shore. I saw one guy down near the general store with about seventeen pounds of camera equipment strapped to his back, wrestling with a trail map. But that's the only stranger anywhere near you at the moment. I think you're safe."

"How do you know all that?" Everly looked startled. She cast a quick look around them, down toward the tourist and his cameras, then returned her attention to Blue. "I mean, I know this is what you do, but I didn't even see you look."

"I always look." He felt himself smile. Barely. "You're not supposed to see me doing it."

He didn't tell her that it was automatic. A survival mechanism, born of all those years when the only things that stood between him and certain disaster were the skills ingrained so deeply he didn't have to think about them. Now that kind of vigilance was like a sec-ond skin.

"I'm amazed at the detail. The camera equipment *and* the trail map."

"I can identify a trail map. And a camera. And a tour-ist who's inevitably going to fall in the water, need to get fished out, and ruin all his brand-spanking-new equipment anyway."

"I'm not questioning you," she said softly, and this time, that real smile of hers was all for him. "I'm thanking you."

Blue realized, abruptly, that he was just standing there. Hanging around the street outside the café as if this were a normal conversation. Some small talk and a pretty smile. Things Blue adamantly did not partake of, ever. He wasn't a casual man. He never had been.

He didn't know what it was about Everly that made him feel new to himself. He knew only that he didn't like it. He was a SEAL, for God's sake. He didn't let anything throw him, and certainly not a *smile*.

He jerked his chin so she would follow him and set off down the winding street, up on the boardwalk, and then back down, aware of every step she took behind him in those silly shoes. But to her credit, she didn't complain. She didn't ask him to slow down or adjust his stride. She followed right behind him, gamely enough, until he reached the place down by the pier where he'd parked her rental.

"Oh." Everly blinked at the car, then at him. "Don't tell me you drove back over that terrible mountain." She shuddered, and he didn't think it was for show. "It was pretty terrifying up there."

"Yeah, about that." He didn't understand why he sounded so flat. So pissed. "Never, ever do something so stupid again."

He expected her to get her back up at that. No one liked being called stupid, especially when it was true.

But Everly didn't look offended. If anything, she

looked rueful, and that was the trouble with her. He couldn't predict a single thing she did. He'd been completely wrong about everything so far, and it was driving him crazy.

"It was stupid," she agreed, because of course she had to make it impossible to dislike her or even stay rightfully furious with her. "*So* stupid. But by the time I realized exactly how stupid it was—and how close to death I was—by which I mean, like, a single half centimeter between me and a sheer drop of I don't even know how far . . ." She shook her head, blowing out a breath while she did it. "I didn't have any choice but to keep going. Because I figured the only thing more stupid than driving over that mountain in the first place was trying to reverse my way back off of it."

"You know what they call that road?"

"Yes. As you pointed out yesterday, I did in fact consult a map. Hardy's Pass. Elevation, way too freaking high, and road conditions, not awesome."

"That's the official name. Everyone around here calls it Hard-Ass Pass. Because only a hard-ass goes up that mountain and makes it back down the other side." Before he could think better of it, or even really think it through, Blue reached out and dealt with that same errant chunk of hair that the wind kept toying with. He pretended he didn't feel the way she went still when his fingers grazed that sweet spot behind her ear. The same way he pretended he didn't feel a damn thing himself. "So I guess that makes you a hard-ass, little girl."

She smiled as if she hadn't shaken before him on an eerily lit porch, or shown him her tears. As if her ears and neck weren't flushed that telltale red. As if she didn't feel that touch the way he did, like an ache.

He reminded himself of that bike, pink and white streamers flapping everywhere. The sheltered kid she'd been back then. But it didn't help. Instead, it made everything in him seem to hum in a kind of recognition he didn't want to acknowledge.

But Everly was smiling at him.

"I can't really tell—because there's a whole growly superhero thing going on, which is very Batman, and of course there's the continued use of 'little girl' in a way that I really don't think is all that appropriate—but I *think* that was a compliment."

"Growly?" He didn't touch her again, and thought that deserved a commendation or two. "*Batman?*"

"I try to like Superman," Everly said in a rush, as if it were a confession, and he watched with that same fascination as another bright red flush spread over her cheeks. "I try and I try, but he's just so boring. He does good for no particular reason and is so bland he can completely disguise himself with a pair of glasses. . . ." She let out a small sigh. "I guess I've always liked Batman better."

"I wouldn't have figured you for a comic book fan. You're too . . ."

"Female?" Everly supplied. A bit tartly.

"Fancy." He raised his brows at her. "Too much of a city girl."

"I like Chicago a lot," Everly told him, and when she smiled this time, he found his gaze drawn to the tiny dent in one of her cheeks. He wanted to taste it. He didn't know how he held himself back. "But my favorite city, obviously, is Gotham."

Blue knew full well they had things to do. Important things. He'd decided to take Everly and her situation on, and that meant he had problems to solve. Lurking asswipes to locate and discourage. A police force to handle and a potential crime scene to investigate in his own way.

But instead, all he could seem to do was stand around on a cool summer morning talking about the local flavor and comic books he hadn't read since high school.

None of this made sense. None of this was who he was.

He didn't get to meet-cute and live her kind of life. He didn't get to go back in time and find a white picket fence to wrap himself in. He wasn't innocent. Maybe he never had been.

Blue made himself take a step back from her, and hated the fact that putting space between them practically broadcast his own weaknesses. He might as well tell the whole town that he couldn't control himself.

Or, worse, that he was entirely too tempted to forget himself.

"Take everything you need out of your car," he told her, his voice too gruff.

"I got my bag last night." Everly gazed back at him, but her green eyes were unreadable. If she'd noticed that he'd touched her and then jumped away like a kid who didn't know his own mind, she didn't show it.

Which, perversely, pissed Blue off.

"Is that everything?"

She studied his face for a moment. "Does it matter? We'll have days and days and days to figure out what's in the car. And whether or not you want to throw it out into the wilds of the Yukon rather than look at it one moment more, which I've already considered. About fifty times a day."

"We're not driving."

"What? What do you mean?"

"Exactly what I said. We're not taking a week to drive the length of Canada, for God's sake. I don't know how you survived it one way. All that sitting would drive me crazy."

"I don't want to brag, but I'm actually really good at sitting. Like Olympic level."

"Are you trying to be cute?"

She made a grand gesture with one hand. "It's a simple truth you can do with as you will."

As if she realized she was babbling, a hint of red appeared on the tips of her ears. Again. There was so much blushing, it surprised him she didn't go up in flames.

Then again, it also surprised him that he didn't.

"Of course," she was saying, "it's a rental car. I have to actually return it. I'm pretty sure it's in the contract I signed."

"We'll take care of your car. You don't need to worry about it."

"But—"

"This is why you came all the way here, Everly," he said patiently. Or maybe not all that patiently, he thought, when her eyes narrowed. "These are the kinds of details you hire people like us to take care of."

She stood straighter then, and the last hint of her smile disappeared from her lips. "Right. We need to talk about what hiring you means."

"It means I'm going to solve your problem. The end."

"You and all your friends look too scarily capable, let's just say, to be cheap. And there's the whole Fortress of Doom on the back side of an impossible-to-reach island where there's no running water but there is, notably, abundant Wi-Fi."

He hated that she made his mouth twitch despite himself. "We have running water. In some cabins."

They also had what Griffin liked to call *all that spy shit*, but there was no need to get into that.

"My point is that I have some savings that my grandmother—"

"I'm not taking your money." He was offended she even suggested it.

"Of course I'm paying you," she retorted, standing even straighter, like she imagined she could go toe-to-toe with him. "As you pointed out, you barely know me. We grew up on the same street, that's all. It never occurred to me that you would do anything for me for free, nor should you. My grandmother—"

"I'm not going to argue about this," he told her. In a tone of voice that had been known to quiet treacherous uprisings and unruly dissidents alike. He wasn't as shocked as he should have been that it had no discernible effect on Everly. "It's not happening. I don't want to hear about your grandmother again."

"Blue. Really. I want—"

"If you have anything left in this car, you need to get it." His voice was calm now, and so was he, because this was the mission. She was the mission. He didn't want to examine what was happening to him around her and all that blushing and that smile that was wrecking him, but none of that mattered. Because *this* was what he did. He needed to focus on that. "We'll go back to the inn and get whatever you left there. And then we're hitting the road."

"Hitting the road?" she echoed. "What road?"

"It's commonly known as the Alaskan Marine Highway. You took the ferry over it already. But we're going to fly."

She digested that. "You have your own plane?"

"This is Alaska, sweetheart. Everybody has a plane."

"Everybody." It was a challenge. "That old guy in the restaurant has a plane, too?"

"Ernie is a bush pilot, among other things," Blue told her. Maybe with too much satisfaction. "Some places, there are no roads at all, not even what passes for a street here in Grizzly Harbor. People use boats to get to town and ride ATVs in the bush. If someone needs to go any farther than that, they use a plane." He nodded at the harbor spread out before them, the boats bobbing on their moorings, and the unforgiving white-capped mountain peaks all around. And everywhere else, in all directions, the seething summer ocean. "In case you haven't noticed, this is the Last Frontier."

Everly looked like she had more to say, but when he nodded toward her car again, more insistently this time, she went over to it, opened the hatchback, and started rifling through it. When all was said and done, she threw her things into a bag on the backseat, and then looked like she wanted to object when he took it from her.

And that was when he got it. The thing that was so different about Everly Campbell.

She didn't seem the least bit afraid of him.

It spun his head around a little, Blue was man enough to admit. At least to himself.

He was used to being . . . problematic. Women who enjoyed a taste of danger were always drawn to him, but they had their own issues, and he could usually see that particular avidness coming at him from a mile away. That wasn't how Everly looked at him.

Everly had called him a hero. She looked at him as if he were still that boy he'd been a million years ago. It was funny, the things he remembered when he'd actively been trying to erase that entire part of his life for years now. That house. The people in it. The one person—his father, who had died when Blue was ten—who had not been in it. He'd worked so hard to block all of that out.

But he remembered this. Everly. Her wide green eyes, fixed on him with perfect, total trust.

She'd looked at him back then when she couldn't have known better. It was worse now, because she should have realized who and what he was.

But she showed no fear. No wariness, even. Just that same solemn certainty he was surprised to realize he remembered, as if she had no doubt at all that he could do exactly what he said he would. As if he could do anything.

She made him want to try.

And that, he knew, was begging for disaster.

Because this was just a regular Tuesday for him, but only the most dire circumstance—witnessing a murder, possibly being targeted to be next—could have brought Everly here to find him. While she'd slept last night, before they'd had their talk on the porch of her cabin, he'd dug into her.

And the thing about Everly was, she was normal. Happily normal, according to all the available evidence he'd accessed on the Internet and through Alaska Force's more back-channel means. Her mother and brother were doctors, just as she'd said. Her father had recently retired after teaching biology at the university level for most of his life. Everly had gone to college at a place that touted itself as the Harvard of the Midwest and then had built herself a nice, safe life in Chicago. Roommates had come and gone, but there had been no glaring incidents with any of them aside from the usual squabbles over housekeeping. Landlords wrote good reviews about her, and employers followed suit. She'd had a couple of equally normal-seeming boyfriends, but nothing serious. Her social media accounts were filled with pictures of friends, the occasional trip or outing somewhere exotic, and the usual selfies—though he noted that wasn't something she did too often, either.

She was just . . . normal. Completely and totally normal, as far as he could tell.

And for a man like him, that was as much a temptation as it was forbidden.

Because *normal* meant innocent. Untouched. Unsullied.

Normal meant whole. No blood on her hands, nothing tainted and twisted, or charred in the place where real people kept their hearts.

It wasn't an accident that Blue lived out here, far away from normal people and their quiet, contented little lives. There was a reason he surrounded himself with men just like him, savage to the bone. Men who still lived by strict codes of honor and still tried to do the only thing they were good at, because that was the only way to survive with the kind of blood they had on their hands.

The kind he had on his.

Blue had always handled what needs he couldn't repress or ignore with the adrenaline junkies, the women who wanted him precisely because of the danger he represented. Maybe that was empty, but no one got hurt.

He'd decided a long time ago that he was done hurting anyone, if he could help it.

It had never occurred to him that he would ever meet a woman who would tempt him to break his own rules.

"You've gone very quiet," Everly said. She looked slightly apprehensive as she gazed up at him. "That doesn't mean you're changing your mind."

She said it like it was a statement, but he heard the question there, hanging in the air.

"I'm not going to change my mind," Blue said shortly, though he knew he should. That if he was even half the man he'd always imagined he was, he'd step away from this particular temptation right here, right now. He'd turn her over to Templeton, Isaac, even Jonas. One of his brothers could handle this, and her, without breaking a sweat.

And, he had to believe, without that unwelcome thing inside him that kept pushing him to act like someone else.

Someone undamaged. Someone unbroken and fit for human interaction, when he knew better.

God, did he know better.

There was a kind of knowledge in her gaze then, and it hit him much too hard, because she shouldn't have been able to read him. She shouldn't have been unafraid of him. She should have cowered a bit. Cried more.

She should have done *something* to make herself less tempting.

"You don't look sure."

"Everly." Blue gritted her name out like it hurt. Because it did, and he didn't know what to do about that, either. "I'm sure."

And that, at least was true. He was sure all right.

That he was boned.

Seven

Chicago had changed in the week she'd been away.

Everly told herself it was the long flight. Or, more likely, the man who'd lounged across from her in the biggest of the plane's three different seating areas, apparently deeply engrossed in whatever he was reading on that tablet of his. Or studying the drawings she'd made of the men in her apartment that night and the ones she'd seen following her on the street. Or conducting almost laughably laconic mobile phone conversations that consisted of him saying single words like *affirmative* repeatedly.

She'd wanted to focus on the fact that she was on a private jet flown by one of the mysterious Alaska Force men, but didn't. Instead of marveling at her surroundings, she'd found herself fixating on that strange, breathless moment down at the pier in Grizzly Harbor when Blue had tucked a bit of her hair behind her ear.

Here, now, in the passenger seat of the SUV that had been waiting for them when they'd landed on an airfield outside Chicago, Everly fought off a shiver. Again. Just thinking about that brush of his fingers—

Her inner voice was stern, as if that might make a difference. *You need to get a hold of yourself.*

Not that she'd paid much attention to her inner voice so far.

Beside her, Blue navigated his way through the usual Chicago traffic as if he drove through congested major cities every day. Everly knew perfectly well the only congestion back in Grizzly Harbor was likely to come from the moose population, and yet Blue didn't seem to be the least bit bothered. He had one hand hooked over the steering wheel, while the rest of his big, rangy body somehow took up twice the room it should have. She had to physically restrain herself from pressing against the passenger door, because she didn't want him to have even the slightest inkling of the effect he had on her.

She didn't want to admit it to herself.

And if she didn't keep herself under control, she was afraid she would give in to the temptation to press herself against one of his absurdly sculpted arms. It was shown to entirely too much perfection in the T-shirt he wore, which strained to handle his biceps at all, and his forearm was a thing of such intense masculine perfection that Everly wasn't sure how she was supposed to *breathe* with it *right there*. It was safer to sit carefully and quietly still. It was better to stare straight ahead, out the front of the vehicle, at the city all around them, gleaming steel and stone in the last of the summer evening.

Everly had always considered Chicago her home, even

before she'd lived within the city proper. She'd spent her childhood and all her college years dreaming of moving here, and she'd made her dreams a reality the minute she'd graduated. But tonight it felt too big. Anonymous and threatening as it loomed above them. Blue inched his way into her neighborhood, and instead of feeling welcomed back or at home at last, she thought there was too much concrete. Everywhere she looked. Too many people jostling for space in the streets, on the sidewalks, and who knew how many of them were out to get her? It was hot and crowded and vaguely sinister. It made her feel as if there were a stone pressing down on her chest, forcing the air from her lungs. Crushing her bones where she sat.

She tried to shake it off.

After all, it had been a long day. They'd been up and chatting on a strangely lit Alaskan porch at one in the morning. Just about twelve hours later they'd taken a seaplane on a quick, beautiful jump from Grizzly Harbor to Juneau, where Alaska Force's private jet had been gassed up and waiting for them.

"Stop gawking," Blue had ordered her in that clipped, hard tone of voice he liked so much, as if he were her commanding officer.

His military background was why she'd sought him out. But it was a stark change from the way he'd talked to her as if they were some kind of almost-friends, there on the streets of pretty-as-a-postcard Grizzly Harbor. At first she'd told herself she'd imagined the change in him. That odd way he'd talked to her in the café and on the street, as if he were worried about her. Her personally, not just her as his next job. She'd lectured herself extensively that she was delirious and still exhausted and *in Alaska*, so of course she was hallucinating things like even the slightest little bit of softening in the hardest man she'd ever known.

But then, after she'd gathered her things from the adorably cozy Blue Bear Inn and had tried to relax in the alarmingly tiny seaplane that was flown by yet another one of Blue's frighteningly competent ex-military friends, she'd changed her mind. It was something about the deliberately curt way Blue spoke to her. Not rude. Not mean.

But as if he'd gone too far before and was dialing himself back.

She'd decided that she hadn't imagined anything after all.

Maybe that was why she'd grinned at him so openly, standing there on a chilly tarmac in Juneau with only the ever-present mountains as witness.

"I thought the whole point of having a private jet was so the unwashed masses would gawk," she'd said.

That gleam in his dark gaze that she was starting to crave too much had gotten brighter then. His hard lips had hinted at a curve, there on that impossibly strong jaw he still hadn't bothered to shave. It was her curse that she liked it that way. She liked *him*.

"You can't fly commercial if you want to conduct missions on any kind of timetable."

She'd nodded sagely. "And also, no one gawks at you if you arrive late from a layover in Cincinnati. Because that makes you one of the unwashed masses yourself."

"There's a lot of *unwashed*, suddenly. Is this your way of trying to tell me you didn't shower today?"

Everly had only smiled wider. "I showered. But someday I'm going to have to go back to Grizzly Harbor and try those hot springs."

Blue had looked at her for a moment that had gone on too long. Lifetimes, maybe, though it was possible only she had felt it that way. And the longer he'd looked at her, the less his eyes had gleamed in that way she liked.

"Are you planning to get in more trouble?" he asked, in a too-mild tone that Everly hadn't really cared for.

But she'd answered him anyway. "Obviously, if I survive this, I plan to get in no trouble of any kind ever again."

His mouth had twisted then, but it wasn't a smile. "Then why would you come back to Grizzly Harbor?"

She'd spent the first few hours of their plane ride turning that one over and over in her head when she wasn't reliving those odd, hushed moments near the pier—and spent the last few hours beating herself up for being such an idiot.

Maybe it was only natural to try to make this whole thing into something it wasn't. Maybe she wasn't so much an idiot as a very scared woman hoping like hell that Blue could really do the things she thought he could. The things she desperately needed him to do when they got back to Chicago.

But she had to remember that this was nothing but a job to him. Another mission, that was all. A favor he was doing her because they'd grown up on the same street, and nothing more.

It was disheartening—or maybe the word she was looking for was *crazy*—how hard that seemed to be for her to remember.

"Do cities make you feel claustrophobic?" she asked Blue as they lurched along in traffic, slowly making their way toward her apartment building.

He made a low noise. Maybe it was a laugh.

"I don't get claustrophobic. I was a SEAL, Everly. Not a great career choice if you get claustrophobic."

Everly had never been particularly claustrophobic herself. But that was what it felt like, returning to Chicago tonight. Driving back into her life, which had felt cheerful and good, for the most part, before that night a month ago. Now everything she'd built here seemed like a nightmare. When they passed her favorite coffee shop, the one she'd stopped at every morning on her way to work for years, it was like an unseen hand wrapped around her ribs and squeezed her tight.

The closer they got to her apartment, the harder and tighter that hand felt.

Then again, she thought when they pulled up in front of her building, maybe it wasn't claustrophobia at all. Maybe it was simpler than that.

Maybe it was plain old terror, sickening and syrupy, rushing back in after the brief vacation she'd had from it in Alaska. Since the moment she'd slammed on the brakes in her rental wagon because she'd recognized the man standing there outside the lodge in Fool's Cove.

She snuck a look—or three—at him as he pulled up in front of her building and parked there, tossing something on the dashboard that looked a lot like a parking pass that police might use. Not that she knew too much about Chicago parking passes without a car of her own.

Blue didn't seem to notice the way she kept looking at

him, as if she expected him to disappear at any moment. He swung out of his seat, slamming his door behind him. By the time Everly unfastened her seat belt and opened her own door, he was there, their bags slung over his broad shoulders as if they weighed nothing at all.

She figured with shoulders like that, he could carry their bags, the SUV, and her without breaking a sweat.

"Into the building fast, head down, no looking around," he told her.

It didn't occur to her to disobey him. Not when he sounded so serious. Not when his gaze never met hers because he was looking to the right and left as if he were sweeping the street, looking for those men who had stalked her. Not when she was still caught in the grip of that terrible fear she'd somehow forgotten about while in Alaska.

Of course she hadn't really *forgotten* it. But she'd . . . put it on hold. And she couldn't say she cared for the way it rolled back in so easily, flattening her, as if it were making up for lost time.

She ducked her head down and sprinted for her front door, a desperate, itchy kind of panic rippling down the length of her spine as she moved. As if she had a target drawn all over her back. As if she could *feel* one of those creepy goons taking aim—

Everly was panting when she pushed through the double sets of doors, into the small lobby that held nothing but tenant mailboxes and a stack of those old paper phone books no one ever used anymore.

"You can check your mail later," Blue said gruffly from behind her.

Right behind her, which made the hair on the back of

her neck stand on end. Because who could imagine that a man that big could move so quietly? Everly couldn't really imagine it and she was experiencing it.

But she didn't say anything. She just nodded and pushed on to the elevator. Despite the grand claims the landlord had made in the rental listing about the *boutique elevator* here, as if that were a perk, it was usually easier to jog up the stairs instead. Tonight the old, creaking thing seemed to take even longer than usual, and Everly didn't know what she was supposed to *do* while they waited for it. Talk? Not talk? Stare grimly ahead the way Blue was doing? Pretend she was perfectly at ease with a brooding commando at her back?

She was ready to sob openly in relief when the elevator finally clattered to a stop before them. Happily, she contained herself as she stepped inside, and then had to stand there while Blue followed her, crowding into what little space was left. And he was so huge and dangerous that she didn't really know what to do with herself except try to keep from gasping for air.

Or doing something much worse, like throwing herself at him again.

Obviously she couldn't let herself do that. Everly stared straight ahead instead. She pretended she couldn't really see him. That she was all alone in the antique elevator. She stared at the arrow that inched from one floor to the next and willed the elevator to move already.

It took forever to rise a single floor. Everly tried to think about something else. Anything other than the fact that she kept finding herself too close to this man, torn between wanting to touch him and knowing that would be . . . very, very bad.

At the moment, she couldn't remember why, exactly.

She breathed in, then out. The fact was, she hadn't been gone very long. A week was nothing. And still she felt like a complete stranger. To herself. Or maybe it was that nothing in her life seemed to fit anymore. It hadn't when she'd raced out of here a week ago, and it certainly didn't now that she was back. With Blue.

"I don't like this elevator at all," Blue said in a low growl when the elevator finally groaned to a halt on her floor and she stepped out. His comment instantly destroyed whatever fantasy of distance between them she'd been fostering. Because she could *feel* that growl, as if his mouth were on her—

Stop it, she snapped at herself.

"We're going to take the stairs from now on," Blue was saying, still in that same burnt-ember way of his.

"I live on the sixth floor."

Everly didn't know why she said that. She usually took the stairs because she didn't have to be a decorated war hero with danger stamped all over her and a mouth-watering pair of forearms to know that the elevator was old, slow, and the last place she'd ever want to be stuck if something bad was happening.

It was possible she wasn't as okay with him ordering her around as she'd thought she was.

Blue craned his neck to gaze down at her, right there in the hallway with their bags across his shoulders. Once again he seemed to take up twice the amount of space that he should. As if shoulders like his were entirely too broad to fit in a narrow hallway six floors above the Chicago streets.

She waited for him to say something. But he didn't.

He just looked at her, steady and implacable, and she felt herself flush.

"You expect me to walk up and down five flights of stairs. Every time I want to come in and out of my apartment."

"I do."

"What if I have heavy groceries?"

"Then you'll get a workout. Also, you're not going to make yourself a target by doing something stupid like carrying heavy bags, right? It's like begging for trouble."

"What if I have a broken leg?"

"Then you won't have to worry about how you get in and out of your building, because you won't be leaving your apartment at all in a compromised state."

"What if—"

"Everly." Her name was a command, and it seemed to land on her, then slide in deep. "A few stairs never killed anyone. But getting caught on that death trap elevator just might."

"But—"

"I'm not going to stand out in a hallway and argue with you."

He sounded so reasonable when he said that. So measured and calm. It made her ears burn and something more spiky than her usual fear storm through her.

She welcomed it. She'd rather be angry than afraid any day.

Everly headed down the hall toward her door, another short walk that felt like an uphill half marathon. But no matter how long it seemed to take, they were eventually at her door. And that terrible hand that gripped her at the rib cage clenched harder. Tighter.

Whatever charge she'd gotten out of being angry disappeared as if it had never been.

"Hey." She looked up at Blue when he gritted that out, blinking to bring him into focus. That dark gaze of his that had tracked this way and that on the street moved over her in the exact same way. Looking for weaknesses and probably finding them. "Breathe."

"I am breathing, thank you." She couldn't tell if she was frozen or furious or just plain afraid. She scowled at him. "And how could you tell either way?"

But she realized as she said it that she really had been holding her breath.

She . . . didn't like that. The fact that Blue could tell whether she was breathing when, as far as she knew, he hadn't even really been looking at her until this moment. He'd been looking at each of her neighbors' doors. At the window down at the far end that looked over the alley. At the entrance to the stairwell beside the elevator shaft. He'd been constantly scanning from one side of the hallway to the other, making whatever calculations it was that he made. As if it was all second nature to him, which she supposed it would have to be.

And he didn't answer her question. He just kept that dark gaze trained on her until her face felt too hot.

Again.

It was more difficult than it should have been to fit her key in the lock, then throw the bolt open. And then it seemed to require a heroic amount of energy to push open her own door and step inside.

The air inside her apartment was dull. Still. Everly tossed her keys on the small table in what passed for a front hall, then moved farther inside. She flicked on the lights from the switch in the hall, realizing as she did that she was holding her breath again, but at least this time she knew it.

But there was no one there when the lights blazed on. Rebecca's door was open, just as Everly had left it. There were no signs of life inside, from what she could see from this angle. No one sang out a greeting or leaped out from behind the sofa, wielding deadly weapons of any kind.

She didn't know whether to be thankful or worried that nothing seemed disturbed.

"Stay right there," Blue ordered her.

This time, she was more than happy to do what he told her. He dropped the bags at her feet. Then she stood in her own foyer and watched as Blue moved around the apartment, shifting from one room to the next, barely making a sound. And that quiet of his was . . . disturbing. Or it got under her skin, anyway.

It was as if her head couldn't quite make sense of it. She could *see* him as he moved, running a seemingly idle hand over her comic book collection in the living room bookcase, then stepping into Rebecca's room to check it out more closely. She heard the refrigerator hum in the kitchen. She flicked the switch on the box on the wall near her and heard the air-conditioning kick in and rush through the vents high on her walls. She heard the closet in Rebecca's room open, then close, but she didn't hear *him*. His feet made no sound on her hardwood floors. Blue was like a shadow, here and then gone.

And when he disappeared into her bedroom, she felt that same obnoxious heat wash over her again, but it was from head to foot this time. And came with a healthy side helping of embarrassment. She opened her mouth to tell him to stop, to stay out of her bedroom, but closed it again.

Because asking him not to look through her things was a surefire way to indicate she found all this a little too intimate. A little *too much*.

She couldn't remember if she'd made her bed before she left for her mad drive, though she doubted it. She didn't know why the thought of him standing there, looking at her sheets thrown to the side and a dent where her head had been on her pillows, made something uncomfortably hot twist in her gut. It wasn't as if she was worried about a man like Blue rooting through her underwear drawer—because she had absolutely no doubt he saw all the ladies' panties he wanted to see, whenever he wanted to see them.

And more to the point, he wasn't that kind of guy. She was sure about that, if nothing else.

Still, she found it was all too easy to imagine Blue there at the foot of her unmade bed. Dark and commanding and silent and mouthwatering all over.

Only, in her head, she was watching him stand there while she was lying in her bed herself.

She thrust that out of her mind. Or tried, because there was no way anything like that was ever going to happen.

Everly didn't know whom Blue typically dated, assuming anyone dated at all in a town as small as Grizzly Harbor, but she was pretty sure that Batman types did not generally go after account managers at midsized ad agencies who were addicted to French macarons, sushi, and reruns of *Friends* they'd already seen nine thousand times. No way.

In fact, she thought when Blue finally prowled out of her room and stood there in her doorway—every inch of him a predator, made of smooth muscle, obvious skill, and that lethal confidence stamped deep into him—she would be very much surprised if a man like Blue Hendricks dated at all.

"Something funny?" he asked, just as curt and growly as ever, which only made it worse.

Everly was obviously a bit punchy, because she told him. "I was trying to imagine you on a date."

Eight

Well, she thought, as Blue stared at her in what looked like a kind of amazement, except a lot less friendly, *that was stupid.*

"A date." He said it as if he'd never heard of something so repellent. "Why?"

Everly waved a hand and told herself she felt effortless. "It isn't the *why* that's interesting. It's more, you know, imagining you storming into some café for a coffee date like you were thundering into battle and ordering . . . I don't know. Some nails to chew on?"

"Why can't I have coffee like a normal person?"

"*Can* you? Or does that require mission parameters and a private jet?"

She couldn't read the look he threw at her, but she could read herself perfectly well. She was flirting with him.

She needed him to save her life and she was *flirting* with him.

What was *wrong* with her?

Blue roamed from her bedroom doorway, across the living room, and into the open-plan kitchen, and she found herself trailing after him. Very much as if this were his apartment instead of hers. But then, she couldn't say the place really felt like hers anymore. She'd spent nearly a month here after that night, and she wasn't sure she'd relaxed that entire time. Not once.

Not until tonight.

Well.

She wouldn't call herself *relaxed*, exactly. But the sun was going down outside and she wasn't sitting with her back to the wall, wide-eyed and panicked. She wasn't listening for any and every noise that might be the men who'd hurt Rebecca, back to finish the job.

It was him, of course. Blue. The simple fact that he'd checked every room in the apartment to make sure that it was safe to be here. And now he was towering over the small galley kitchen as he rummaged through her refrigerator, as if everything were perfectly normal. Everly pressed the heel of her hand to the center of her chest and recalled how, only moments before, she'd stood outside the door in her hallway and felt as if something were crushing her.

It was gone now. He'd made her feel safe. Here, where she'd thought she might never feel safe again.

"Should we order some food?" she asked. "There's a great pizza place down the street."

Blue straightened, then looked at her over the open refrigerator door. "Unless you're some kind of culinary genius who can whip up something delicious from a couple moldy old apples, three cheese sticks, and a six-pack of Diet Coke, I don't think we really have another choice."

"How dare you? That's what I call a feast."

He muttered something. Then he swung the refrigerator door shut, and it was instantly clear that Everly had let herself drift too far into the kitchen and was now standing entirely too close to him. That was the problem with this place, and galley kitchens in general. There was never any real space, just a long, narrow strip of very little floor and too many appliances, tucked on one end of the living room.

And there was even less space in her kitchen now than there usually was.

It took her longer than it should have to notice that the way Blue was looking down at her was . . . not exactly friendly. Again. Which didn't make sense, because she was no longer babbling inanely about *dates*.

Another thing that made no sense was that she found it fascinating the way his dark brows pulled together. The way he seemed somehow less icily contained and controlled than he had when they'd walked in here.

It made her imagine things she shouldn't.

"You came all the way to find me in Alaska, so I assume you actually want to survive," he was saying, and he didn't sound clipped or commanding. He sounded ticked off. "But survival isn't just finding some bad guys and handling them. That's my job, and I'll do it. You need to take care of yourself. It doesn't look to me like you have the slightest idea how to do that."

That stung, and she frowned up at him, crossing her arms in front of her in a way she knew, even as she did it, was much too defensive. She did it anyway, because her hands couldn't be trusted.

Besides, she felt pretty freaking defensive. "I'm alive, aren't I?"

Everly really didn't like the way he looked at her then, as if that were a subject for debate.

"You're too skinny," he said flatly. "It looks like you barricaded yourself in this apartment and didn't come out for weeks. Is that about right?"

"I have a job. So, yes, I went out. When I had to." She pointed at him, because she wanted to do something like punch him in his chest, but she wasn't that foolish. She knew she'd hurt her hand if she tried. "And don't talk about my body. It's none of your business."

He let out that laugh that wasn't remotely amused. "As the bodyguard you just hired to—guess what—guard that body? Yeah, it is. And there's no point wasting my time saving your life if you snap in half at the first hint of a breeze."

"I didn't snap in half while driving across the Yukon to find you."

She hurled that at him like the punch she didn't dare throw. And the good news was that the paralyzing fear hadn't returned. The bad news was that she was filled with righteous indignation instead, and it made her feel reckless. Invincible. Not a smart way to act around a man like this, she was pretty sure. He could snap her in half with his pinkie finger. But she kept right on, because she didn't think he would.

No matter what she did.

"I think I'll probably be fine eating a few cheese

sticks and chugging some Diet Coke to stay awake while I wait to see if I live through the summer. But thank you for your concern."

"I'm not talking about your weight, Everly. I'm talking about your health. If you want to look like a scared stick figure every other day of your life, knock yourself out. Not my circus, not my monkeys. But this?" He did something with his chin that seemed to encompass her, the apartment, and everything she'd ever told him. In one economical gesture that she felt like a harsh conviction. "This is all my business until your problem is solved. What if we have to run and you can't because you haven't eaten a goddamn thing in three days?"

"First of all, I ate breakfast in your presence this morning. Second, I knew I was leaving for a week and I cleared out my refrigerator."

"I don't believe you."

She hated that he knew she was lying. As if he'd watched her stand right where he was and decide she couldn't be bothered—and was entirely too anxious—to go get any new food. That a few cheese sticks and cans of whatever would do. "Third, when I'm stressed, I'm not hungry."

"I don't really care if you're hungry. I care that you can handle yourself in any given situation, and I hate to break it to you, but that requires fuel. And adequate sleep. And not doing insane, suicidal things like driving over Hard-Ass Pass or trying to sustain yourself on crap and chemicals."

There was no reason why this should bother her so much. She kept telling herself that, but it didn't make her any less bothered. "I thought the point of you being here was that you'd handle any situation that might come up."

"Sure. In a perfect world. But I have to tell you, sweetheart, I've been on a lot of missions in my time, and not one of them has ever been perfect. Not one."

Everly wanted to hurl things at him then, mean and vicious things if she could think of any, but she bit her tongue. Because she was making this personal, and it wasn't. It might be about her actual person, but that didn't make it personal. Not on his end, anyway. He was here to protect her, not compliment her or be polite or worry about hurting her feelings.

This wasn't some kind of weird, extended extreme date.

"If you don't want to order a pizza, Blue, you could have just said so." Everly was proud of her voice, calm and cool. Or close enough. "I'm sure we can find a place to deliver a bucket of Paleo horror, with a kale and coconut-oil smoothie to wash it all down."

"I like pizza. I particularly like cheeseburgers and greasy fries, now that you mention it. But I limit how much garbage I eat, because I need my body to function at peak performance levels."

"You have my congratulations." Everly didn't buckle when he scowled. "Listen, I'll make an effort to eat, because you make a good point about maybe needing to run. But I'll eat what I want."

"This isn't a fight. I don't care what you eat." There was something different in his gaze then. She could feel it. Everywhere. On some level she knew that she should be alarmed, but she couldn't bring herself to do anything about it. She didn't step back. She didn't think she moved forward, either, and yet somehow, he seemed closer.

"You just told me I was too skinny," she said, and she knew it was a mistake. It was the way she'd said it. Not exactly petulant, but not the way a grown woman talked to a person she'd hired to perform a very specific and dangerous task.

On cue, she felt herself flush, because that was all she did around him, apparently.

"Let's be clear about what's happening here," Blue said then, all business, which made her feel even more embarrassed and overbright. "This isn't playtime. This isn't a game. If you think otherwise, there's no reason for me to be here."

"We're standing in the apartment where I saw two men possibly murder my roommate. I've never thought this was a game."

"This is either life-and-death or it's not. Which is it?"

"*My* life. *My* death. Not yours."

"I'm glad you're confident about that. I have no intention of dying, but it doesn't always work out that way. So let me say this one more time. I'll take care of you as best I can. But you have to take care of yourself, too." She started to speak, but he plowed right over her. "I get it. Something horrible happened, and you hunkered down here, just trying to survive. You've been gone for a week, so your refrigerator is empty. I'll buy that. But everything in this apartment tells me the same story."

"Is it the story of a very scared person with bad guys after her?" She straightened her shoulders when he raised a brow at her tone. "I don't understand why you're making such a big deal out of a couple of cheese sticks."

"It's not just the cheese sticks. It's the shoes."

They both looked down.

"You don't like my shoes?" Everly was baffled.

"This is what I have to ask myself," Blue said, almost conversationally. And Everly might not have been able to tell if he was breathing, but she was pretty clear on the fact that despite his easy tone, there was nothing but that dark tension flaring between them. "Who gets in a car, knowing they have a long, thankless drive in front of them, through parts of Canada that are never really too far from winter no matter what time of year it is, and thinks, *Hey, I know. I'll wear the most impractical shoes I can find*?"

Everly shook her head in confusion. "They're my favorite shoes. And I was in the car, not trekking my way across the Rocky Mountains."

"They're the only shoes you brought."

"They're completely practical. The perfect travel accessory, in fact."

"They fold."

"That's obviously *why* they're practical."

"And you wonder why I think you're not taking this seriously."

Everly didn't snap, exactly. But something inside her seemed to crumble. As if she'd propped everything up on slender, fragile little matchsticks, and they'd all given way at the same time, in a big rush and tumble.

For a moment she thought she might topple over and explode into dust herself, but she didn't. Of course she didn't.

She didn't know what to do. She apparently never knew what to do around this man. So instead of standing there and letting him read that all over her face, she turned around and headed for her bedroom. Because the other option was saying something else she'd regret.

But she couldn't help throwing a look over her shoulder when she got to her doorway.

He'd followed her out of the kitchen, but he'd stopped there at the other end of the living room. Which was good, because if he'd still been too close, she might have taken one of the fists she hadn't known she'd made at her side and tried to whack him with it. Suicidal, obviously, but all those matchsticks had snapped, and she had nothing left but rubble.

Some part of her just wanted to make it worse. To see if it was possible that things could actually get any worse than they already were.

"What's the matter with you?" She fought to sound if not exactly calm, not crazy and over-the-top, either. "You don't have to be nice to me, I guess. But would it really kill you to be polite?"

"This is polite."

"Do you have any idea what I've been through?"

She threw it at him, only distantly aware that she was loud. Too loud. That this was probably what snapping felt like. But for once, she didn't care.

"Oh, I know," she said, when he began to say something. "Nothing I could possibly have gone through in the past month compares to anything you've been through out there, saving the world."

She thought he looked stiffer and more grim than he had a moment before. "You're right. It doesn't."

"I'm sure that's true. But you were trained for what you did. Bad things didn't just show up in the middle of the night, waking you from a sound sleep and changing your life forever. I was never trained. I have no tools to use in a situation like this." She made herself pull in a breath, and hated that she was now *aware* of her breathing, or lack of it. It made her temper kick up harder. "I don't know if you get scared for your life or not, but I did. I am. I'm *afraid*, Blue. Do you understand that?"

The air seemed to pull tight between them, thick and sharp at once.

His dark eyes blazed. "More than you will ever know."

Something about that scratched at her in ways she really didn't like. Everly felt ashamed of herself, and she liked that even less.

"I'm sorry," she made herself say, though she didn't know if that was true. She didn't know anything anymore. "I'm tired. I'm overemotional. I'm not sure I know what I'm saying."

"I think you do," Blue said, and whatever intensity she thought she could see on his face, it wasn't in his voice. He just sounded cold. "You want it both ways. You want all that superhero shit. Batman and Gotham and whatever else you were talking about earlier. And at the same time, you want to pretend that I'm still that kid who lived across the street from you."

"I'm not pretending anything," she said, but her voice was barely more than a whisper.

"Neither of those people exist," Blue told her, his voice hard. "I'm just me. I'm not that pathetic, angry kid, and I'm certainly not a hero. What I am is the only person who can keep you safe."

"Blue . . ."

"Here's how this is going to work." It was as if she hadn't spoken. "I'm going to chalk tonight up to exhaustion. But going forward, you do what I tell you to do. No discussion. No debates. And definitely no emotional outbursts, like I'm some douchebag boyfriend telling you to put on a few pounds to keep him happy."

It was like he'd slapped her. And the way his gaze bored into her, she thought he knew it. That it was deliberate, like everything else he did.

"I'm not your boyfriend," he continued when she didn't respond. Because she couldn't seem to form words. "The only interest I have in you is keeping you alive. Do you understand me?"

Everly understood him too well. She couldn't tell if it was shame or humiliation that wound around inside her, burning like a red-hot cramp. But all she wanted to do was crawl off into her room, curl up into a ball, and pretend none of this had ever happened.

Of course, the reason he was here was that doing that hadn't worked the first time.

"I'm going to need you to respond with words."

"I understand," she managed to force out.

"Good." He was unyielding. So unapologetically ruthless, even just standing there. And she knew this was why she'd sought him out and would be the only reason she lived through this, *if* she lived through this, but it didn't make it any easier. It didn't make that great, endless embarrassment inside her ease any. "Now, I'm going to order some food. When it comes, I expect you to eat it. If you need to stamp off to your room and have a tantrum between now and then, that's your call. I won't judge you."

Everly reminded herself, because she clearly needed some reminding, that this wasn't any kind of normal situation. If he had been her boss at the agency, or one of her coworkers, and he'd spoken to her like that—well. She would have ripped off a piece of him and fed it to him without thinking twice. She would have told him where he could take that attitude of his, and precisely where he could shove it.

But this was what he'd been trying to tell her, she understood in the next moment. He wasn't a normal guy. And this wasn't any kind of typical, normal, palatable social interaction. He wasn't some strutting, arrogant wannabe alpha male, trying to assert his dominance because he wished he was a big man.

He *was* a big man, in every sense of the term.

More than that, he was in charge because he knew what to do and how to handle this kind of thing. *This kind of thing* was what he did. Even if she hadn't known the bits and pieces of his résumé that her brother had shared with her, she would have been able to see his skill all over him. It was evident in everything he did. It was who he was.

She might not like it right this minute, but she was going to listen to him.

Or there was no point at all to her insane drive to Alaska. She might as well have stayed right here and let those men do what they wanted with her.

She felt a deep revulsion move through her at the very idea. Because she wanted to live.

She wanted to live.

And if Blue kept her alive, did it really matter what he said or did or how he treated her? It was ridiculous to imagine that she should feel comfortable in a situation like this. She could hardly remember what *comfortable* was. What mattered was that he made her feel safe, even now when she was mad at she didn't even know what. Even now, when she felt vulnerable and exposed, all broken matchsticks and too much embarrassed heat.

As if, given the opportunity and some space, she would cry for a week.

Maybe that was why she felt so safe. Because she knew Blue could handle whatever happened. He could and he would, and that gave her room to feel all the things that had gotten shoved aside. She hadn't shed a tear no matter how frightening it had all gotten—until she'd been with him.

"Are you all right?" he asked, and she wondered how much he could read on her face. Did he know every thought that had scrolled through her head? Or only some of them?

She had a sudden flash of that moment near her car, down by the docks in Grizzly Harbor. The aching, impossible beauty of the water and the quiet forests standing all around. The proud mountains, capped with snow from the winter that was never truly over, austere and remote.

And Blue, so bold and bright in the middle of that cool, gray morning. The brush of his fingers against her ear, and the dizzy shivers that had spread through her at even so innocuous a touch.

Something clicked then. This was deliberate, this methodical putting her in her place. He wanted her furious. He wanted her focused.

He wanted her to stay alive. Maybe as much as she did.

She had no words to describe the giddy sensation that wound around inside her, faster and faster, like some kind of internal tornado, because if this was a deliberate ploy, that meant it was entirely possible that he wasn't as remote and forbidding as he wanted her to think he was.

And that meant . . . but she couldn't let herself go there. Not quite.

Not yet.

"I'll get you some take-out menus," she said quietly instead, as if he'd cowed her.

And when his eyes narrowed at her, she smiled.

She ignored how wobbly her legs felt as she walked into her bedroom. She could smell her own familiar scents in here, as if they were new. The lotion she used on her face at night. Her favorite laundry detergent, clinging to her clothes and the comforter kicked down to the foot of her unmade bed. She took a moment to think about how strange it was to have been so far away that her private, personal space should feel strange and small, too.

She moved over to the desk she kept against the far wall, and reached for the top drawer where she kept her favorite menus, but then stopped dead.

Everly didn't think she called Blue's name. She didn't think she did anything but stare, but then he was there, standing beside her with a particularly alert look on his face.

"What's the matter?"

She didn't—couldn't—speak. She just pointed toward her desk.

Blue scanned it, then looked at her again, blankly. And somehow that kicked her back into gear. She reached over and pointed at the piece of paper lying on the top of her desk, in between different stacks of bills.

It was card stock, as if someone had torn off the top of a folded greeting card to use it as a makeshift post-card. And it had only one sentence on it.

Gone on trip with new guy—back soon.

"That's Rebecca's handwriting," Everly managed to say, as if her heart weren't a sledgehammer in her chest. "And, Blue. It wasn't here when I left."

Nine

Blue had never intended to return to Chicago. He hadn't been avoiding it, necessarily, but he hadn't made any effort to visit his hometown. He'd been too busy with the SEALs and then doing his thing with Alaska Force—but he knew that wasn't the truth. Or at least not the whole truth.

He liked the city of Chicago well enough. There were pros and cons to any urban sprawl. The pros were usually the good food, with more variety to choose from; all hours or more hours of entertainment; and always more people around to make a life feel anonymous. But the cons were all those same people, everywhere, and the traffic they made. All the concrete and the trash. Cities left a man with no space to breathe.

Blue wasn't sure he was cut out for any city after all his years in the service. He didn't like crowds. He knew too much to relax in them. The problem with

Chicago, specifically, was that it was much too close to his family.

Blue didn't want to deal with family. He didn't want to talk to his mother any more than he already did. A call every now and again, when he wasn't on a mission, kept up the mirage of the mother-son relationship they'd never had. The truth was, they had nothing to say to each other. Blue had gone off and done his thing. His mother had stayed right where he'd left her. He'd made his feelings on that pretty clear when he'd been a teenager stuck in that same house with her and her bad choices. Why belabor the point now?

He had zero interest in speaking to the man she'd married a scant year after Blue's father had died. The seven years he'd spent under his stepfather's roof had been more than enough. Blue knew his stepsisters were both fine, in their way, now that they were grown up and off on their own, because his mother liked to fill the silence in their phone calls with random chatter about what Kelsey was doing these days over in Akron, or what Lauren had gotten up to lately in Milwaukee. Blue didn't have anything against either one of them. He just didn't have anything *for* them.

Blue never thought about any of this stuff. Deliberately. He didn't give it any head space because it wasn't an issue for him. He didn't care if he had a relationship with his family. He didn't appreciate the fact that being back in Chicago made him feel like he was backsliding, way back into those dim high school days when he'd wanted to escape but hadn't understood how he could make that happen. When he'd had no perspective and hadn't realized how easy it would be to simply leave home and never go back.

Coming back to Chicago was like signing up for an unpleasant trip down memory lane, but that wasn't the only problem.

The other, bigger, unsolvable problem was Everly.

He hadn't quite gotten a handle on her situation, which pissed him off more by the day. The letter from the missing roommate, with handwriting Everly insisted looked like Rebecca's, was a curveball.

The note wasn't the only indication that Rebecca might still be out there. It had taken Blue only a couple of calls to the Chicago PD the following morning to discover that there had been a lot of activity in the previous week. In addition to the note on Everly's desk, there had been an e-mail to Rebecca's workplace, talking vaguely of a last-minute leave of absence, for personal reasons left undisclosed.

"Not to mention," the detective Blue had spoken to had said, "dead girls don't generally update their social media."

Rebecca had done just that. Or she'd appeared to do it. There were three posts in the last week, all similar. Short, vague, cheerful. With a few gauzy promises that all would be revealed in time. And no replies to any questions asked in the comments.

"I don't want to tell you how to run your life," the detective told Blue after he'd identified himself as a representative of Everly's legal team, in a tone of voice that indicated she wanted to do exactly that. "But your client is a nutcase."

"I'll take that informed opinion under advisement," Blue had replied dryly.

And he was tempted to leave it at that, suggest Everly seek out intensive therapy and good drugs, and haul his ass back to Grizzly Harbor as fast as he could.

That right there was the issue.

Because Blue couldn't explain the flurry of messages from Everly's lost roommate, but he knew people. He knew straight-up panic when he saw it, and that was exactly what Everly had been trying so hard to hide when they'd arrived back at her apartment. That was the part he couldn't reconcile.

If she really was the nutcase the police thought she was, he'd expect a whole lot more drama. Grand gestures like the one she made by driving out to Alaska, sure. Anyone could fake a good story, he supposed. Even to a dubious, suspicious audience like Blue and the rest of Alaska Force. Anyone could be fooled, given the right set of circumstances. He knew that.

But it was a lot harder to fake the physical manifestations of fear. The way Everly had held herself, as if she were trying to make herself smaller. Less of a target. He'd seen the hair stand up on the back of her neck when she'd walked toward the front of her building, and when she'd looked at him, her pupils had been dilated. A fine sheen of sweat had broken out on her lip as she approached her own front door, though the hall had been air-conditioned and cold. And then there'd been the quick, shallow breathing she'd fought to keep quiet.

She kept thinking she could hide things from him. She kept trying to cover up her responses, even when they were obvious, and he didn't think it was part of a game she was trying to play with him. He'd expect that level of manipulation from someone in his line of work, maybe. But Everly didn't have a drop of special ops instinct in her body.

So when Blue's first knee-jerk response to the notion Rebecca might be alive and sending notes all over the place was to pack up and get the hell away from Everly, he found it . . . disappointing.

Because the only reason he had for wanting to do that made him a giant dick.

Literally.

Blue knew the truth about himself. He didn't pretend to be the hero people usually didn't try to call him more than once. But he did try to be the best man that he could be at any given moment, and that did not include jumping the bones of a scared, desperate woman who was caught up in the middle of something neither she nor Blue himself could understand.

He couldn't believe it was even an issue.

But there was something about Everly Campbell that was lodged beneath his skin whether he liked it or not. She seemed to get in deeper each day he spent with her. He didn't like anything about it, and camping out in her apartment, waiting for the next shoe to drop, didn't make it any better.

He told himself it was that Everly reminded him of a past he didn't want to think about. She'd been a part of that past, now they were near their old hometown, and it was all too much. Too many ghosts. Too many memories.

The only way Blue could think of to deal with that was to want things he couldn't have.

Because sex would make things simple. He could scratch an itch, vanquish a ghost, and be done. He could move on, do his job, and forget about Everly all over again.

He told himself it could all be that easily handled.

But he knew better. Deep down, he knew better. He doubted there would ever be any forgetting Everly, and the fact that she was all tangled up in his memories made it worse.

That was why he wanted to call this thing solved right now and leave. He didn't want to *feel* all this old, ugly crap. He didn't want to feel anything.

And certainly not *this,* he thought, about twenty-four hours after they'd touched down in Chicago, as he stood there in Everly's pretty, overtly feminine living room, all sage greens and soft, inviting creams, looking down at her as she sat on the brightly colored sofa and scrolled through Rebecca's posts.

He watched her cycle through hope, then suspicion, then despair, and he was too tense. As if he were feeling it all *for* her. He wanted to jump in and fix it, fix her, fix whatever the hell put that broken look on her face. And maybe slap it around, too, while he was at it. He wanted things he didn't know how to name.

He *wanted.*

That was the problem with this whole thing.

"You must think I'm crazy," Everly said quietly. She set his tablet beside her on the sofa as if she thought it might bite her if she picked it up again, and she laced her fingers together on her lap. "I'll be honest with you. I kind of think I'm crazy, even though I was here and I know what I saw, because that's the only explanation. Isn't it?"

She was sitting in the dead center of her couch, stiff and still. And her knuckles were turning white, telling him she was gripping herself much too hard. Something about it—about her—made his chest hurt.

"I don't think you're crazy."

He wasn't lying. He didn't think she was crazy no matter what the Chicago detectives thought. But there was a big part of him—and bigger by the moment—that wanted to accept that explanation.

It was the part of him that had joined the navy and never looked back, he realized with a sudden jolt now.

He really, really didn't want to make that connection. But he'd never tried to fix things with his mother or anyone else in that house. He'd never tried to find a way forward with the only family he had left. He'd just disappeared.

He wanted to do the same thing now. And not because he didn't think he could help Everly. But because helping her was the least of the things he wanted when he looked at her.

He wasn't thrilled with what that said about him. What any of this said about him.

Everly was still talking. "But that's the thing about a psychotic break, isn't it? Would I even know if I was having one? Isn't that the whole deal? You just . . . break? And the next thing you know, you're imagining murders and driving across the Yukon?"

"I'm pretty sure *I'm* not having a psychotic break." Blue had to cross his arms over his chest to keep from going to her and doing something that made absolutely no sense. As if touching her would make that haunted, broken look on her face go away. Or was he hoping it would make that ache in him disappear? "And I don't have to be a computer genius to know that anybody could have left a note here. Just like anybody could have sent an e-mail or posted a few things online. Proof of life has been suggested, not established."

"I don't know if that's comforting or terrifying."

Neither did Blue. But he didn't think it would exactly inspire confidence to admit that.

"Here's the plan," he told her instead. "You'll jump back into your normal routine tomorrow. We'll just . . . wait and see what happens."

"Okay." She looked at her hands, still threaded there in her lap. "So if I turn to you one day and tell you I see a dragon in the corner, psychotic break it is."

"If the dragon in the corner is some idiot with a gun, maybe it's something else. Either way, I'll take care of it."

She studied him for a minute, those green eyes of hers too intense. Too sad, as if she already knew this would all end badly.

It killed him how much he wanted to promise her it would all be okay—but Blue wasn't sure if he'd be talking about this situation of hers or himself.

"Tell me what a normal week looks like for you," he said instead, and it felt like his jaw was made of granite.

"Pretty boring," Everly replied. She lifted her shoulders, then let them sink down again. "I work long and irregular hours. Then I come home, where I eat food I suspect you would not approve of and watch television that I feel, in my heart, you would hate."

This would be a lot easier if he didn't find her entertaining. "I don't have to like your routine. I'm not here to improve your life, Everly. I'm here to make sure you have a life to waste on bad food and mindless reality shows."

"And what a life it is," she said softly. "Isn't it funny that it only takes a few near-death experiences to make you contemplate how lucky you are to have a life of long hours and late-night television binges in the first place? I had no idea how much I'd miss it."

"*Funny* isn't the word I'd use." Blue was still standing there, but he couldn't let himself move. Not until he knew which way he planned to go. Toward her or away from her? "As you pointed out to me, you didn't choose this. When this is over, you get to jump right back into the life you had. Or change it if you want a different one. You can do whatever you want."

There was a kind of recognition in her gaze that made Blue feel something like itchy. *Bothered*. He had to force himself to stand still.

"I take it that doesn't apply to you."

"The truth about the world is that there are monsters pretty much everywhere," Blue told her, far more fiercely than necessary. "There have to be people to hunt them, or they win. But it turns out the only way to fight a monster is to become one."

She was shaking her head before he finished, those finely cut strawberry blond strands dancing toward her shoulders. "I don't believe that."

"The thing about the truth is that it's just as true whether you believe it or not."

"Every person on this earth has a hundred reasons at any given moment to consider themselves a monster. You don't have to believe it, Blue."

She was so earnest. So sincere. It made him feel like his skin was on fire. He didn't know whether he wanted to wrap her up in protective material and try to keep her safe from all the nightmares in the world, himself included. Or if he should take the opportunity to show her what a monster really was.

But it wasn't about him. None of this was *about him*.

"You don't know what you're talking about," he told her, his voice even. "And that's good. You shouldn't. I spent a lot of years fighting in a lot of wars so that civilian girls like you never, ever need to know anything about it."

And she was such a fragile thing. Too bony, too weak. He was afraid he wouldn't be able to protect her. That one of those goons she'd seen before would come back at her and snap her in half before he had time to react. He'd dreamed about it as he slept fitfully out here on the couch, jolting awake with images of her broken body plastered all over his mind.

At least it was an upgrade, of sorts, from the crap that was normally plastered there.

She was small and she was scared, but he had to remind himself of that when she pulled herself up to her feet. She closed the distance between them and then stood there before him, closer than he should have allowed her to get.

It took him a long, shattered kind of moment to understand that she was placing her palm over his heart.

"No one is a monster here, Blue," she told him, soft and solemn, her green gaze steady on his. "Unless they want to be."

And then she padded off toward the kitchen, seemingly unaware that she'd cut him in half.

Ten

Everly resumed normal life the next day, just as Blue wanted.

She woke up that morning and decided she would play the best version of the Everly Campbell she'd been before, back before all this had happened. She would view it as a voyage of discovery, hour by hour, as she tried to re-create the life and times of the person she'd been. Way back when she hadn't been scared, she'd simply . . . lived.

Her alarm went off at six, the way it always had. She shuffled to the bathroom to shower and let the hot water wake her. She did her makeup the way she always did on workdays, using enough mascara to look appropriately awake and energized without tipping over into something better suited for the stage. She dressed in one of her favorite work outfits, a dress that was funky and professional at once, as befitted a creative person in a corporate environment, or so she'd always told herself. And she was ready to step out the door at seven on the dot, so she could stop by her coffee shop and then walk the twenty minutes or so to work.

Every step of that was part of the typical Everly Campbell morning routine—except the fact that there was a huge, entirely too beautiful man crashing on her sofa.

He'd already been awake and fully dressed when she'd come out of her room a few minutes after six, which was much too early for that shrewd, dark look he'd thrown at her as she'd mumbled something, clutched her robe tighter around her, and barred herself in the bathroom. By the time she was out of the shower, he'd had coffee brewing in the coffeepot Everly had forgotten a previous roommate had left in her kitchen, making her apartment smell like it was someone else's. His, possibly.

A notion that she hadn't found calming.

By the time she was dressed and ready to leave, armed with her makeup and favorite dress, she'd already had more interaction with a ridiculously attractive male than Normal Everly could expect in months.

It didn't help that Blue stared at her when she emerged from her bedroom. And then kept right on staring as she walked over to where he sat at a stool on the living room side of the open kitchen counter.

And it was hard enough to dress herself this early in the morning. It wasn't fair that he looked so effortlessly *good*. He had on jeans and a T-shirt, both of which did things to his perfect body that should have been illegal. It certainly felt illegal inside Everly.

On top of his T-shirt, he wore a shoulder holster. Complete with a very large, very dangerous-looking gun. In case she'd forgotten why he was here in her apartment, making her jittery and silly without even trying.

But he was still staring, so she jerked her attention away from the very real, not-at-all-fake weapon, and concentrated on him.

"Do I have something on my face?" she asked. Defensively.

"Yes. Makeup."

Everly relaxed. Slightly. And kept her eyes averted from the gun, looking down into her bag instead. "Well, of course I do. I can't go to work without makeup. I'd terrify people."

It was a throwaway comment, so she was surprised when she looked up from a quick rummage through her bag to find him still studying her. With a look on his face that made her chest . . . hurt.

"No." It was all he said. In a low mutter, as if the words were being torn from him against his will. "You wouldn't."

And Everly had to turn away to conceal the little pop of something like joy that burst in her at that. Luckily, she could mask her response by making for the front door.

"You always walk to work?" Blue asked, getting to his feet. She heard the stool scrape against the floor. But he didn't follow her toward the door. "In those?"

"Those . . . ?" She frowned down at her feet. "These are wedges, Blue. My favorite wedges, in fact."

"They're four inches high and completely impractical."

"If they were rickety stilettos, I might agree with you, but they're not. They're like wearing tennis shoes." She pivoted around to shake her head at him, and her eyes locked on the gun he'd hidden beneath a light jacket. "Would you like it if I lectured you on the appropriate handguns to use in your harness?"

"It's a holster, not a harness, and I didn't lecture you."

"The lecture was implied in the commentary. I get it. You don't like any of my shoes."

"I don't have any feelings about your shoes one way or the other," he growled at her, and it dawned on Everly that she was . . . getting to him. Why else would he look so annoyed with her? "My only concern, as always, is how you're going to handle yourself if the situation deteriorates. Can you run in those shoes?"

Everly took a breath and let herself savor the fact that she was managing to burrow under the skin of Mr. Tall, Dark, and Icily Remote. Right here in her own home. Simply by walking out of her bedroom wearing shoes.

If she could have marinated in the moment forever, she would have.

"Two things," she said after a beat or two, because she might want to enjoy this, but she was also close enough to see the temper he was clearly fighting back. She didn't *really* want to tempt fate. Too much. "One, I don't think you actually know what a practical shoe is or isn't. Because, two, I could run a marathon in these wedges, the same way I could in those flats you also hate."

"Somehow," Blue said, hard and low, "I doubt that."

"I believe you know a lot about a great many things. But ladies' shoes and their varied uses are not among them."

"Great," he clipped out at her. "I'm wrong. Noted. Let's hope we don't get ambushed and need you to run that marathon, after all."

Everly didn't comment on that. Because she bit her tongue to keep from commenting on it.

And it was all hilarity and wit until they were in the stairwell.

Because Blue wasn't cranky or grumpy or fighting off his temper as they took the five flights of stairs down to the lobby. Or if he was, he hid it—because he was working.

The switch in him made every hair on Everly's body seem to stand straight up.

It reminded her—a little too forcefully—that while she might feel she was playing a role today, Blue wasn't. This was who he was. It was why he was here.

He was the man who prowled ahead of her down the stairs, blocking her from whatever might lurk in wait with his body. He was the trained operative who melted soundlessly down one flight into the next, every part of him honed and ready. He didn't have his gun out, but Everly had no trouble imagining that if he needed to draw it, he'd have it in his hand in a flash.

She felt a whole lot less entertained when they pushed through the doors in her lobby, out into the street. It was a typical summer morning in Chicago, not too hot but muggy. Everly felt that same prickling sensation, as if someone was watching her, but forced herself to simply walk.

Blue roamed there next to her as she walked down the block toward her coffeehouse, which made it difficult to pretend any of this was actually routine. She thought it would be less noticeable if she were prancing around with a lion on a leash. And potentially less dangerous, too. For her.

By the time she had her daily skinny mocha latte in hand, she'd managed to get herself back into the right mind-set, she thought. It didn't matter what she felt. All she had to do was play the part of herself, as if she hadn't seen what she'd seen in her living room.

She told herself it was simple.

Blue, on the other hand, was complication on a whole different level.

"This is how you walk to work every day?" he asked as he kept pace with her, making their way toward her office building, located on the other side of her Lincoln Park neighborhood. One of the only Chicago ad agencies she knew of that had settled outside the Loop, the city's central business area.

"In the winter I walk up to Fullerton and take the bus," she told him, and then tried to imagine a man like Blue, all threat and portent, on a Chicago Transit bus during rush hour. She bit back a smile. "Because it's not Alaska or anything, but winter here is no joke. So when the weather's nice, I walk."

He gave her that intense look he used when he was considering things, but said nothing. He only escorted her to her office and left her at the security checkpoint in her lobby.

And because she was only playing the part of Everly Campbell, she had a good day. Because any day that involved her alive and not in a crumpled heap somewhere was good by definition. She hardly minded it when she had to suffer through a tense meeting with her boss ten minutes into her first day back at work, because it turned out that the week of sick leave she'd taken with no warning had not exactly pleased him. Or anyone else.

"Tell me why I shouldn't fire you for leaving us in the lurch," he demanded.

"Trust me, Charles, I was doing you a favor," she replied, with the confidence of someone who really had spent the last week waiting for death, if not precisely in the form she'd claimed. "You would not wish this stomach flu on your worst enemy. I hope I'm not still contagious."

Charles, a nitpicker of the highest order, who could milk a grudge for years and often did, backed down at that.

If she'd been herself, actually located inside her own skin, lying to her boss might have worried her. Upset her, even, because she'd never been a liar. She prided herself on doing her job well and following the rules, not bending them to suit herself.

But it was hard to care about things like office rules and the right way to talk to her prickly supervisor when she didn't know if she'd make it home tonight. Or live through the night. How could she care about any of the tiny things that had consumed her before when she honestly had no idea if she'd live long enough to see the leaves change?

"It's surprising how much easier everything is when you don't care about it," she told Blue that evening. "Pleasant, even."

"What don't you care about?"

"Everything. Except, you know, staying alive."

He was waiting for her right where he'd left her, down

in the office lobby. He leaned against the wall with a pair of Ray-Bans on and that fierce set to his mouth. Everly saw more than one woman nearly trip over her own feet at the sight of him. She was pleased that her extended exposure to him had prepared her, so she walked in a straight line.

Her pulse might have gone crazy and her stomach might have hollowed out and plummeted to her toes, but she didn't trip.

"Staying alive is good," he said, and she wished she could see his dark eyes.

But his sunglasses were mirrored, and all she could see was herself. Her cheeks, which were too red. And her eyes, which were much too bright.

She shoved her own sunglasses onto her face and followed him outside.

Out on the street, twilight was just bleeding in as the sun inched toward the horizon, and the temperature was dropping. There was a breeze coming in from Lake Michigan, stirring up the heavy summer air and suggesting that Chicagoland's typical thunderstorms couldn't be far behind. She could feel the charge of coming storms in the air, making her skin feel too tight for her body.

Then again, that could just be Blue, walking beside her like a caged thing, ready to burst free at any moment.

Everly didn't think that could possibly look anything like her *normal routine* to anyone who might be watching her—and who had seen her actual normal routine over the course of the previous weeks—but she wasn't complaining.

Instead, she talked, as if Blue were picking her up

from work because he wanted to and not because he was trying to keep her safe.

"I shrugged my way through what should have been an upsetting business meeting or four today. I told my boss I had the stomach flu last week and was so convincing I almost believed it myself. There's a woman I work with who's had it in for me for years, and she didn't bother me the way she usually does. She said her usual passive-aggressive things, and I just smiled and asked if she'd gotten enough sleep."

"Is that supposed to be an office takedown?" Blue sounded aggrieved. "You might notice I've gone out of my way to live a life that never, ever involves stray office chatter, Everly. If you start talking about intrigue over a watercooler, I might punch myself in the face."

"I'm sorry not everything can be life-and-death and Alaskan retreats."

She didn't realize how tight a grip her temper had on her until she almost ignored the changing lights at a busy intersection. It was Blue's hard hand on her upper arm—hauling her back a step—that saved her.

Everly wondered who saved him. If he let anyone try. He was so lethal, so hard and tough—but she could still feel the way his heart had kicked there beneath her palm last night. She knew it was there, whatever he did to convince the world, and maybe himself, otherwise.

But she was wise enough not to say something like that, out here on a Chicago street with commuters streaming all around them.

Instead, she smiled at him. And saw only herself reflected back at her in the mirror of his sunglasses. That and the faint line between his brows.

"I'm trying to say that everyone in the office treated me much better than they would have if I'd cried or gotten emotional or apologized all over the place."

Whatever happened, she thought, she would always remember Blue in that moment. The late summer evening spread out around him, air thick with coming storms and the usual humidity, and his mouth a grim slash in that jaw he still hadn't shaved.

He took his time letting go of her arm, never looking away from her. She'd never felt so safe. And, at the same time, so *seen*. Because she knew he didn't miss a thing. Not the state of her hair and makeup after a long day at work. Not the fingernails she'd chewed on today despite her attempts to beat back the habit. Not even the glob of salad dressing she'd tried to scrub off her dress after lunch, which even she would have had trouble seeing if she didn't know where it was.

She knew he saw all of that and more, everything happening around them. The street and the traffic. The man next to them on his phone. The two women doubling over with deep belly laughs and clinging to each other as they did. A pack of college students, probably involved in nearby DePaul's summer sessions.

If she asked, she was sure Blue could tell her about every single one of them.

"Never apologize for things you're not sorry about," he told her now. "That's rule number one."

"There are rules?"

"Everly." There was a hint of a curve in that hard mouth then, and it made her pulse quicken. "There are always rules."

"Rules for what, exactly?"

But she didn't care about that, either, for once. The rule-following good girl who'd never quite been good enough had died with Rebecca a month ago, and Everly wasn't sure she missed her. Too much had happened since.

She wanted the summer evening to last forever and this walk home to go on even longer than that. She wanted to walk beside him, carefree and much too giddy, until her feet gave out. And Everly didn't want to remind herself how stupid it was to get her heart involved in a situation that was all about fear.

Or how fleeting her time with this man was going to be, whether she lived to see fall or not.

"Rules for being a badass, obviously," Blue told her, as if that should have been obvious. "That's a side benefit to my being here. You stay safe, and I teach you how to be even safer."

That curve in the corner of his mouth widened, becoming a grin. And her heart did a flip in her chest that she was sure she could see in the mirror of his Ray-Bans. And the truth was, Everly couldn't bring herself to care. She didn't even blush.

She was pretty sure what she did then was surrender.

Completely. To whatever came next.

"In fact," Blue said, sounding like he knew it, "we're going to start with a few lessons tonight."

Eleven

An hour later, Blue was feeling pretty great about his decision to teach Everly a little down and dirty self-defense. It made sense to give her a few tools she could use to combat her own fear—and, if she had to, stun a bad guy in the unlikely event one got to her before Blue could.

He continued to feel great about it as he pushed the furniture back in the living room and made a space for training. And then Everly walked out of her room wearing nothing but yoga pants and a sports bra, and he about swallowed his own tongue.

For a beat, there was nothing in his head but a kind of . . . sizzle.

Every last drop of blood he had in his body left whatever it was doing and pooled exactly where he didn't want it. She kept walking toward him, clearly oblivious to the effect she was having on him. Her strawberry blond hair was scraped back in a ponytail at the nape of her neck. She was barefoot.

Blue registered those details, but really, all he could focus on was the pale, freckled expanse of her abdomen now exposed to his view. He wasn't a complicated man. He just wanted a taste. Of the indentation of her navel. Or the place where her hips flared out from her waist.

Just one taste—

But he shut that down, because he was a professional. He'd been a SEAL. He wasn't a fifteen-year-old kid about to embarrass himself in front of the first girl he'd ever laid eyes on, no matter how it might feel. He was going to have to suck this up and deal with it, because it didn't matter that he couldn't remember ever wanting a woman the way he wanted Everly. He couldn't have her.

She stopped in front of him. And was eyeing him strangely, which suggested Blue's expression was giving too much away. He cleared his throat and tried to school himself into impassivity. Something that had never before been a stretch for him.

"I'm going to teach you how to defend yourself," he intoned, stiff and weird like it hurt him, and wasn't surprised when she frowned.

"I thought—"

"That I was going to protect you," he finished for her. "I am. This is part of it."

"If you say so." She nodded at his own athletic clothes, the exercise pants and T-shirt he'd packed so he could keep his fitness at performance levels. His plan involved waking up at four a.m. and doing a solid ninety minutes of tailored resistance exercises out in the living room every morning, but he didn't tell her that. A man needed to preserve some mystery while he was slowly losing it. "This looks a lot more like a workout class I didn't sign up for. What's next? Claims that salad is a form of self-defense?"

"It's never going to hurt you to eat something green."

She looked wounded. "And so it begins. Karate from the inside out. I'd rather eat cake."

Blue had a sudden, remarkably dirty vision of her lounging around with a cake and nothing else on, giving him access to all kinds of dessert—

And he shut that down, too. Because he wasn't an animal.

Or anyway, was trying his hardest not to be where she was concerned.

"I want you to pay attention to this, if nothing else," he told her, very seriously. Because he couldn't let himself get distracted by cake. Or that sweet, soft belly of hers, with freckles like the sprinkles on top. "If someone chokes you, you have six seconds. Tops. It takes about three seconds for you to start seeing stars, and once you hit five or six seconds? Lights out. What do you think happens then?"

"You appear in a flash of sound and fury and save the day?"

"That's the plan. But plans have a tendency to go awry. A better plan is not to pass out in the first place."

She swallowed. Audibly. "I just want to clarify. You honestly think there's a possibility of me getting choked out?"

Blue shrugged as if that very scenario wasn't high on his list of personal nightmares. "It would be the most efficient way to move you from point A to point B, if that's on the agenda."

He didn't mention that there was something worse. That being no need to move her somewhere, because whoever was after her planned to finish the job right here.

"I would rather that hurting me not be an agenda item," Everly said.

"I hear you." He refused to let himself get swayed by that look that was still all over her pretty face, as if the various ways she could be hurt had only just occurred to her. "But it would take six seconds to choke you so you pass out, another second or two to toss you in the backseat of a waiting car. If I'm more than seven seconds away? If I'm handling one of their friends, for example? It's game over."

"That . . . would not be ideal."

"No," he agreed, aware he sounded a lot more abrupt than necessary. He didn't like the picture he'd painted any more than she did. Blue shifted, sliding one foot behind the other and then bringing his hands up in front of him, palms facing outward. "This is lesson one. Get your hands up."

And for an hour, that was what she did. Blue taught her a fighting stance. Palm strikes that could inflict a whole lot of damage without requiring great skill on her part. Where to kick to incapacitate an attacker. How to operate within her fear rather than run scared because of it.

They both worked up a sweat. Blue found he was a lot more patient than he usually was when he was teaching things like this. He told himself it was because she wasn't some guy hopped up on his own testosterone and fantasies of epic butt-kicking. But he thought it was actually just . . . her.

Everly made him want to slow down and take his time. She made him want to be certain she not only understood each move that he taught her but could execute it. Because when she did, her green eyes lit up and she laughed.

As if learning how to use her own body to protect herself was a deep, abiding joy, and one she'd never experienced before.

He couldn't remember ever wanting another woman. He could barely remember what other women looked like.

His whole world was that smile of hers, wide and delighted. Especially when she landed a good strike or managed to evade an attack.

Blue wasn't sure his battered old heart, black and cold for years now, could take it.

"Will this really work?" she asked him after he taught her a particularly vicious move that would leave an attacker reeling, possibly blind, and definitely on the floor at her feet.

"Absolutely. All you have to do is commit."

"Even if it's someone five times my size?"

"I'm five times your size and you just threw me," he said calmly, already rolling to his feet. "Why not someone else?"

And he didn't know, later, how he'd managed to let her wander off with that thrilled, amped-up look on her face. How he hadn't suggested a way to work off all that adrenaline. How he'd sat out in the living room, listening to the shower run, and contented himself with blistering sets of angry push-ups instead.

That night he dreamed about fighting. Feats of bravery and daring with Everly at his side as she kicked and punched and took down all the shadowy creatures that dared come at her. Until it all shifted, somehow, and the attackers weren't shadows any longer. They fused into Blue, and he wasn't attacking her. It was a different kind of struggle.

Hotter. Sweeter.

Dangerous in an entirely different way—

And when he woke up, his heart was pounding, he'd broken out in a sweat, and he had to take an ice-cold shower at three forty-five in the morning to get his heart rate under control.

The other part of him that needed controlling required his hand.

The days rolled by. He walked Everly to work, picked her up, and taught her his dirtiest and most effective street-fighting and self-defense tactics every night. That was when he got to indulge himself. Her hands on his body. Seeing that smile. The things she chattered at him, as if they were friends. As if this was their life.

During those stolen hours, he was tempted to pretend it was.

Even though he knew better.

But the rest of the time, he did his freaking job and dug into her roommate's life. Rebecca Lambert had been born in Winnetka, one of Chicago's most exclusive suburbs, to an unmarried single mother who had no visible means of support that Blue could uncover. And he was very, very good at following money trails.

Rebecca had gone to a private boarding school in Massachusetts, then a snooty college in Vermont, and had spent her summers in other fancy East Coast places like Cape Cod and the coast of Maine. But she'd come back to Chicago after college. And as far as Blue could tell, she hadn't been able to hold down a job for more than a few months at a time for years. She'd taught yoga for six or so weeks at an upscale studio. She'd spent a season interning at a magazine. She'd spent a summer working in a museum, which couldn't possibly have paid her rent.

"How did Rebecca pay her bills?"

"Hello, Blue," Everly said dryly, and he could practically see the look that went with that tone through the phone. "How nice to hear from you in the middle of the day. Are you well? I am, too, thank you for asking."

Making Blue realize that he'd treated her like a member of the Alaska Force team, calling her at her job and firing questions at her without bothering with the niceties.

He refused to apologize.

Everly made a humming sound that it took him a minute to realize was her. Thinking.

"Uh . . . She works in PR. *Worked*, I mean."

"That wasn't the only thing she did."

"I think she used to do a bunch of different things. I got the impression she had a trust fund or something."

"Did she tell you that?"

"No." He heard Everly shift in her seat, then the sound of her fingers tapping on a keyboard. There was no reason he should feel that as something intimate when it wasn't. He knew it wasn't. And yet . . . "It's that thing that happens. Everyone's going along, doing the same things. Entry-level jobs, first apartments. And then suddenly *some* people start taking extended European vacations. Or sort of flit from job to job without ever seeming stressed about it. Or they randomly buy property out of nowhere. Or even just wear really, really nice clothes you could never afford. And you realize that it's not that they're doing so much better than you. It's that they have other means of support."

Blue had never had any support but himself. It was something he'd always prided himself on.

"Your parents must be doing pretty well," he said. "If your mom is a surgeon and your dad was a professor."

"My parents are doing great," Everly agreed, an edge in her voice. "And they spend their money on themselves, as they should. They're currently on an extended French wine tour. It involves châteaux. And they're very supportive of whatever my brother and I want to do, but they expect us to do it ourselves. I thought Rebecca probably had some extra money, but I didn't. I don't."

And Blue told himself he had no reason to feel like an ass when she claimed she had work to do and hung up.

He tried to push Everly out of his head. He sat back in the chair in Rebecca's room, her laptop open in front of him, and tried to figure her out instead. He didn't see anything that looked like a trust fund in her financials. Still, no matter what job she took, she always had a nice, fat, comfortable balance in her bank account. It certainly wasn't her salary that kept her account so flush.

As far as Blue could tell, it was cash infusions every week. A few thousand every time.

Anonymous, untraceable cash.

Lately, Rebecca had actually managed to keep a job for almost a full eighteen months, which was a record for her. It was the kind of PR agency that catered to celebrities who needed fires put out left and right. Blue wondered if she'd gotten herself caught up in a blaze that burned too hot, but so far, he couldn't see how. Rebecca had worked at the firm consistently, and her coworkers seemed to like her, but she hadn't been in charge of any clients. Which he figured made it unlikely that one of them would have taken her out.

"Rebecca didn't handle fire drills," the vice president of the firm told him when he wrangled a meeting with her a few days later. Angela Martin was an overdone woman who was trying her best to cling to her early fifties and a shade of blond that didn't become her. She was also the only one who would talk to Blue, and only after he hung around during her lunch hour and tried to channel Isaac's sort of easy charm. "She was better with the celebration afterward, when it was all champagne and quiet donations to worthy charities. That was her niche. That and attractive young men with very nice cars, that is."

"I wasn't aware she dated."

"Oh, honey." Angela let out a husky laugh. "I'm not sure I would call it *dating*."

Blue kind of wanted to put himself out of his own misery after an afternoon spent listening to what qualified as a "fire drill" to people who trafficked in famous people's worst moments and public shame, but no matter how he tried, he couldn't come up with a convincing narrative to suggest why someone might want to kill Rebecca for being caught up in anything the agency handled. The usual triggers—affairs, embezzlement, drugs—were the agency's stock-in-trade.

And apparently, Rebecca's idea of an entertaining night out. Though whatever she got up to, she tended to keep it out of the apartment she shared with Everly.

"I guess I forgot that while I was busy out there trying to defend the American dream, these people were back here crapping all over it," Blue griped at Isaac in one of their daily status-update calls.

"That's what civilians do," Isaac agreed cheerfully. "Pretty much as their full-time job."

Blue agreed. But he had his own full-time job, and he needed to do it—and fast, so he could get out of Chicago and away from the woman who was making him crazy.

It took him longer than it should have to find a number for Rebecca's mother, which he couldn't help but think was yet another red flag.

He left Annabeth Lambert a message on her voice mail, asking her to call him because he had information about her daughter. It was the kind of message that usually got a call back within the hour.

But Rebecca's mother didn't take the bait.

Blue accepted that he was going to have to hunt Annabeth Lambert down. She was another woman with financials that didn't make any sense, and he needed to see if two puzzle pieces that didn't make any sense apart made sense together. He bet they would.

And in the meantime, there was Everly, who was on track to drive him around the bend long before he got to the bottom of what had happened to her roommate.

"I have to have an explanation for who you are," she

announced that night when he picked her up from work.
"It's been a week."

One week was edging toward a second, in fact, and
all Blue had discovered so far was that Rebecca Lambert
lived beyond what ought to have been her means with
money he couldn't explain. As far as he could tell from
scouring the laptop in her bedroom, she hadn't been doing anything more illicit than streaming movies for free.
If she was secretly a call girl or selling her organs, he
couldn't find any evidence of it. The Alaska Force computer geniuses couldn't, either—and they could find anything.

"It's not normal to have a bodyguard," Everly was
saying.

Blue stopped trying to figure out Rebecca Lambert
and focused on Everly instead. Tonight she was wearing
one of those outfits of hers that he thought was designed
to cause him actual grievous bodily harm. A pair of
trousers in a cute pattern that showed off entirely too
much of her legs and butt, with more of those high
wedges she ran around in that made her calves look like
heaven. He could torture himself for hours imagining
those legs tossed over his shoulders or wrapped around
his hips—and did. Add a frilly blouse that offered the odd
impression of her lacy bra beneath and he was barely
able to stand upright.

But he managed. Somehow, he managed, even though
every day he thought she was so pretty and so *cute* it
might actually succeed in taking him apart. When all his
years in the navy, under attack by enemy forces, hadn't
cracked him.

"It's not anybody's business who I am," he said now.

Clearly she was no longer in awe of him, because she rolled her eyes. "It's not about whether or not it's someone's business. It looks weird. Because it is weird."

He'd spent enough time in this lobby over the past week. He could tell when the people walking by were her coworkers by the side-eye and speculation they threw her way as they headed outside into the summer evening. And she wasn't wrong. There were more of them by the day.

"I get that your office is a little out-of-the-box," she said, as if she were trying to manage him. He was almost entertained. "Try to imagine how you would react if suddenly one of your friends showed up with some other, random person who was always *right next* to them. I think you'd find that strange."

"Then make up a story," he suggested. "Tell them I'm your—"

"Brother?"

"Sure," he drawled, because she was turning pink. Watching her blush was one of his new favorite things, and he never seemed to get enough of it. "Call me your brother if you want."

"That would never work." She sounded fuzzy, and Blue liked that, too. "Everyone knows my brother is a doctor who lives across the country. He would hardly have time to follow me around like a shadow. I mean, maybe for one day. As a visit. But not, you know, for weeks on end."

"Then tell them I'm your boyfriend." He let his mouth curve. "And I'm possessive."

The pink turned to red, and that was even better. "Who would believe *that*?"

She laughed. Nervously.

Blue did not. "You don't think I look like boyfriend material?"

"I think that the term *boyfriend* implies the kind of relationship that is significantly less intense than . . . this." Everly waved her hands at him. "You don't look like the kind of man who becomes a boyfriend." As if she were afraid that might hurt his feelings, she hurried on. "To me, I mean."

He studied her flushed face. "What's wrong with you?"

"Too skinny, for one thing," she threw back at him, too quickly. "A stick figure, I think you said."

"Let's clarify something," he drawled, though he shouldn't have. He knew he shouldn't touch any of this with a ten-foot pole or two. "I said you looked too weak to fight off bad guys. I didn't say that was unattractive. Particularly if a man wasn't looking for a fight."

Everything went still, and it was as if the whole of the world fell away, leaving nothing but Everly. But if Blue was honest, that had been true since the moment she'd roared up in her car and changed everything.

He told himself he knew what he was doing. He was tired of fighting her; that was all. He'd fought his whole life—he'd made a career out of winning—but he couldn't fight this. He couldn't fight her. Not anymore.

Everly let out a kind of sigh. She looked down, then away. She swayed toward him, resting her hand on his abdomen, just below his ribs.

Gently. So gently.

He'd had actual sex that got to him less than that light touch, not that he could recall a single detail of it now.

There was only her. There was only this, as inevitable as a summer thunderstorm on a Chicago evening.

She smiled at him, and inched even closer—

And then she stopped short. She went stiff.

He saw fear. Panic. Ice.

"What just happened?" Blue demanded.

But he was already scanning the lobby. He had his back to the wall, but she'd looked off to the side, where there were people walking in and out of the lobby doors. Three women and two men engaged in the kind of conversation that suggested a business dinner. A businessman in a three-piece suit.

With a face he recognized.

"Don't look now," Everly whispered. "But they're back."

He got it then. He'd last seen the guy loitering near the exit—supposedly engrossed with whatever was on his phone—in Everly's sketchbook.

And Blue had a split second to decide on a course of action. He could rush the asswipe, but that would leave Everly unprotected in this lobby, and his own words flooded through him.

Six seconds. That was all it would take.

He couldn't take the risk.

So he did the next best thing.

"Run with this," he ordered her gruffly.

Then he hauled Everly toward him and took her mouth with all the hunger and greed he'd been repressing since the day she'd reappeared in his life.

Twelve

His taste exploded over her, through her, like a tidal wave.

It was that huge. That devastating.

And that good.

Everly went from one extreme to the other in the space of a heartbeat. She was already too comfortable with Blue waiting for her every evening. And on their walks home, where he scanned the streets for killers and she got to pretend . . . things that she knew better than to let herself imagine.

She knew how dangerous it was to get carried away. How temporary this arrangement was and how deeply it was going to hurt when he solved her current problem and disappeared off into the Alaskan wilderness.

But her heart had clattered around the way it always did when she stepped out of the elevator and saw him with his back against the wall, there on the other side of security.

And then he'd thrown out the word *boyfriend*, which was such a silly word. A ridiculous word, really, when she thought about trying to apply it to a man like Blue.

It was like calling the ocean a puddle.

But then everything had frozen when she'd looked over her shoulder and seen one of the faces from her nightmares. Not ten feet away.

She understood then, with a horrible lurch, that she'd . . . forgotten.

Well. Not *forgotten*, exactly. It was more complicated than that. It was impossible to forget what had happened, particularly with Blue here. Living in her apartment. Teaching her self-defense every night until her fingers ached. And she never knew, standing in the shower afterward, if they ached from the strikes she'd landed on his tough, hard body or from her endless, insatiable urge to touch him in a whole different way.

She'd been lulled into a false sense of security. She'd understood that in a sudden, sickening flash—the presence of the man she thought of as Goon Number One brought it all back.

But now everything was changed. Again.

Because Blue was kissing her.

For a moment, Everly couldn't make sense of it. His hand had gripped her upper arm, on the outside bit of her shoulder where her frilly, puffy quarter sleeve left her skin bare. She'd had a split second to register the intense heat and power in that hard palm of his, and the fact that he was *touching her*, and then he was pulling her toward him.

And she certainly wasn't fighting him.

Then Blue's mouth came down on hers and ruined her forever.

Everly expected him to be fierce, like the warrior he was, and he delivered. But there was something lazy in the way he took her mouth. A kind of deliberate, confident sampling that spiraled through her like a heat all his own. But at the same time, softer and more persuasive than she could possibly have imagined.

Branding her. Changing her.

This time, when she flushed hot and red, it had nothing to do with embarrassment. It had everything to do with Blue.

"Kiss me back," Blue muttered, pressing each word against her lips like some kind of sensual tattoo.

Everly obeyed him. Happily. She let herself melt against him, winding her arms around his tough, hammered-steel torso. She tipped her head back, and couldn't help letting out a moan when he angled his head to get a better fit, using one of his big, hard hands to cup her jaw and move it where he wanted it.

It was blistering. She felt as if he singed her, head to toe and back again. He licked his way into her mouth, his tongue dancing with hers, over and over and over.

And when he pulled away, Everly wasn't certain she knew her own name.

Until Blue said it.

Three times.

"I'm sorry," she managed to say at last. She was tingling, everywhere. Her legs felt weak beneath her, and she was at a complete loss to describe the chaos winding around and around inside her.

A sweet, delirious sort of chaos that she knew had altered everything.

They could never go back. *She* could never go back.

"What did you say?" she asked.

It took her much too long to blink away the fog before her eyes, and when she did, her heart sank.

Because Blue wasn't looking at her with any of that heat or fire she still felt storming through her body. On the contrary, Everly had never seen him look so cold or forbidding. And that was saying something.

"We have to go," he said again, stern and harsh.

And he didn't wait for her to respond as he slid a hand around to rest impatiently between her shoulder blades. She looked around for Goon Number One and didn't see him, which made something jostle unpleasantly deep in her belly. But Blue was hustling her out of the lobby of her office building and into the street, so there was no time to explore her reaction.

Her lips felt swollen. *She* felt swollen. Everly didn't know how to put that into words, so she simply followed where Blue led her, distantly amazed at the fact he'd had the presence of mind to pull out his cell phone and summon a car.

She doubted she could answer her own phone right now, much less use it to *do something*.

The car was there when they got to the curb, and Everly was grateful for the simple set of tasks before her. Open the door. Climb into the backseat. Throw herself to the far side of the car, so Blue could follow after her. Simple, easy things that didn't require thought. She didn't have to worry about it; she just had to do it. She didn't have to analyze the whys and hows.

She didn't have to wonder what the hell she was going to do now.

"Blue—" she began, aware as she spoke that her voice was much too husky. Too revealing.

"Not now."

Terse. Dismissive.

And it was a measure of how thrown she was, half-giddy and half-hollow, that she didn't push him.

Instead, she sat there beside him in a daze as their driver navigated the evening traffic and delivered them to the front door of her apartment building in what felt to her like record time.

Though it could have taken a lifetime. She didn't think she'd be able to tell the difference.

Once inside her building, Blue was all grim, focused business as he hurried her across the lobby and into the stairwell.

And still, Everly didn't think to stop and have it out with him. Not out in the open.

She didn't even pause. She ran up the stairs the way she'd been doing every day, waiting at the top of each flight until Blue—always there in front of her—nodded to let her know it was safe to proceed. She did the same at the heavy metal door that led to her hallway, and waited an extra beat for her breathing to calm down. She could have pretended that it was the stairs that had gotten to her, but she knew better.

Walking up the stairs often left her winded—it was true—because she wasn't a career warrior like Blue. But tonight she'd been winded going into the five-flight climb.

And that kiss replayed in her head, over and over, in

case she was tempted to tell herself she didn't know why.

She could still taste him, she thought, as he jerked his head to indicate that the hallway was clear. She could still feel the way his palm had fit there on her jaw, as if he'd left a mark.

But all she did was follow him down the hallway. Then she stood there mutely as he fished out the keys he'd made copies of one day while she'd been dutifully pretending she was the same Everly Campbell she'd always been, and let them into the apartment.

My apartment, she reminded herself. Because she'd managed to forget that lately.

The way she was forgetting too many things, it seemed.

She stood inside the door, the way he'd taught her. She didn't watch him as he roamed from room to room, checking closets and looking under beds the way he did every time they returned home. She stayed where she was and tried to control her breathing before Blue commented on it, the way he liked to do.

But her heart was still pounding. Her pulse was still elevated and wild.

And there was a fire in her, burning almost too bright to bear, one she had no idea how to put out.

Blue appeared in her bedroom door, always his final stop. He propped himself there with one hand on the doorjamb and his gaze darker than usual when it met hers across the living room.

"Good job," he said.

Everly hardly registered the words. It was his tone that got to her, because it was so . . . *neutral.*

Aggressively, bizarrely neutral.

"Thank you," she replied, almost by rote. She straightened, there in the foyer. "Which job do you mean?"

"It's good to know you can think on your feet," Blue said in that same tone. It wasn't a slap, she cautioned herself. It just *felt* like a slap after they'd shared a kiss like that. As anything would. "You went with it in that lobby, and it worked."

That comment, on the other hand, felt like he'd used his fist. Her heart slammed against her ribs, hard, and she was surprised it didn't knock her to the ground.

"Oh?" She sounded distant. Far away to her own ears, but Blue didn't seem to notice. "In what way did it work?"

"There's no way a bargain-basement 'roidhead like that looks at me and doesn't know exactly who and what I am. He probably clocked my military training before he walked through the glass doors."

Blue moved from her bedroom door to the space beside the couch where he kept his things, stacked so neatly it felt like he was making a statement, and squatted down beside his bag.

Busy busy busy, Everly thought. Not nicely.

Because it was almost as if he was trying to keep himself as busy as possible rather than look at her again.

"And that works, because I'd prefer he go back and tell whoever he works for that you got yourself a dangerous man as a lover, not a bodyguard."

"A lover." Everly echoed him as if she'd never heard that word before.

She was still standing a foot or so inside the front door. Frozen in place. Because she thought that if she allowed herself to move, she knew just enough self-defense that she might imagine she could hurl herself at him and hurt him.

He could incapacitate her in a few seconds and without much effort, she knew. Oh, she knew. But maybe it would be worth it if she drew some blood first.

Blue slid a dark look her way, as if he could read her every murderous thought, and then returned to whatever the hell he was doing in his duffel bag.

"If it causes some confusion, good. That's what we want."

"Let me make sure I'm following you," Everly said, very carefully. Very deliberately.

Possibly also very aggressively.

Blue sat back on his heels, his eyes narrowed. "Don't start down this road, little girl. You don't want to go there."

"Little girl," she repeated. And there seemed to be no containing the incredulous laugh that burst free of her then. "You do realize that every time you say that, it does the exact opposite of what you think it does, right?"

"You have no idea what I think."

"I'm sure it makes you happy to believe that," she said through clenched teeth. "But every time you go out of your way to diminish me, it makes me wonder why you think that's necessary. And guess what, Blue? I can only come to one kind of obvious conclusion."

She could see he didn't like that. *Good.*

"I'm not trying to diminish you, Everly. I'm trying to save your life. If you're not happy with the way I'm doing that, I'll remind you that you're the one who drove three thousand miles to find me."

"And you're the one who decided to act like we were in a bad thriller and throw the bad guys off our trail with a big, bad kiss. Has that ever actually worked?"

Blue stood. It was more of an unfurling, rolling up from where he'd been squatting, and Everly certainly didn't miss the inherent threat in that.

She just didn't care.

"I did what I had to do to confuse the issue and buy us some time," he said, sounding like he was delivering a dry military report. And managing to imply that she was being . . . something. Unreasonable. Childish. *Something*.

"Why can't you just admit that you wanted to kiss me, so you did?" she demanded. "Would it kill you?"

"What I want or don't want has no place here." He was coiled tight and about to explode. She could feel it. But she refused to let that stop her. "This is the job."

"You're such a liar." She was whispering, because she was too mad to keep her voice level, but it didn't matter. He jerked as if she'd shouted it directly into his face. "If you were in the exact same situation with a six-foot-four, burly truck driver as a client, would you have solved the problem in the same way? Would you have run through all the available scenarios and come up with that particular solution? I don't think so."

"You want to think you're special," Blue said in an even, placating kind of way that made every part of her stiffen in outraged resentment. "And I get that, Everly. I do. But if you want to survive this, you need to get your head on straight."

"Right. Or I might find myself accidentally kissing more random men in the lobbies of office buildings and pretending that it's crack detective work. Huh. I wonder if anyone will believe that excuse?"

"What do you want me to say?" Blue threw at her, no longer sounding even or placating.

It struck her that it was a remarkably foolish thing to do, to push a man like this until he cracked. What did she think she was doing?

But she knew. This was what she wanted. Exactly this.

Blue reeling and uncontrolled. Blue outside himself and uncertain how he got there.

Just like she was.

"Tell the truth," she suggested, not backing down, though if she was smart, she'd run and hide. "Maybe there was a tactical, strategic advantage to kissing me like that. But that's not the whole reason you did it. Just admit it."

Blue looked at her for what felt like an eternity, a solitary muscle flexing in that rough jaw of his, and too much fire and electricity in the space between them.

"You want things from me that I can't give," he said eventually, dark and low. "I don't know how. And I don't want to learn."

And Everly found herself taking a step toward him. Then another one, temper and something like betrayal too forceful inside of her to ignore.

"Is this the part where you let me down easy?" she demanded. "Don't patronize me, Blue. You don't know what I want from you. Neither do I. The difference between you and me is I'm not playing games of make-believe with my own intentions."

"That's not the difference between you and me."

His voice was harsh. Unyielding. "You have no idea the kinds of things I've done. And I'm not planning to clue you in. All you need to know is that you drove three thousand miles to hire a monster to chase after other monsters. That's what I do."

"You are not a monster. I thought we covered this."

His lips twisted, and something inside her did, too. "You can put your hand on my heart and tell me pretty things, but it doesn't change the facts. You want tonight to mean something. You want a kiss to be a fairy tale. Well, wake up, Sleeping Beauty. There's no fairy tale here. There's no happy ever after. There's me, solving a problem and then getting the hell out of your sweet, soft civilian life. The end."

Everly made herself breathe before she keeled over. But she ignored the pounding of her heart, focusing on Blue instead.

"Cinderella. Little girl. Now Sleeping Beauty." She didn't realize she was moving again until she'd made it within reach of his hands. And she could feel the danger coming off him in waves. What was the matter with her that it didn't terrify her? But it didn't. He didn't. "What would happen, I wonder, if you let yourself see me as a grown woman for a minute? Not a kid who lived across the street from you a hundred years ago. What then?"

Blue let out a hollow laugh. "Believe me, you don't want that."

"I keep trying to tell you that you don't know what I want."

"And I keep trying to tell you that you don't know *who I am*. The fact that I see a pudgy kid in pigtails on a pink bike is the only reason I'm here, Everly. That little girl is what's keeping you safe. Not from them." He jerked his chin toward the windows, and she knew who he meant. But he didn't take his eyes off her. And she couldn't bring herself to look away. "From *me*."

Everly knew it was stupid, that all of this was stupid and self-defeating at best, but she just couldn't seem to stop herself. He wanted her to run from him—she just knew it—and she wouldn't. Or couldn't.

Instead, she stepped forward, ignoring that dark glittering thing in his gaze and the way every muscle in his body turned to stone right there in front of her. And she kept going, until she was so close that she had to tip her head back to look up at him, the way she'd done in that lobby earlier.

"Of course I want to be safe from the men who killed Rebecca," she whispered, trying to make him hear her. See her. *Listen* to her, the way he had on that porch in a brooding blue Alaskan night. "But not from you, Blue. The last thing I want from you is too much safety."

And it didn't matter what he said then, because she could see the truth stamped all over him. She could see it in the way he held himself, stiff and hard as if the slightest bend would give him away. She could see the wildness in his eyes, and all over his face, and it was almost as if she could scent it in the air between them.

She knew he wanted her as much as she wanted him. *She knew.*

But she would be damned if she begged him. She would be damned if she put herself out there like that, when he refused to admit what was happening between them. No way.

Not tonight.

She might not recognize what had become of her life. But she still had her pride.

"Well?" she asked, challenging him. Daring him. Lifting up her chin like a prizefighter and wordlessly asking him to take a swing.

And she wasn't surprised when he didn't take that dare. When he stepped back, his face shut down into something dark and unreadable.

She wasn't surprised, no. But she discovered she was disappointed all the same.

"You should eat something," he gritted out, back to playing the father figure she didn't want. And certainly didn't need. "And get some sleep while you're at it."

"It's eight o'clock at night. And news flash, Blue. I'm not a child."

"So you keep telling me," Blue retorted, a swift hit she didn't see coming. It rocked her, though she fought to hide it. "Anytime you want to prove that, go right ahead. You could start by not throwing down challenges left and right."

"Why? Are you afraid?"

"Careful, Everly." And for a moment she wasn't sure she recognized him, so dark and forbidding did he look. "Be really careful. Your mouth is writing checks your body can't cash."

She wanted to scream. She wanted to rage at him. Throw herself at him, maybe, because she knew he wouldn't drop her. Not even tonight, when he looked as if, given the opportunity, he might consider killing her himself. Of course, she knew he wouldn't.

Everly knew that no matter what she said or did, she was safe with this man.

Whether she wanted that or not.

But he insisted on calling her a child. And she understood on some level that there was a huge part of him that expected her to react that way. To fling herself against the wall he represented, throw a tantrum, have a fit.

Anything to touch him, a knowing voice, deep down inside, whispered.

And nothing Blue had said to her tonight shamed her, but that unpleasant moment of self-awareness did.

So Everly did what she could. The only thing she could think to do. She drew herself up, trying to appear serene and unbothered—or as close as she could get to it on the outside.

He didn't have to know that she was torn up inside.

Then she turned, very slowly, and walked calmly into her bedroom.

Where she closed the door, staggered over to her bed, and spent a lot longer than she wanted to admit with her face in her pillows.

Not screaming or sobbing, though she wanted to do both. *Wanted to*, but she'd told him she wasn't a child, so she refused to let herself act like one.

Instead she relived that kiss again and again, hoping against hope that, at some point, it would affect her as little as Blue claimed it had affected him.

Because she had to stop obsessing about him. She knew that. She had to let this go no matter what her treacherous heart was telling her—and get back to the far more important business of fearing for her life.

Thirteen

Blue woke up like a switch being flipped.

It was a particular kind of jolting, immediate awareness he recognized from too many missions to count. He
went from sound asleep to alert and wide-awake in an
instant, shifting into battle mode seamlessly, because
some skills never died no matter where he found himself.

He didn't move. He stayed where he was, stretched
out on the couch in Everly's living room. Without changing his breathing or shifting his position, he eased open
his eyes and began scanning the apartment around him
to see if he could pinpoint what had woken him up.

One breath, long and deep like he was still asleep, in
case someone was watching him. Then another.

He heard it then. A soft clicking noise that didn't
sound like much by itself.

But Blue recognized the sound for what it was.

Someone was trying to pick the lock on the front door.

Before he fully finished the thought, he was moving.

He hit the floor soundlessly in his bare feet and moved swiftly to Everly's bedroom door. He could admit he was surprised she hadn't locked the door behind her when she'd marched away from him earlier, ripping him up in ways he refused to acknowledge—especially right now. But she hadn't.

He was inside and at her bed in two steps, then went down on the mattress beside her, hauling her into his arms with his hand tight over her mouth before she had time to react.

There was no time to think about how warm she was, sleepy and sweet. There was no time to catalog every last way her lush body fit with his, or what she was— or wasn't—wearing. There was no time to act like the horny teenager Blue hadn't been in years, not until her, when there was someone at the front door.

Everly woke up fast and scared, if the wild pulse in her neck was any guide. And she did his heart good by instantly trying to fight him off, as if she hadn't noticed that he was bigger and stronger and already pinning her to the bed.

Because that was what he'd taught her. It was never over unless you were dead. And if you weren't dead? You fought.

She was brave and determined, and it hurt like hell when she kicked him in the shin. He couldn't have been prouder.

"It's me," he said against her ear, ignoring the way his body responded to getting that close to her, no matter the pain in his shin. "Nod if you understand, but stay quiet."

He felt her shudder. When she nodded a moment later, he eased his hand from her mouth.

And then they were staring at each other in the dark. In her bed. Something that only the direst circumstance—like the one happening right this second—could get him to ignore.

He felt like a saint. An aggrieved, pissed-off saint of lost opportunities, victim to an irritating hero complex. As far as he could tell, it had resulted in nothing so far but a whole lot of battle scars and a misplaced sense of honor that, bonus, matched his current level of sexual frustration.

And it wasn't the time or place to think about any of that nonsense.

"Someone's at the door," he told her in a low voice, barely a whisper. "They're picking the lock as we speak. I want you to barricade yourself in here. If anyone tries to get through your door who's not me? I want you out that window again. Get dressed, put on some shoes, and take a different route to the police station in case they have someone watching the street. Got it?"

Everly didn't speak. She didn't point out what he assumed she must know—that if someone else was coming through her door, it would be over Blue's dead body. She just nodded once. With certainty.

Because he might have stood there in the other room and shot off his mouth about what a child she was, but he knew better. That had been a self-serving diatribe at best, to divert attention away from how much he wanted to get his hands on her. Everly was more courageous than she should ever have had to be.

And he hated himself for lying about that. For making it seem as if he didn't know it.

But there was no time for his crap.

Blue knew he was a dick, full of mixed messages and deserving of every last accusation she'd thrown at him, but he couldn't help himself. He leaned over and pressed a hard, swift kiss to Everly's mouth anyway, because she'd called him a liar and she'd been right.

And if he died out there, he didn't care if she knew it.

Everly made a small sound in the back of her throat that Blue thought he'd carry with him forever, and he'd never wanted anything more, in all his life, than to stay right where he was.

But his time was up.

He forced himself to roll away from her, then up and onto his feet. And he didn't look back.

Blue heard her scrambling out of her bed behind him as he headed back into the living room, keeping his ears pricked for the sound of her locking that door the way he'd told her to do. When he heard it a few seconds later, he went over to his bag and grabbed his gun, then moved quietly and quickly across the living room floor to the kitchen. Thanks to the apartment's open floor plan, he could wait in the shadows and position himself behind whoever came in as soon as the intruder crossed the foyer.

He heard the front doorknob rattle. He controlled his breathing and got his heart rate down, plastering himself to the wall.

He heard a louder noise and knew the dead bolt had been breached.

And he waited.

For a moment or two, nothing happened. Blue knew that whoever was at the door was doing the same thing he was. Waiting. Listening. Trying to figure out if anyone inside had heard them pick that lock.

Everything was quiet.

That they didn't come thundering in told Blue a few things about their operation. The choice of stealth over force was interesting, given what he'd seen of the goon squad so far. But he filed it away to think about later, once the current threat was neutralized.

He heard the door swing open. He watched the light from the hall outside sweep over the floor, then disappear.

It was go time.

Blue tossed aside everything careening around inside him. The taste of Everly's mouth beneath his. The look on her face when she'd tried to confront him about it. The way her green eyes had flashed when she'd called him a liar. And how soft and sleepy she'd been when he'd climbed into that bed beside her.

He had to let it all go.

Along with everything that could go wrong in the next few minutes, leaving her exposed and vulnerable. He would not put her at risk. He would not let her down.

But he had to shove that aside, too.

His adrenaline kicked in hard. But Blue waited for the next beat, and that cool, deep calm that washed over him as sure as night followed day. It focused his attention. It made him who he was.

A lethal weapon, courtesy of the United States Navy.

Aimed straight at whoever was foolish enough to bust into this apartment tonight.

He heard the faint brush of a foot against the wood floor in the foyer. It was tempting to jump out and handle the situation there and then, before this animal got any closer to Everly, but he held back. There was no point rushing in until he had all the information.

Until he knew how many asswipes had come to this little party, for example.

There was almost no light in the apartment with the front door shut, but Blue's eyes had long since adjusted. He stayed where he was as the intruder eased farther in. Then waited to see if there was anyone else with the one bulky figure who crept into the open living room. Concealed in the shadows of the kitchen, Blue didn't move when the man threw a look this way, then that. He even held his breath on the off chance the guy was sharper than he looked.

Blue could tell the second the asswipe's eyes adjusted to the dark, because he picked up his pace. And he didn't even glance toward Rebecca's room, which seemed like a pretty good indication that he'd been in the apartment before. He knew Rebecca's room was empty because he'd helped make it that way.

He headed straight for Everly's door. No hesitation.

And still Blue waited.

The intruder was the man who had been in Everly's office lobby earlier this evening. Blue could tell by the set of his shoulders, the way he walked, and the fact that he was still wearing the same suit that didn't quite fit him. As if it was an old one that the guy had pulled out for the express purpose of stalking a woman he'd expected to find scared, alone, and defenseless.

Everly was none of those things. Not anymore.

And she currently had one of the finest military weapons ever forged at her disposal, aimed and ready to play.

Blue eased himself out of the shadows, leaving his gun behind on the kitchen counter, tucked behind the toaster oven, because he didn't want a firefight in close quarters. Not when a stray bullet could punch through the thin walls and hit Everly. He moved across the living room floor in the intruder's wake, making no sound, focused entirely on this piece of garbage who thought he could break in and come after Everly like this.

In the middle of the night. With a gun in his meaty fist.

Hell no.

"You shouldn't have come alone, douchebag," Blue said into the stillness of the apartment around them.

He launched himself into the air as he spoke, landing a killer kick on the man's right forearm even as the asswipe whirled around. And tried to raise his gun the way Blue knew he would.

The intruder yelped at the kick, or maybe the way his weapon spun out of his hand, but he didn't go down. Instead, he threw himself at Blue.

He was a big guy. A gorilla of a man, huge and snarling. But Blue didn't have to study his face in the dark to get a handle on who this guy was. He could tell by the way the guy fought—or tried to fight. Big guys like this were used to bullying anyone smaller than them. Reveled in it, probably. Blue figured he might have boxed recreationally, then loomed around playing a bouncer outside clubs and the like, hoping his size and brawn would do the fighting for him. Blue pegged him as a gym rat with lofty aspirations.

But he was about to discover that going to the gym was not the same thing as training in martial arts and combat.

Blue set out to teach him that lesson, as brutally as possible.

He took a punch to the gut and let the goon throw him. He heard the other man's wheeze of triumph, and hoped he savored it. But it did what Blue wanted it to do. It made his opponent sloppy.

The intruder rushed Blue the way big men with no fighting prowess liked to do, because they thought their bulk could get it done. It often could.

But Blue wasn't a drunk outside a club or a much smaller female.

He rolled up from the floor in a single swift movement, then executed a combination of strikes with pinpoint accuracy. Groin, throat, back of the head.

The bigger man went down with a thud Blue thought might have rocked the building to its foundations.

Blue found the man's piece on the floor and kicked it into the farthest corner, then turned to finish the job.

But the gorilla was scrambling across the floor on his hands and knees. He was heading for the door, panting in a loud, anguished way that told Blue how much damage he'd done. He hauled himself onto his feet in the foyer, then threw himself toward the door.

Blue followed him, but the other man was crashing through the door and staggering out into the hall.

And he could have chased the douchebag into the stairwell and further expressed his feelings about stalkers and low-rent thugs all over the other man's battered, ugly face, but he didn't. For one thing, Everly's neighbors were opening their doors and squinting into the hallway.

And for another, Everly was still in the apartment and like hell was Blue leaving her alone to see if thug two, three, or four showed up.

"Go back to sleep," Blue barked out, using his best military voice to silence everyone in the hallway. "The problem is solved."

And he waited there, grim and steel-eyed, until one by one, the neighbors each shut and then loudly relocked their doors.

Blue stepped back inside Everly's apartment and did the same, though he thought it was a wasted effort at this point. If the lock could be picked once—or twice, if he counted the night Rebecca had been killed, or taken, or whatever had happened to her—it could certainly happen again. But he couldn't worry about that now.

He pulled the table in the foyer over and planted it in front of the door. It wouldn't stop anyone who really wanted to get in, he knew. What it would do was give him a few extra minutes of reaction time. Because he was fairly certain that when these people came back, they would come in force, and they wouldn't make the same mistake this first guy had.

They knew Blue was here now. He had to assume they'd come prepared. But he also figured it would take them some time to mobilize, since Blue had been here a week and today was the first time they'd made a move.

He grabbed his gun from the kitchen and the intruder's from where he'd kicked it, stashing both safely in his bag. Then he crossed to Everly's room and knocked twice on the door. "It's me."

She threw the lock immediately, indicating she'd been standing right there on the other side of the door. Possibly even pressed against it.

"I barely heard a thing," she said, craning her head to look past him.

"That's because I handled it," Blue told her, too gruffly.

Because she wasn't dressed the way she should have been. He saw her jeans on her bed behind her and a pair of Converse next to them, but Everly was still wearing nothing but the T-shirt she'd been sleeping in.

Blue knew exactly how little was under it because it had been hiked up around her waist when he'd rolled into that bed with her.

Which he was definitely not thinking about, because he was a grown man who could control himself.

Everly pushed past him, her head swiveling wildly on her neck as she looked around the living room, like she expected to see evidence of the fight imprinted on the floor. She switched on the light next to the couch, and that didn't help matters. Maybe she could see better. But the trouble was, so could Blue.

The light gave him a much better view of the long sweep of her legs, for example, in case they weren't already burned into his brain. Perfectly formed. Just as pale and freckled as her belly, God help him. And worse, the hint of her butt right there where the hem of her oversized T-shirt flirted with the tops of her thighs.

She was killing him.

The puffed-up gym rat hadn't been much of a challenge, but there was a distinct possibility Everly Campbell was going to take him down with a nightshirt.

"Do me a favor," Blue gritted out before he well and truly lost it. "Go back to bed. Try to get some sleep. Because in the morning, we're out of here."

She was still staring out at the living room. At Rebecca's door, Blue realized in the next second. As if she were reliving what had happened there all over again. What she'd seen that had caused all of this in the first place.

"I guess using me as bait worked."

"I guess it did."

"But you didn't catch him."

"I hurt him." Blue didn't work very hard to keep the satisfaction from his voice. He heard the little breath Everly pulled in at that, but if she thought he was a violent savage, he couldn't really bring himself to care. Because he *was* one, and proud of it. "And the thing about a guy like that is that he's never alone. He'll be back, with friends. You can set your clock by it. We need to be somewhere else tomorrow night."

"That's comforting, thank you."

Everly took her time turning back to face him, and Blue braced himself for what he was sure he'd see on her face. Because it was easy to talk about heroes in the abstract. The same way it was easy to support wars that took place overseas, out of sight, where no one had to face the consequences of daily engagement with the enemy. Everybody loved a decorated war hero in uniform when he returned from battle unharmed and stoic. Few people wanted to deal with the physical and psychological cost veterans paid when they were back home, out of uniform, and alone. Blue had lost as many friends after their tours of duty had ended as he had in battle, because some wars never ended. Some wars stayed with a man. And a lot of his friends had fallen on that internal battle-field, supposedly safe at home, as surely as they would have to an IED.

Heroes were much better on paper.

Everly had come to him because she wanted the kind of hero who looked good in comics and in the movies. Blue knew she had no idea what that actually meant.

He'd told Everly he was a monster. She should have listened.

But when she finally faced him, her expression wasn't what he was expecting. She didn't look disgusted or hor-rified. She looked . . . worried, almost. Everly reached over and ran her fingers over the back of his hand, then took it in hers, and Blue had to fight to keep from jerking it away from her.

She looked up at him, and it dawned on him that this woman wasn't worried about any gorilla thugs coming back tomorrow night. She was worried about *him*.

Something inside him seemed to shift. As if he lost his balance, though he knew he hadn't. He didn't.

"Are you hurt?" she asked softly.

"Of course not."

But the truth was, Blue hadn't stopped to take an inven-tory. He did it then. There was a tender spot on his jaw. A little bruising and some scrapes on his knuckles where he'd landed a few good blows. And a faint hitch in his thigh, where the douchebag had landed a kick. That was it.

He got hurt a lot worse regularly in Isaac's gym of pain.

"This guy was low-level muscle at best. Too dependent on his gun, which didn't help him much when I relieved him of it. And he was used to his size solving problems to his satisfaction, which also didn't help when I took him down."

Everly was still holding his hand between her palms, as if she were inspecting it for signs of worse damage.

And maybe if Blue kept telling himself this was a clinical moment with medical overtones—not that Everly had ever indicated she had any training in that area—it would start to feel that way.

"He could have killed you," she said, in a hushed, solemn voice that made him feel even more off-kilter than before.

"Always a possibility." He didn't know why he was talking in that low voice just because she was. As if this were intimate, this discussion that shouldn't have been anything but an exchange of information. If that. "The truth is, I'm hard to kill."

She shuddered, and something seemed to scrape through his gut, leaving him hollow. He wanted to call it weakness, but he didn't feel even remotely fragile. He wanted to rip apart every creature who had ever dared threaten her, in the next fifteen minutes, if at all possible. He wanted to make them pay for frightening her. More than that, he wanted to tattoo her fingerprints on his hand where she'd checked him over to see if he was okay. He wanted to bundle her up and keep her safe no matter what it cost him, even if *safe* meant keeping her the hell away from him.

He looked at her and he *wanted*.

For the first time in his life, Blue wanted . . . everything.

"I hate the fact that you know that," Everly whispered, fiercely, and her green eyes were shot through with an emotion he couldn't identify when she looked up at him. "And I hate that you had to put that to the test tonight. Especially for me."

And before he could brush that off, change the subject, and fight his way back to solid ground, she made everything worse.

She threw herself at him.

He could have handled it if she'd thrown a punch. His whole life was about functional responses to violence. How to contain it, survive it, combat it. He was good at all those things. He'd even have said he lived for it, if asked. He could have had her down and handled in a heartbeat if she'd tried to hit him.

But Everly wasn't trying to beat on him.

On the contrary, she wrapped her arms around him. Then leaned in close, nestled her head against his chest in a move that made his entire body ache like some kind of sudden-onset arthritis, and hugged him.

Tight.

And didn't seem to understand she'd disarmed a decorated Navy SEAL who was used to winning every battle before him.

Without landing a single blow.

Fourteen

Everly was only going with an instinct that she didn't entirely understand.

And her own deep, abiding need, if she was honest. To get her hands on him. To feel that he was alive, flesh and blood. Warm and real.

Not another casualty of this battle that she'd woken up to find herself fighting.

Maybe she also just wanted to touch him. *Needed* to touch him, to make sure that no matter what he said in his tough guy way, Blue was really and truly okay.

"It was like reliving a nightmare but knowing I was awake," she whispered against the hot, hard wall of his chest, without stopping to question whether it was a good idea. "This time I knew exactly what was happening. I knew what those thumping sounds meant. I was so afraid that I'd open the door and it would be you this time, broken and bloody and—"

"Stop," he said, but he didn't sound pissed at her. Or as if that were an order he expected her to obey like the good little soldier she wasn't. "That's not going to happen."

"Not tonight," she agreed, feeling ferocious and relieved at once. And something else that pounded through her, edgy and dark, spurring her toward a shimmering that yawned there ahead of her, just out of reach.

Something wild and dangerous in a different way. Something irrevocable.

She held him tighter, and she felt it in every part of her when his arms finally—finally—closed around her.

And Everly knew she wasn't imagining *this*. She wasn't making this up in her head. This wasn't a simple physical reaction to the man who'd broken in here or the fact Blue had fought him off. She knew, like it or not, that they were both caught up in the grip of the same thing.

That they had been all this time. Since the moment she'd found him again after all these years in the cool shade of the towering pines behind Fool's Cove.

She wasn't sure she could handle it. Not and stay in one piece. She kept her head turned to the side so she could catch her breath. So she could try to figure out what she should do next. Whether she should climb in bed and go to sleep the way he'd told her she should, or whether she needed to surrender, once and for all, to this *thing*.

And maybe throw herself at him while she was at it.

Because whatever else might happen, she knew that Blue would catch her.

He's already caught you, a voice inside her pointed out slyly, as if she might have missed the deliciously heavy weight of his sculpted, honed arms around her, cradling her body against his, as if she'd been put on this earth for exactly this purpose. To fit against this man, just like this. *What are you waiting for?*

And it was as if everything crystallized inside her at that.

During the drive to Alaska, she'd told herself that all she wanted was to get her life back. But if the past few days were a test run, the truth was that she hated it. This whole long week of baiting a trap, she'd had the feeling that she was merely playing a role in her own skin, and she didn't think that had as much to do with what had happened to Rebecca as she'd wanted to pretend.

For good or ill, her desperate drive to Alaska had woken her up.

And there was no going back now. She was sleep-walking through a job she'd stopped finding exciting a long time ago, living for the clock to tick over to the precise minute she could escape and race down to the lobby to find Blue again. She was ignoring texts and calls from her friends and older brother, because she had some notion that pretending they didn't exist would keep them safe. And also because she didn't want to waste a single second she had left with Blue.

She existed for that walk home in Blue's company. For the hours they spent training together in her living room. For the dreamy, too-hot showers she took afterward, when she could lose herself in vivid fantasies about his hands all over her, but without the workout clothes this time . . .

Everly knew what she wanted.

What she'd always wanted, if she were being honest.

She'd been fascinated by Blue when she was a little girl, too young for crushes in any meaningful way. She was seven when he graduated from high school, but she'd followed him around for years before that, because she'd thought he was *wonderful*.

She still thought he was wonderful. But now she knew precisely what she could do with all that wonder.

Everly couldn't understand why she was wavering. Why her heart was pounding much too fast and she was on the verge of pulling away, then running off to hide. Why was she worried about staying safe now? The past month had taught her that no one was safe, least of all her. Safety could be stolen from anyone in a few seconds.

It could be taken in an instant. In her sleep.

Do or die, she told herself.

And there were only so many nights left before somebody killed her. Or before Blue solved everything, made her life safe again, but then disappeared off into the Alaskan wilderness.

Any way she looked at it, whatever happened, she was running out of time.

Why not spend this one night the way she'd been imagining since that first night in Alaska?

She tilted her head back and smiled at him, reveling in that hard mouth of his. That beautifully stern expression. And that bright, hot gleam in his dark eyes, which she chose to believe was all for her.

Everly stopped dithering. It was like a key had slid into a lock, and everything suddenly made sense. She rose up on her toes, pressing herself against him as if she were stretching like a cat, and looped her arms around his neck.

And it was *awesome*.

In this position, she could feel him in a way she never had before, not even when they'd been grappling in some or other lethal hold. She wasn't wearing a bra beneath the T-shirt she'd been sleeping in, and it only now occurred to her that she wasn't wearing her pajama pants, either.

Thank God.

Because she could feel him everywhere. *Everywhere.* Pressed up against her, hard and hot, and entirely Blue.

"You don't need to do this." His voice was low. Gravelly.

But what she noticed most was that he didn't push her away. He didn't step back. The gleam in his gaze went . . . molten.

And she did, too.

"But I do," Everly said quietly. "I really, really do."

And this time, she was the one who kissed him.

She set her mouth to his and indulged herself at last. She tested the shape of his firm, beautiful lips. Then she teased them apart and slipped inside, and drowned herself in all that sweet, hot fire.

And she felt it everywhere when he growled a bit, as if he liked that as much as she did; angled his head to one side; and took control.

It was a breathless catapult, wild and slick.

He took her head between his hands. He kissed her and he kissed her, and she fought to get closer. To go deeper. To taste every part of him she could.

Blue kissed her as if he had to. As if he couldn't get enough. As if she'd broken something in both of them, and now they both had to pay the price.

The sweet, hot, glorious price.

Everly had the distant thought that she'd happily bankrupt herself if it meant she could have this.

His hands moved, one threading into her hair to hold her head still, leaving her mouth and neck bare for him to sample at will. And he did, a touch of fire, a faint hit of steel. The other hand slid down her back, slow and certain, then beneath the hem of her T-shirt to mold itself to her hip.

Then lower still, as if he couldn't help himself. As if he needed to test the shape of her bottom, full against his palm.

Everly shuddered. Blue muttered something, hot and male and explosive.

Then everything shifted. He lifted her up and swung her into his arms as if she were weightless. Or maybe she just felt that way around him. She was captivated by the span of his mighty shoulders. And that wide, sculpted chest with a dusting of dark hair. And that intense, deliriously focused look on his face, as if she were the only thing in the whole of the world.

Everly was afraid her heart might claw its way out of her chest.

Or maybe the truth was she didn't mind what happened next, as long as it happened with him.

She thought he might head into the bedroom, but there was something desperate in him. In her, too. She felt nothing but grateful when he carefully laid her down on the couch and then came down after her, covering her with his long, hard body.

"The bed—" she gasped.

"Too far."

He settled between her legs at last, and it was her turn to frame his face with her hands. She ran her palms over the rough surface of his unshaven jaw, thrilling to the faint abrasion against her skin. It seemed to wind its way deep inside her until it pooled like a new fire between her legs.

He let out another sound, something like a sigh.

As if this were magic for him, too.

"I need to taste you," he said, his voice like its own caress, there in the dark.

And all Everly could do was make a noise, helpless and greedy at once. She didn't know what it meant. But Blue seemed to.

He reached down and took the hem of her T-shirt in one fist, then lifted it, tugging it up and over her head.

And then she was naked, save the skimpy pair of panties she wore, stretched there beneath him.

Open. Vulnerable.

Completely exposed to the most gorgeous man she'd ever seen in her life.

But Everly thought she'd never felt more beautiful than she did with Blue's dark, hot gaze all over her, as if she were an altar and he had a mind to get his worship on.

He bent down, his hands smoothing their way over her as if she were precious beyond measure, so he could lift her breast to his lips. He licked her until she squirmed, and then he sucked.

And when she cried out, he started all over again on the other one.

Everly simply tipped her head back, surrendered herself to his hands and his mouth, his teeth, and his low, stirring laughter, and let him drive her wild.

She was breathing loud and heavy when he moved down farther, and she squirmed beneath him. His big hands circled her hips and held her still as he tested the depth of her navel, then licked his way down farther still.

"Stop fidgeting," he said against her belly, halfway between her navel and the part of her that ached for him the most.

"I can't help it."

"Try."

Everly could feel him smile. And his words were like coals, hot and glowing, pressed deep into her. She couldn't stay still. She couldn't stop smiling, her head tipped back like she was at the very top of a roller coaster and about to take flight.

"Or what?" she managed to ask.

"Oh," he murmured, the scrape of his jaw against her tender skin, his head much too close to that melting place between her legs. "I'm sure I'll think of an appropriate punishment."

Everly couldn't wait.

Blue's fingers curled into the sides of her panties, then peeled the scrap of lace out of his way. He shifted as he tugged them down her legs, then tossed them aside.

She thought she said his name, but she couldn't hear herself over the racket of her own heartbeat and her raw, desperate breathing, so loud she worried she might wake up the neighbors.

But she knew Blue was laughing, because she could feel it when he pressed a kiss to one hip bone. The way his mouth curved. The way his big body shook with delight.

"Hold on, baby," he told her.

Everly heard that. And she thought the way he said *baby* might throw her over the edge, right there and then. She felt herself tremble, so hard and deep it made her throat feel tight.

Blue laughed again, then moved lower on the couch, wedging his shoulders more securely between her outstretched legs.

Then he leaned forward and set his mouth between her legs.

And everything . . . *lit up*.

She was on fire. His mouth was hot, masterful, and sure, and Everly couldn't stand it. She couldn't take it—

And she couldn't get enough.

Blue licked into her, and she lost herself. She felt too hot to bear. She rocked against him, lifting her hips toward his mouth like an offering. He wrapped his arms around her hips, and she didn't know if he was moving her or she was moving herself, rocking herself against his clever mouth in a kind of blistering rush, lost in the wild sensation stampeding through her, flinging her arms up over her face as she began to fall—

And too quickly, too easily, she shattered into a thousand pieces, all of them ablaze.

She didn't know how long she lost herself out there, too many pieces thrown too far apart. Too much fire, not enough breath.

Too much need and longing wringing her dry where she lay.

When she came back into herself, she was still naked on the couch. Blue was crouched there beside her, as if he'd been rummaging in that bag of his.

His gaze met hers and held, dark and unyielding, and, God, she loved how uncompromising he was. Even now.

"Sorry," she managed to get out, smiling at him. She reached out and fit her hand to his remarkable face. "I think I died."

And she watched that ruthlessness in him soften, just the slightest bit, right there before her.

"Not yet," Blue drawled. And this time, when his mouth curved, she felt as if it were wired to different parts of her body. Her mouth, certainly. And better yet, that tender place between her legs that seemed to have a heartbeat all its own. "Want to see what we can do about that?"

She couldn't seem to keep herself from smiling wider.

Blue tossed something on the coffee table, then stripped off the athletic pants he'd been wearing. Everly hardly had time to admire him the way she wanted to, tall and sculpted to ferocious perfection.

But then she didn't care, because he was settling himself between her legs again, and that was better. That was everything.

She could feel him, huge and hot, against her hip.

"Blue . . . ," she whispered.

"Tell me what you want, baby."

Everly smoothed her hands over the parts of his wide back that she could reach. "I just did." She smiled at him again and thought the smiling might break her face in two. But she couldn't seem to mind. "You. I just want you."

He made a noise that on another man she might have called desperate. But from Blue, it was like music to her ears.

And then he was kissing her again, deeper this time. Rougher and hotter, and somehow sweeter for it.

She wound herself around him, and for a long time, lifetimes maybe, they explored each other. Red-hot and breathless, there in the dark.

And when they were both shaking, he reached over to the coffee table and grabbed the foil packet he'd dropped there. He ripped it open with his teeth, sheathed himself with a single, practiced movement, and then, finally, held himself there at the entrance to her body.

And for a moment, they were suspended there.

Everly's heart was a drum. She could feel Blue's pound, too, with his chest tight against hers. He seemed almost . . . wary. And she couldn't stand it.

She slid her hands to his face again. She traced his beautiful mouth with her fingertips. She held his dark gaze and she smiled, so wide and sure it made her eyes water.

"Blue," she told him, solemn and soft at once. "You're not a monster. You're a man. And I've never wanted anyone more."

He let out a sound, as if she'd torn it from him, and then he was pushing his way inside her.

She was melting, shivering, and still, it took a moment or two for her to accommodate him. But then he was lodged inside her, sunk down deep, and Everly knew she'd never felt anything like this, so good and so right, in her life.

And that was when he began to move.

And every time he slid inside her, it was better. Impossibly, unimaginably better.

Blue set a pace. First slow and steady, then deeper. Determined.

And Everly was there with him. She clutched at his shoulders, and she didn't simply take his thrusts—she met them.

She felt like liquid.

She felt like his.

And with every roll of his hips, she felt made new.

Part of him. Changed. Electric and free.

He dropped his head to her neck, and pressed his mouth there. His thrusts became wilder. All she could do was hold on and meet him.

Again and again, she met him.

Until she thought the fire might burn them both alive.

"I need you to come again," he muttered against her neck, and Everly shuddered. "Now."

And she obeyed him. Once again, she obeyed him.

She drowned herself against him, she whispered his name, and she let herself go. Over and over she tumbled, losing herself in a new shattering, and this time, he was with her.

This time, he called her name, and followed.

And when Everly woke up again, it was to a crashing noise and the sound of glass shattering.

Which was terrifying enough.

But then the walls caught fire.

Fifteen

"Fire!" Everly cried out, still tangled up against him on the couch.

And Blue was in motion again before he fully registered what was happening.

There was the crash. Shattering that he understood came from Everly's window before he fully put together that something had come through it. And a deep sort of *whoosh*ing sound that he knew, on a deep level that had everything to do with his years in hell, spelled death. And fast.

Blue rolled to the floor, taking Everly with him and twisting so that he took the brunt of the impact. He rolled her carefully to one side, then sat up to assess the situation and the damage as best he could.

Firebomb.

They'd thrown it into Everly's bedroom window, where they clearly expected her to be sleeping—and now burning to a crisp—but he couldn't allow himself to think about what might have happened if she'd been tucked up in her bed where she belonged. They'd had good aim, too. The flames were already dancing along the length of the bed she should have been sleeping in, and licking at the walls.

Blue didn't have time to explain himself. He scooped up her T-shirt and tossed it at her as he lunged for her bedroom doorway.

"Cover your face," he ordered her. "And call nine-one-one. Tell them the address and hang up."

He didn't wait to see if she would obey him. He wrapped his hand in his own T-shirt as a precaution, then reached out to grab the doorknob and slam the door shut. He turned back to face her as the apartment's smoke detector began to shrill.

"We have to get out of here," he told her, loud enough to be heard over the insistent shrill from above. "Now."

Everly looked pale and a bit sick, but determined. She was clutching the apartment's landline phone in one hand while she pulled on the T-shirt he'd thrown her with the other, but she only nodded at his latest order. Blue realized he expected her to argue. But she didn't. Instead, he heard her belt out her address into the receiver, then toss it on the table, just as he'd asked.

He headed back to the couch, shrugging into his own T-shirt. He shucked on his athletic pants, stamped his feet into his boots, and grabbed his bag with his other hand. By the time he turned around again, Everly was across the living room floor near the kitchen, throwing open the utility closet that he knew by now contained an apartment-sized washer and dryer, stacked on top of each other.

"Now, Everly," he bit out, eyeing the bedroom door in case it exploded.

She didn't react, but she didn't stop what she was doing, either. She yanked a pair of jeans out of the dryer, then stepped into them. She hooked them up over her hips, then raked her hands through the rest of the laundry in the dryer, finding a handful of what looked like panties. Nothing else. By the time Blue made it to the foyer, Everly was ready, meeting him there and sticking her feet into another pair of Converse she'd left by the door.

These were bright red, he noticed. And he couldn't have said why that little detail, combined with how focused and calm she appeared in this latest crisis, made something in him clutch. Hard.

The girl next door had grown up into the perfect woman, but this wasn't the time to throw himself into that minefield.

Will there ever be a right time? something in him asked. *Will you ever face what's been happening here?*

But Blue didn't really want to look into why his instant response to that question was negative.

"Stay behind me," he told her curtly, because he wasn't sure he even knew what might come out of his mouth around her. It was something he planned to be deeply pissed about—once they were safe.

"I will," she said, in that same quiet, resigned way. As if she'd woken up to a firebomb a thousand times.

He hated the fact that it had happened to her even once. Blue was the one who'd been trained for this crap. Everly was supposed to . . .

Stay seven years old forever? that same obnoxious voice asked.

Blue gritted his teeth and shrugged his holster back on and into place. He hauled the table he'd left in front of the door back to its usual place in the foyer. Then he pulled his gun out, clicked off the safety, and eased the front door open.

He took a quick glance out into the hallway, fully expecting to find a gun in his face. Maybe more than one.

But the hallway was empty. He stepped out, then motioned for Everly to follow him, and he knew he should have reprimanded her when she tucked her fingers in the waistband of his sweats. He shouldn't have encouraged that kind of thing, but the truth was, he liked knowing where she was.

Then they were on the move, a solid three minutes, maybe four, from impact. Blue moved swiftly down the hall toward the stairwell, and pulled the building's fire alarm as he passed.

He sorted through the information he had as he jogged down the stairs, Everly right there behind him as he went. It seemed like an extreme escalation. Stalker to hit man to firebomb in the course of a single evening after all these weeks of nothing. Who did that? Who went from game playing on social media to explosive devices tossed through windows?

Blue turned that question over and over in his head as he heard the rest of the building start to come awake around them. There were shouts and slamming doors on the floors as they ran past them. The usual reactions to fire alarms in city buildings.

But he had the two of them out of the stairwell, then headed toward the side door of the building that let out into the alley beside it, before he heard the fire trucks in the distance.

"We're going to head for the SUV," he threw over his shoulder when they reached the door to the outside. He eased his way out, checking the alley for lurking scumbags, but it was clear.

"I thought you got rid of it days ago."

Everly sounded a shade too monotone for his peace of mind, which suggested she was in shock, but there was nothing Blue could do about it now.

"I moved it from the front of the building days ago. Rule number two is always, always have a getaway car." She slipped out behind him and closed the door carefully, instead of letting it slam shut, because she wasn't just a pretty face. Not this one. "Or, you know, a handy seaplane. A boat. Whatever works."

Instead of heading toward the front of the building and the busy street, he took her elbow and led her in the other direction. There was a fence in the middle of the alley, separating one property from the next, but Blue didn't pause. He threw his bag up and over the chain-link barrier, then turned to Everly.

"Can you climb it?"

She was too stiff when she stopped moving. Pale and fragile-looking, to his mind. But there was a kind of grim acceptance in the way she stared at that fence. It ate at him.

"I can climb it."

"Because if you can't, I can—"

"I said I can climb it."

And then she did. Not particularly gracefully. Not fast or with any skill. She looked like what she was—a scared woman climbing over a city fence in the middle of the night because she had to. Because she'd decided she would, and so she did.

Blue waited where he was, making sure no one was coming up behind them. But when she reached the top of the fence and threw her leg over, she let out a long, shaky breath, and he found himself looking at her instead of keeping watch.

"You okay?"

She didn't quite smile. Her mouth looked too soft and too vulnerable for that, and Blue's problem was that all he could think about, then, was tasting her all over again. Getting his mouth on her and who cared where they were or how much danger they were in?

He was even more pissed than he had been before, because whoever was chasing her had ruined that, too. He could have woken up with her. He could have taken his time. He could have—

"I'm okay," she said, snapping him back to this alley. This moment. And the things he should have been doing that weren't fantasizing about getting his hands on her again. "I'm alive, right?"

And for a moment she looked more than simply *alive*. The security light from the building behind hers made her strawberry blond hair look like some kind of halo. And it made Blue feel alive in ways he couldn't explain to himself.

As if she'd flipped a switch in him. One he hadn't known was there.

One he didn't like knowing was there, especially

when he felt lit up, a lot like that impossible red halo and her soft mouth as she looked down at him. Then swung her leg over and climbed down the other side.

Leaving him . . . outside himself and out of sorts and not at all okay with pretty much anything.

He was almost glad he had concrete things to think about. Getting her away and to safety. Figuring out what hornet's nest he'd kicked and how to find it again, with an exterminator this time. Then removing himself from the Chicago area and all these damned ghosts before it was too late.

Whatever *too late* meant. He shoved that to the side, too.

Then shoved his gun in his shoulder holster so he could run and flip himself over the fence. He landed in a crouch, then grabbed his bag with one hand and her with his other.

He wasn't thinking about the way her fingers laced with his or the fire that raced in him at even so little contact, because that was unacceptable. Unacceptable in every way, and yet he took a moment to let the heat really settle in him.

Because her mouth was so soft and her eyes were so big and he was a sucker for her in ways he was afraid to list, even in his own head.

And then they ran.

This was the girl who'd complained about potentially having to climb five flights of stairs, but she didn't complain tonight. Everly gripped his hand and ran beside him, her breath ragged and loud, but she didn't slow down. She didn't stop. She followed him out the other side of the alley to the street behind hers and across three more blocks before he finally led her to the SUV, which he moved to a new spot in the neighborhood every day. Just for the possibility of an occasion like this.

He bundled her into the passenger seat, then circled around, looking for potential danger in every shadow— but there was nothing there. Just the relative quiet of a city night. They were three blocks away from her building, and there was still no sign of whoever had thrown that crap through her window.

Something worse than temper cracked in him at that, but it still wasn't time to take that on. Not when they were exposed like this.

There was all the time in the world to get pissed about the intentions of asswipes, Blue thought as he climbed behind the wheel and fired up the engine, but not while Everly was out on the streets. Unsafe and unprotected.

"We need to find a safe house," he said tersely as he pulled the SUV out of its parking spot and gunned it down the street. "And then we need to reassess this situation."

She didn't say anything. One minute dragged by. Then another. He slid her a probing sort of glance as he turned the corner, but he couldn't see any obvious issues. She was sitting gamely enough in the seat next to him. Not shaking. Not crying. Her hands were folded neatly in her lap. She was maybe too quiet after everything that had happened tonight, but that was the only indication that something might be amiss.

"Are you all right?"

Everly laughed. It was a wild, jagged sound. She clapped her hands over her mouth, as if the sound had shocked her.

She stared at him over the tops of her hands, and then dropped them slowly. "I'm sorry. That feels inappropriate, but the truth is, I can't really tell."

"Don't lose your shit now, baby," Blue said in a low voice as he circled the next block, making sure the sedan in his rearview mirror wasn't tailing him. "I know it's tempting to fall apart, but this is the time to keep it together."

"Together, absolutely. I'm totally together. Though it did just occur to me that a giant bomb, or whatever that was, right there in my apartment, isn't something they can clean up before the police get there. So I guess that's progress?"

"They firebombed us," Blue said tightly. He should have said *you*. But he didn't correct himself. "They threw it through your bedroom window, and let's be clear. That was deliberate. They expected you to be in that bed. They knew you had someone watching out for you in the living room, so they targeted you directly instead of worrying about where I was."

For a long moment she didn't say anything. A quick glance told him she was still sitting there, staring out at the road ahead of them.

"I get it," he said roughly. "I remember the first time I was in a situation that wasn't a drill or an exercise, when it was suddenly clear to me that someone was trying to kill me. Me, specifically."

And then he had to sit there wondering why the hell he'd brought up something like that.

"Did it make you feel sick to your stomach?"

"Yes."

"A little dizzy?"

"Yes." He stopped at a red light and kept his eyes on the dark street behind them. "That's normal."

"I'm betting you didn't curl into a ball and cry until the weird, targeted feeling went away."

He couldn't help himself. That made him grin. "Not exactly. I did my job."

She sighed, shuddery and long, and he spent more than a few moments lecturing himself about why it wasn't smart to reach over and put his hand on her. Because it sent the wrong message. Because despite the game he appeared to be playing here, he wasn't that guy.

Then he did it anyway. Just a hand on her leg, to let her know she wasn't alone.

The next breath she took sounded different. More . . . wistful.

"I'm sure that at some point it's going to hit me that I probably just lost everything," she said after a moment.

She slid her hand over his and held it there, and Blue started telling himself a whole lot of lies about it. Like that he'd have reached out to anyone in the same situation. Like that he couldn't feel the heat of her skin through her jeans. Like that he couldn't remember that slick, perfect slide deep inside her.

"Things are replaceable," he said. "You're not."

She settled back in her seat and he took his hand back, because it was that or do something even more stupid.

"Right now the only thing I can think about is how happy I am that no one can accuse me of lying," she said. "About this, anyway. Is that crazy?"

"I don't think there's any set behavior for how to act when someone blows up your life."

Everly rubbed her hands over her face. "I hope no one

else gets hurt. I don't know how I forgot that the whole building could burn down. I don't think I could live with that."

"You can live with anything," Blue told her, his voice curt. Harsher than it should have been. "That's the price of surviving sometimes. You don't honor anybody's memory by wasting the life you get to live when they lost theirs. Remember that."

Sixteen

But if Blue was expecting Everly to react badly or crumple or finally collapse into jagged, emotional pieces, she didn't.

Instead, she let out a laugh.

"That's what I love about you," she said.

She laughed again, but with a sharp edge to it that he knew was the kind of shock that could tip over into tears or hysteria if she let it. He figured that was why she didn't mind throwing around the word *love* like that.

And more, why he didn't drive the car off the road at the sound of it.

"You're always there with exactly the right thing to say to make everything better," she was saying, with that same edge but without any apparent collapsing. "Good job, Blue. I feel much better."

He found himself smirking against his will. He wouldn't have blamed her if she'd lost it back in her apartment. If she'd been useless and sobbing and he'd had to cart her out of there on his back. But Everly didn't break. She'd handled this whole situation on her own for weeks. She'd driven all the way to Alaska and then over a treacherous mountain pass that made locals shake and grown men cry. Regularly.

There was no doubt about it. Everly was a badass.

Even now, he kept waiting for some kind of reaction to take hold of her, but if it did, she didn't show it. She pulled her feet up onto the seat so she could wrap her arms around her knees, but that was it.

She didn't cry. She didn't start hyperventilating. She didn't have a well-earned panic attack, right there on the floor of the SUV.

Blue couldn't tell if that was a good thing or a bad thing.

For her, that was. He already knew it was a terrible thing for him. He didn't need any reasons to like this woman more than he already did.

"I need to think about why this happened," Blue muttered out loud, after he'd put some significant distance between them and Everly's neighborhood with no apparent tail. "I'm going to drive around a while longer to make sure no one is following us. Then we're going to have to find a place to hunker down for a while. Until I can figure out who the hell is throwing Molotov cocktails through your bedroom window."

Everly checked out her side mirror, as if the fact they could be followed hadn't occurred to her. And as if she maybe expected to see something *right there*. "Do you think someone's following us?"

"I think they wanted us to go up in flames, and hopefully, they'll think we did for at least the next hour or so. But I wouldn't be surprised if they had a couple of people watching the front door. I don't think anyone saw us go out that alley, but you never know."

He heard her take another one of those long, steadying breaths. "What makes a good hiding place?"

She wasn't focused on her own potential death, he noted. Just on the next step. That same thing he was devoting all his damned energy to ignoring kicked at him. Again.

And harder this time.

"We're not hiding. We're beating a strategic retreat while we gather intel."

"Okay. Where's a good place to not hide?"

"Somewhere untraceable with an armed guard would be nice," Blue said darkly. "But I'd settle for off the radar. That means cash only, in case they're tracking your credit cards. Or mine, which is a lot less likely but not impossible."

Though if they did try to run him through any kind of database, it would set off alarms back at Alaska Force HQ. Which could be its own fun—but not with Everly in tow. The kind of fun he wanted to have with her didn't involve a firefight.

"I would typically head for the last place anyone who knows me would expect me to go," he told her. "But I don't know who these people are. I don't know what they know about you. I still don't know why they took out your roommate. The truth is, I expected them to escalate a lot slower than this, so tonight is squarely on me."

Everly was quiet for a moment. Blue switched lanes, then took a quick right, still scanning the road behind him as he went. He hadn't seen any sign of a tail yet, but he couldn't rely on that. Not in a situation like this, where he'd already been wrong.

And, worse, had let these scumbags catch him and Everly naked.

Literally naked.

"I don't think you set my bedroom on fire," Everly said mildly.

Too mildly.

"Well, I might as well have."

"You were right there on the couch with me. Unless you're confessing that you set my bed on fire and then ran back to the couch before I woke up so I would think—"

"You're my responsibility," Blue managed to get out, stiff and harsh. "This night is my failure, no one else's."

They stopped at another light, and the passing head-lights of other cars played over Everly's face, but she didn't look at him.

Which meant Blue had nowhere to push the unpleas-ant weight that was pressing down on him like it wanted to pound him into dust. He was familiar with the sensa-tion. He'd felt it before, on other missions that went epi-cally wrong.

But he'd never felt it like this. Not sitting next to the woman he—

Stop. The voice inside him could have been a com-manding officer's, it was so complete an order. *Now.*

"I know where we can go," Everly said when the car started moving again.

Blue shot her a dark look she didn't appear to notice. "Yeah? Because you have to think about the fact these guys are too bold already. They showed up at your work. And your apartment, repeatedly. You need to assume they know everything about you."

"Then they know I only go back home to visit my parents very rarely. For Christmas every year, sure. And sometimes for my mother's birthday, but that was two months ago."

"They'll look at your parents' house first."

"Right now?" she asked, and Blue wasn't sure he liked the pushback. Meaning, he definitely didn't like it. "Tonight? First they'd have to realize I'm not already dead, right?"

"That's not going to take as long as you might think."

Everly seemed unimpressed. "My parents are in Europe. I know where they keep the spare key. At the very least, we could grab a hot shower while we figure out where to go next."

"Out of the question." He was . . . agitated. He tried to keep it out of his voice, with little success. "It's too obvious."

She shifted slightly in her seat then, and Blue couldn't say he really enjoyed the sensation of her sharp green gaze against the side of his face, with more of that pushback.

"You're probably right," she agreed, but she sounded too mild again. He tensed in foreboding. "Wouldn't it be great if we had access to a house that was right near my parents'? A house that, as I recall, has an attic that someone could hunker down in and watch my parents' to see if any bad guys rolled up. The way you seem to think they will."

Blue didn't say anything, because he was stunned.

Speechless, in fact, in the face of such a crazy suggestion.

Everly folded her arms over her chest, kept her gaze trained on him, and did not back down. At all.

"Imagine if we had the opportunity to hide in plain sight like that," she continued in that same way of hers, so calm and rational it made him want to start breaking things. Only the fact that he was a goddamned professional with twenty years of keeping his cool kept him from it. "Because these people might know everything there is to know about me. They've clearly spent all kinds of quality time in my apartment, leaving cute little notes and whatever else, and who knows what happened to Rebecca or what they knew about her? But there's no way they know anything about *you*, Blue. After all, we're not friends. We're not even friends in the usual, run-of-the-mill online sense. I haven't laid eyes on you since I was seven years old. And if they don't know you, there's no way they know anything about your mother's house, either."

There were a thousand things he could have said to that. Including his knee-jerk reaction to her assessment of their relationship—which was crazy, because he agreed. They weren't friends. They wouldn't *be* friends. They weren't anything.

That he could still taste her sweetness in his mouth was neither here nor there.

Blue settled on the easiest response. "No."

"Okay." She sat back in her seat, just as calmly as she'd done everything else tonight. *Except come all over you.* That wasn't exactly polite, but it chilled him out some. It reminded him that she was just as wild underneath as he was. "But I need you to tell me something."

"Do I think that the shock is getting to you? Yes. I do."

She ignored that. "Do you not want to go to your mother's house because you think it's actually a bad idea? Or because you're afraid?"

He thought his jaw might break in half. "I am not afraid."

"Or let me guess. You think you have to take responsibility for every bad thing that's ever happened, anywhere. From my apartment tonight to—I don't know—your entire childhood."

"Everly. Stop. This is not something that's going to happen."

She shrugged in the seat next to him—that was all, so Blue had no reason to feel it like a court-martial. Then she started to rub her palms up and down her arms, as if she needed the heat.

And she didn't argue with him, which was worse. He could have handled an argument. Hell, he was jonesing for one, the louder and meaner, the better.

But all she did was sit there next to him, pointedly saying nothing, and that meant he couldn't seethe and fume and formulate responses to her. He had to think.

And he couldn't help thinking, despite himself, that her idea was brilliant.

Much as it killed him to admit that.

He wasn't afraid to go home, he assured himself. He just didn't *want* to—which wasn't the same thing at all.

He grabbed his phone and called up Isaac's number,

letting the SUV's sound system put the call on the speakers.

"Talk to me."

It was Isaac's standard greeting. Especially when an Alaska Force brother was out on some kind of mission and was calling back to Fool's Cove in the middle of the night.

"There's been an escalation," Blue said, matter-of-factly, and then filled Isaac in on the night's events in the same tone. The break-in. The fight. The fact the punk had run off—and Blue had let him.

And then they'd tossed a firebomb through her bedroom window.

Isaac didn't pause. Or offer any reaction. "Status?"

"We're both alive and well," Everly said from her place beside him. Dryly. "But thank you for your concern."

There was a pause. Then Isaac let out a short bark of laughter. "Glad to hear it. I mean that."

"I think these guys are a little too motivated for my tastes," Blue said, getting the conversation back on track. "We could lay low at Everly's parents' house out in the suburbs, but I have a bad feeling they'll track her there."

"Your bad feeling has saved my ass a time or two," Isaac pointed out. "I'd be inclined to listen to it."

"There's an interesting second option," Blue said stiffly, though it cost him. "I could set up shop across the street, and see if they have the stones to chase her that far out of the city. It's an hour away. A different world, really, and there's always the possibility that this is just a localized issue."

Though Blue thought the firebomb suggested otherwise.

"Run-of-the-mill intimidation is one thing," Isaac said after a moment. "I think blowing up an apartment takes it all to a different level."

"Agreed."

"Can you secure the new location?" Isaac asked.

He meant, could Blue keep Everly safe? And Blue couldn't give the answer he wanted. Which was that he would figure out how to do it or die trying.

"To an extent," he said instead. Gruffly. "It's not perfect."

"That sounds good to me," Isaac said. "I trust your judgment."

Then Blue heard a sound that he identified instantly. It was Isaac sitting up in his bed, which meant that even though it was past midnight in Alaska, he was going to work. And would likely pull everyone else in, too. Because Alaska Force was all for one, one for all. Brothers-in-arms, always.

He would rather punch himself in the face than admit that it made him feel a certain warmth inside.

"In the meantime," Isaac said, "we'll reach out to the Chicago police and see if we can finesse some of this. We don't need your name in it. Or Everly's. And you can expect reinforcements tomorrow."

Blue muttered his appreciation, and that was it. Isaac hung up, and Blue headed for the expressway that would deliver him to the last place on earth he wanted to go.

He expected some gloating in the seat next to him. Triumph, at the very least, and he wasn't sure he'd handle it well, so he didn't look. He drove for a while instead, making sure he was hyperaware of every other car in their vicinity. And mapping out his childhood home in his head, trying to recall every entry point, every weakness, every window and stair.

And the next time he glanced over toward the passenger seat, Everly's head was tipped to one side and her eyes were closed. And the way she was breathing, deep and long, told him she'd fallen asleep.

Just like she had back in Alaska. All that adrenaline and the way she'd managed to hold herself together throughout the whole of this ordeal had worn off, fast. It was a surprise she hadn't dropped like a stone earlier.

But that meant that he was left with nothing but his own dark thoughts as he drove out of the Chicago city limits and into the suburbs. It was a drive he hadn't taken in some twenty years, and bonus, with Everly asleep beside him and no one chasing him, there was nothing to concentrate on but the past.

Exactly what he'd been trying to forget all this time.

He didn't want to think about his early childhood, when his father had still been alive. He didn't want to think about that loss and all the ways it had affected him, then and now. He didn't want to think about his mother's remarriage or what it had been like to be ten years old and left to feel as if he were the only person on earth who remembered his dad.

He didn't want to think about the ways he might have hurt his own mother's feelings, or how resolute he'd been about keeping his distance ever since.

He didn't want to face any of this crap, which was why he hadn't.

But here he was, taking the same exit he remembered from way back when. He thought there were more trees now, higher and greener in the summer night. And as he wound his way through streets that felt both familiar and strange to him at once, he couldn't deny that Everly hadn't been so far off after all.

Blue knew too many men who pretended they were never afraid of anything, but he wasn't one of them. Fear was a motivating factor. Fear of death, fear of capture, fear of drowning, fear of the enemy—it all worked. It fused into action and made a man unstoppable.

But that didn't change the fact that fear came first.

And it was more complicated than that. Because he wasn't afraid of enemy combatants tonight.

It was his own flesh and blood he didn't want to face—or maybe, if he was more honest than he'd ever wanted to be before, it was himself.

You think you have to take responsibility for every bad thing that's ever happened, anywhere, Everly had said. *From my apartment tonight to—I don't know— your entire childhood.*

But what she didn't know was all the crap he'd *not* taken responsibility for. It was yet one more reason he wasn't the hero she seemed to keep wanting to believe he was.

Blue knew the truth. He always had.

He turned down the street where he'd grown up. The houses were enough the same to make him wonder what year it was, though some of them sported different coats of paint. There were additions here, some new landscaping there. Trees he remembered climbing were gone, while new fences took their place. The world moved on, he supposed. Even in a place that had stayed forever preserved in his memory.

But his stepfather's house looked exactly the same. He pulled into the driveway, then pulled the SUV around the back, where it couldn't be seen from the street. He switched the engine off, looking at the woman who still slept there beside him. As pretty as she was when she was awake, there was something about her sleeping that caught in him.

The way it had that afternoon in Alaska when he'd carried her to the empty cabin and waited for her to wake up.

It was much worse now.

He'd barely had his fill of her. He hadn't even had time to bask in the afterglow before those bastards blew the place up.

And much as he wanted to do it all over again, what he really wanted was something he refused to acknowledge.

He refused.

So he did the next best thing. He climbed out of the car, easing his door shut so as not to wake her. The sun was just starting to peek up over the edge of the world. It was that odd, in-between time just before dawn, hushed and soft.

And Blue was standing in his old backyard, breathing in that peculiar combination of scents that would always be this exact place to him. Newly cut grass. Those sweet flowers that grew in the neighbor's backyard and sent petals soaring over the fence at this time of year. The thicker smell that reminded him of car engines, like the ones his stepfather had tinkered with but never fixed.

His mother's geraniums in the window boxes that were her pride and joy. The rich, green fragrance from the vegetable garden near the back porch.

It was crazy the things a man forgot. And then remembered too well.

Blue shook himself, then went around to the passenger side and pulled Everly out without waking her up. He lifted her in his arms and held her there when she murmured something unintelligible against his neck. When she settled, he turned, shutting the car door behind him with his foot and starting for the house.

And when the back porch light went on, flooding the yard and hitting him square in the face, Blue simply stood still.

He watched with a certain sense of foreboding, or inevitability, as the back door swung open.

He recognized the people standing there before him, both much older now. Both more frail than he wanted to accept. Something clenched inside him, and he wondered how he'd forgotten that part. That they would age. That everybody aged.

He knew he had. He remembered every year and every painful indication that he was no longer the sleek warrior he'd been at eighteen. Twenty. Even thirty.

But they'd gotten even older than he had.

"Dear God," the man muttered.

Blue's attention was on the woman. On a face he knew better than his own. Even lined with time and blurred with sleep, it was far more like his than he'd ever allowed himself to recall.

He knew her eyes. He knew that nose, though the one on his face was bigger and had been broken a few times. He knew her hands—how they felt against his forehead when she'd checked him for fever and how they looked when she fidgeted with her rings the way she was doing now, as if she couldn't help herself. And he knew that if he got closer, she would smell the way she always did, of lavender and fresh air.

A week ago he would have insisted he couldn't remember any of this. And, more, didn't want to.

Blue held Everly closer and reminded himself that he'd survived wars and some things that were far worse. He could handle a couple of nights back in this house, with these people. It might be uncomfortable. It was certain to be, in fact.

But he didn't *think* it would kill him.

He realized they were still all staring at one another, so he made himself smile.

At her. He wasn't ready to deal with anything but her.

"Hi, Mom," he said, as if he'd been away for a few days. Not his entire adult life. And as if nothing had ever separated them but that time. "Do you mind if we come in?"

Seventeen

The previous night was something of a blur. She'd fallen asleep hard and deep in the car at some point, so hard and so deep she wondered if, really, she'd passed out. The way she remembered doing only once before, three thousand miles to the west. It made something deep inside of her shake a bit to think it was Blue who had taken care of her in both instances.

And all the other times in between.

Last night—or early this morning—she'd had small, jumbled flashes. She'd had the impression of Blue's parents' backyard, so much like the one she'd played in as a child, across the street. Two faces in the doorway, staring out at them. But nothing more.

If there had been a conversation between Blue and the family he'd been avoiding all these years, she'd missed it.

Blue had carried Everly upstairs, all the way to the third floor without so much as a heavy breath. She'd noticed that part. She'd vaguely noticed sloping ceilings all along the top floor of the house, divided up like a railroad apartment. One room led into the next, and Blue deposited her on the old twin bed in the bedroom at the farthest end.

"I'll be in the sitting room," he'd told her, which hadn't made a whole lot of sense at the time. "It's right down the hall. So is the bathroom, if you need it."

And then he'd disappeared, leaving her in yet another guest room that felt entirely unused. Everly couldn't tell if she was simply seeing patterns and circles everywhere she looked because she was tired or because they were there. She'd curled up on the bed, her mind racing as she decided what to do next. She'd start with a shower. Or maybe she'd go find Blue and have the necessary post-whatever-that-was conversation. . . .

And then she got caught on the whatever-it-was for what felt like a long while. Until she'd fallen asleep—and then everything in her head had been fire. Glass shattering. Running, except this time, there was no getting away from the dark shadows that had followed her. All the alleys had led to higher flames and fewer chances to escape. All the fences had towered too high and, more, had been wreathed in barbed wire.

And it had stopped only when a big, rangy male form had climbed onto the narrow bed next to her.

"It's okay," Blue had said, his mouth against her ear.

And Everly had known it was him. Instantly. Even in the dark, even in a strange house, even torn apart by terrible dreams, she'd known him. She'd been surprised to find that her face was wet. With tears, she thought, though she didn't remember crying. She didn't care. She'd simply curled up into Blue on that crowded but comfortable bed, let his heavy arms keep her safe, and drifted back to sleep.

And this time, she didn't wake up until light streamed into the room from the curtainless windows and the air was stuffy and thick, reminding her it was still summer outside.

Everly sat up on the bed, then blinked around at her surroundings. She'd expected to see Blue, even though she'd known he wasn't in the bed with her anymore before she'd opened her eyes. But he wasn't in the room. There was nothing here with her but dust motes.

She was still fully dressed in the jeans and T-shirt she'd worn to flee her apartment, and she could smell the smoke on herself. Which had to mean anyone else would think she smelled like a mountain range's worth of wildfires. She had no other clothes. No phone. Not one single thing from her life except the clothes on her back.

She sat there and let that sink in.

But it felt a lot like drowning, and Everly hated it when her throat started to feel thick. She padded over to the dormer windows to look out at the street she thought she knew so well. But she'd never seen it from this angle before.

It was one more way to drown, maybe. Sinking into a different perspective on a place she'd thought couldn't possibly surprise her after all these years. The cherry tree in her parents' front yard looked different from this angle. Smaller, when she remembered lying beneath it in those long-ago springtimes and marveling at how it took over the whole of the sky.

And there was something about the fact that she was

in Blue's bedroom that got to her, right there in the place where she'd last seen him, all those years ago, when she'd been a little girl who hadn't known the world could be scary. Not like this. It scratched at her. It made something deep in her belly turn over.

But she told herself she was just hungry.

She pushed open the bedroom door, and then stood there a moment. The next room in the railroad stack was really more of a hallway. There were clothes on portable racks, wrapped in heavy plastic and storage bags. Padded boxes that looked as if they contained wineglasses or china. A collection of old fans. The usual things people stored in their attics.

But she could hear Blue's voice. She followed the sound, vaguely remembering what he'd said about sitting rooms and bathrooms. She found the bathroom through the next door, splashed cold water on her face, and then had to wipe her hands on her jeans when she realized there were no towels.

Somehow, she found that grounding.

Then she pushed through the door on the far wall into the last room. The stairs leading to the rest of the house were there, so she must have come up this way, but she hadn't seen the daybed shoved against one wall, with an armchair across from it. There were bookshelves everywhere else, filled with old paperback science fiction and fantasy novels, as well as some of her favorite comic books.

And Blue was over by the windows, on the phone.

He turned as she came in. His dark gaze met hers.

And suddenly everything was electric. Bright and hot,

skimming over her skin and settling deep inside her. Where she began to throb with longing.

For a moment she was back on that couch in her apartment and Blue was above her, inside her, surging in so deep she'd shaken apart from the inside out. She'd forgotten who she was and why she shouldn't cling to him the way she had, as if he were the only solid thing in the universe. She'd been lost, so deliciously lost, and he'd brought them both home.

Thrusting deep inside her, changing everything—

Everly blinked, afraid she was swaying on her feet right there on the top floor of his childhood home. And felt herself flush hot and red in response, because of course she did.

Because she always did, especially around him.

But she wasn't sure she minded in the next moment. Blue muttered a few monosyllables, ended his call, and then looked at her.

Just looked at her. And sure, his hard mouth curved while he did it, but it wasn't anything special, she cautioned herself. It was just a look.

But her cheeks were so hot it hurt, and she could feel him. Everywhere.

"Did you finally get some sleep?" he asked.

And maybe it was just because they were in this place that had once been his. Whatever it was, everything felt intimate. As if it wasn't random small talk to ask her how she'd slept but something more. Something different, something—

You're an idiot, she told herself harshly.

There was zero doubt about that. She was tired, covered in smoke and God knew what else, and probably still scared for her life, if she allowed herself a minute to think about it. She certainly wasn't herself, anyway. This wasn't living her best life—this was hiding out in Blue's parents' attic from bad guys they still hadn't identified.

Maybe she could forgive herself for reading all kinds of things into this situation. Blue wasn't trying to kill her. That was pretty much all it took for her to develop softer feelings at this point.

She decided to do both of them a favor and not mention anything that was happening inside her—

But Blue didn't get that directive, clearly. Because he reached over and ran the backs of his fingers over one hot cheek.

Everly managed to keep from jolting by actually biting down on her tongue.

"You look a little red, baby," he said, as if the whole thing amused him.

As if any of this was *amusing*.

Maybe, she thought dimly, it was all actually hitting her. The fact that someone had broken into her apartment. The fact that someone—maybe the same someone—had thrown a bomb through her window. The fact that between those two events she'd *had sex* with Blue Hendricks. And now was standing in the only possessions she had left, in an attic in her hometown—

"Breathe," he ordered her. He dropped his hand.

She didn't know which part of that bothered her more.

"What if I don't feel like breathing on command?"

"Then you'll make yourself pass out." Blue shrugged. "I'd probably catch you. But I might not."

Everly understood that if she did even one of the

things stampeding around inside her head just then, it would not end well. He was the one who'd taught her those moves, after all. He'd know exactly how to counter them.

She smiled to make the bloodlust dim. "Do we have a plan?"

"Find the bad guys. Make them stop. The usual."

"So nothing concrete. More baiting traps and waiting to be blown up."

Blue's eyes narrowed. "You okay?"

"I'm great. Just perfect. Everything I own blew up in a fire last night, and I'm thinking it might be time to *actively try* to catch the people who did it. Before they come up with something worse. You know, like something that might actually kill me."

Blue only eyed her, much too calm. Much too patient.

Everly felt herself flush again, deeper and redder.

Damn it.

"I better get you some coffee," was all he said.

Everly didn't know how she was supposed to feel about that. Chastened? Or pleased that he was going to handle her caffeine requirements without her having to ask?

Blue didn't give her the opportunity for debate on the topic. He just sauntered past her as if he didn't have a care in the world and headed for the stairs, and she followed him, because that was what she did now. She didn't even question it.

Because whether she was cranky today or not, this was the man who'd saved her, just as she'd hoped he would.

The other things he'd done didn't—couldn't—matter.

She had to find a way to forget that anything had changed between them.

Because, dummy, nothing has, she snapped at herself.

She assumed that a man who looked like Blue had sex all the time. It likely meant as much to him as getting her latte every day meant to her. Delicious and perfect while it lasted, but no need to elevate one latte over another when there was always, always another on the way.

Everly was frowning as they walked into the kitchen— definitely not at the idea of Blue with his next interchangeable *latte*, because that would be crazy—but she had to sort out her expression almost instantly, because Blue's mother was there.

Everly only vaguely remembered seeing her earlier. Here in the bright glare of a summer afternoon, she much more closely resembled the woman that Everly had always known growing up. Regina Margate was trim and athletic, her dark hair glossy and straight and cut into a tidy bob. She was sitting at the table with the newspaper spread before her, but her smile looked strained when she aimed it their way.

"Hello, Mrs. Margate," Everly said, because she might be grown up now, but she was incapable of addressing adults she'd known as a child by their first names.

"I see you're both up," Blue's mother said brightly. "You must be starving."

"I can't imagine what a shock this is," Everly began, apologetically.

"She's fine," Blue said, as if that was the end of it.

He went over to the kitchen counter with the ease of long practice, which told Everly that the coffee machine was in the same place it had been years ago. She didn't know why it pierced her heart to think of teenage Blue getting himself coffee in this same kitchen, but it did. He poured two mugs and brought them both over. He plunked one down on the table beside her, but then looked surprised when Everly took a seat.

"I've been collecting your parents' newspapers," Mrs. Margate said to Everly, with a smile that seemed more natural when she looked away from her son. "Their trip sounds like so much fun. I told your mother she's going to have to show me all her pictures when she gets back."

Everly felt her shoulders go down a few inches, telling her how tense she'd been that she hadn't even noticed they were hunched up around her ears. "She loves nothing more. My father had to force a cell phone into her hand, because she vowed she'd never use one. Now she never puts it down, because she's taking a million pictures with it all the time."

"I don't think there's a thing your mother can't do," his mother said, and laughed.

"Okay." Blue's voice was flat. "Enough. We're not here for pointless small talk."

Everly set the mug she was in the process of lifting back down on the table, afraid her hands would start shaking. Because Blue's voice felt like one of the blows he'd taught her, sharp and lethal and designed to maim.

For a moment that felt like it lasted forever, she found herself staring wide-eyed at Blue's mother.

Who did not curl up into a ball the way Everly would have. She straightened her shoulders. For a split second, she looked hurt, but then a resigned sort of expression took over her face. She laid her hands on the table before her, very neatly, one on either side of her newspaper.

"Benjamin Lewis Hendricks," she said, a kind of deep fury—or hurt, maybe, Everly couldn't tell—making her voice shake, though she didn't look away from Blue. "I haven't laid eyes on you in twenty years. You show up here before dawn, and do I ask where you've been? Do I question you on why you're back, and with the neighbor's daughter, no less? No, I do not. Because I love you, no matter how you break my heart. And I'll remind you that this is not the first time I've seen this kind of cloak-and-dagger nonsense."

"Don't."

But Regina Margate ignored her son's terse, angry monosyllable. She stood up, pushing back her chair as she rose but managing to make the scratch of it against the kitchen floor seem almost regal.

And this time, Everly was aware that she was holding her breath.

"I don't think it's asking too much for you to keep a civil tongue in your head while you're in this house," Mrs. Margate said. "However long you plan to remain in this house. That's my only requirement."

"It's not your requirements that were the problem," Blue bit out.

"You stop right there." His mother sounded more furious than hurt. "This is *his* house. You're not a child any longer. You're a guest, not a dependent. If you don't want to stay under his roof, Blue, no one is forcing you to stay here another minute."

But Blue didn't say another word. He simply turned and walked out of the kitchen, and Everly had to sit there in silence, staring awkwardly at his mother as they both listened to him take the stairs two at a time.

Everly knew her face was red. She was surprised to see that his mother's was colorful, too. Flushed, anyway, and her eyes got glassy the more the silence dragged on.

"In my head he was still seventeen," Mrs. Margate said when Everly had begun to think she wouldn't speak at all. That she might stand there, frozen in place, forever. "Isn't that funny? I know how old he is, of course. I knew he wasn't still a teenager. It's almost funny, the tricks time plays on a person."

She focused on Everly then, which made Everly wonder if she'd forgotten she wasn't alone.

Everly racked her brain for something to say that might explain what had just happened, but there was no need. Mrs. Margate smiled politely, murmured something about her laundry, and walked out.

Leaving Everly to fortify herself with another cup of coffee before she slowly marched back up the stairs to that third-floor sitting room to find her . . . whatever Blue was to her.

She found Blue with his tablet in his hands again, sitting near the windows that overlooked her parents' house. And this was the trouble with feeling all this *stuff* about a man she thought she ought to know but didn't. It swirled around inside her. It felt like wonder, as if she might burst wide open if she didn't *tell him*—

Everly bit her tongue again. Hard enough to hurt this time.

She had the sudden, unwelcome memory of her own voice in that car last night, using a word she should never have used.

It had no place here. Not inside her. Not with him.

God, she already knew what he'd say. He'd get pissed.

Or, worse, turn pitying. He'd mansplain her own heart to her, and it wouldn't matter what she said. He was going to leave anyway, the moment she was safe. She knew that, and even if she hadn't, that scene downstairs just now would have clued her in.

She wasn't in love with Blue. Of course she wasn't.

Because that would be . . . hopeless.

"Are you going to stand there and stare at me all day?" he asked without looking up. "I can't say I like it."

A smart woman would fade off into the bathroom and shower for a while. At least until he started looking less outwardly belligerent.

It turned out that Everly wasn't that smart. "What was all that?"

She thought he would pretend he didn't know what she was talking about. She'd even braced herself for it. She wondered if she'd actually push him if he dug his heels in, and thought that yes, she would, because she knew how to protect herself with her own two hands now. She could protect him, too. Even if it was from himself.

Especially then.

But Blue leveled a hard look at her. "I don't think it takes a rocket scientist to figure out that I didn't come back here for years because there's stuff I don't want to talk about. It turns out I still don't want to talk about it."

"What other cloak-and-dagger stuff did she mean?"

"I'm pretty sure I just said I don't want to talk about this."

"Give me a break. That woman loves you. You can read anyone and anything, but you can't read your own mother? You must know—"

But there was something so cold on Blue's face then that Everly choked on her own words. He took his time standing up, every inch of him a threat.

And she immediately understood the difference. That he was aiming all that brawn and power *at* her, for once. That he wasn't doing a single thing to protect her from all the lethal ruthlessness that was stamped deep into his every last bone.

"Do you really think that because we had sex, that means you get to dig around in my life?" he asked, in a voice as frigid as the expression on his face. "Or tell me what to do? It was sex, Everly. Just sex."

It felt like he'd punched her in the stomach.

But it took only another moment to realize that it was meant to feel that way. It was meant to leave her winded. He likely expected her to slink off somewhere to lick her wounds and have a good cry.

In which case, he should have picked on a woman who hadn't survived two assassination attempts in the past twelve hours. A woman who hadn't run all the way to Alaska to find him. A woman he hadn't taught the fine art of palm strikes and eye gouging.

And he definitely should have picked a woman who wasn't in love with him.

"Wow," she said, drawling it out for effect. "I guess that really hit you where you live. Did I ask you to marry me, Blue? Did I tell you that we were now joined forever because we had sex? Or did I ask you a not unreasonable question about your family situation after watching you fight with your mother?"

"I did not have a fight with my mother."

"No, you didn't," Everly agreed. "You were rude, to

make sure she knew how you felt. And then you couldn't yell at her when she called you on it, because at heart you're a man of honor. So you did the next best thing and left, then tried to make me feel like crap. Does it feel better now? Do you?"

"You're the one who suggested we come here," he reminded her, something fierce in his gaze and his hands tight at his sides. "I never said it would be pleasant. I don't know what you expect from me."

"Right. Because I forced you to come here. You didn't clear it with your G.I. Joe friends or anything."

"G.I. Joe was in the army, Everly. Isaac was in the marines. And there are things you can't possibly understand going on here."

"I didn't see your poor mother trying to blow you up. I saw her trying to pretend everything was okay when it clearly wasn't."

"Let me tell you something about *my poor mother*." He threw the words at her as if they cut his throat on the way out. "My father was a navy pilot. He died when I was ten in a stupid training accident. And my poor mother mourned him so deep and so hard that she was remarried within the year."

"I don't know your mother very well," Everly said quietly. "But I do know that you can never really know someone else's heart."

Blue stalked toward her, but she held her ground. She ignored the trembling sensation deep in her belly, which seemed to reverberate down into her knees, and let him come at her.

Because whatever this was, whatever was happening,

she knew without a shadow of a doubt that no matter how mad this man got at her, or near her, he would never hurt her. The same way she knew her legs would carry her forward when she decided to walk. The same way she knew her neck would hold her head up.

She knew this man like she knew her own bones.

You love him, a little voice whispered inside her.

Maybe she'd loved him already, but she knew that right here, right now, in the attic of his parents' house in their old hometown, she was seeing more of the real Blue than she'd seen so far. More than he'd shown anyone else in a long, long while, if she had to guess.

She couldn't pretend it wasn't what she'd wanted.

"She got two daughters and a new husband," Blue was seething at her. "A big house. And I got Ron. Good old Ron, who thought he could make a man out of me."

Everly knew his stepfather, too, of course. She remembered Ron Margate as a man who cooked a decent hot dog and told incredibly corny jokes. And, in the years since, had been a neighborhood staple. Always had his Christmas ornaments up over Thanksgiving weekend and tucked away again on New Year's Day, things Everly's father had always appreciated and commented on.

That didn't mean he couldn't have been an awful stepfather to a grieving kid.

"Blue, I don't think—"

"You don't *know*, Everly. You were across the street riding a pink bike up and down, clueless and sheltered. You have no idea what it was like growing up in this house."

"Did he . . ." She wished she'd never started down this road, but she had. Now she had to deal with it. "Was he abusive?"

"He wasn't my father." Blue threw it at her like a right hook. "And he didn't like it when I reminded him of that fact. Over and over and over."

"Did he get physical with you?"

Blue muttered something under his breath. "The man is a dick. The end. Why are you dragging all this up? All you need to know is that I learned to do without my mother a long time ago. I'm glad that she took the opportunity to lecture me on my manners, because it reminded me that nothing ever changes. She made her choices."

"She loves you," Everly whispered, as if that could change anything.

Something washed over Blue, intense and wild. His eyes blazed.

"Don't talk to me about love. My father loved my mother. He died because he loved his country. And look what kind of loyalty that got him."

"It looks like he has your loyalty," Everly said softly. "Doesn't that count for something?"

She had never seen this man look so . . . undone as he did then. And she would have gone to him, put her arms around him, tried to hold him the way he'd held her in his old twin bed last night—but she knew, somehow, that he would never allow it.

That he got something out of standing there solitary and wounded and forever alone. He wanted it that way.

She could see it all over him.

And she told herself that the hollow sensation in her

chest had nothing to do with him. It wasn't her heart breaking. It wasn't anything.

But even the lies she told herself weren't working today.

"I don't lie awake at night wondering where it went wrong with the woman who abandoned him the minute he was gone," Blue told her. "I wonder how I can ever be even half the man he was, knowing full well I can't."

"Well, of course you can't," she said. "He's a ghost."

And for a moment, everything between them seemed to light on fire, just like the walls last night. She'd never seen this stoic, composed man look the way he did then. Not just undone but furious on top of it, and all of it aimed straight at her.

Everly told herself she could take it, though she wasn't entirely sure that was true.

But just when she thought she might actually be charred from the inside out, he wrenched his gaze away from hers.

"I'm an idiot," he ground out.

"You're not an idiot," she assured him. "A lot of people carry all kinds of things—"

"Everly." His gaze hit hers again, but he was the Blue she knew again. Cool and hard. As if nothing had happened. "Do not psychoanalyze me."

"But—"

"This conversation is over. I just realized the only thing that changed in the past twenty-four hours."

And Everly was certain he didn't mean the fact that they'd slept together. Or the fact that they were here in his childhood home, the very last place on earth he wanted to be.

"It's Rebecca's mother." Blue shook his head. "I can't believe I let all this extraneous crap distract me. I called her yesterday and left a message. What mother doesn't respond to someone calling about her missing kid? I think she's the key to all this."

Everly felt like the world was spinning too fast and uneven beneath her, but she forced herself to ignore it.

"Great," she said, tilting up her chin against the objections she could already feel coming at her, like he was firing them one after the other from that big, ugly gun of his. She even crossed her arms in front of her, like that might make her bulletproof. She pretended she was. "Let's go find her."

Eighteen

Blue was off his game, and he didn't like it.

They were back in the SUV, Everly in the passenger seat at his side, because he'd lost that fight in a hurry.

When had he started losing fights? But he already knew the answer. It was coming back to the same place where he'd last lost fights, when he'd been a kid and almost entirely powerless.

He wasn't enjoying the déjà vu.

"How are you going to keep me safe if you're not here?" Everly had asked him. In that new, challenging way of hers that made him hard.

And also made him want to tie her up and lock her in a closet, just to keep her safe.

But that was the trouble. Teach a woman to fight, and a man was pretty much guaranteeing that, sooner or later, she'd fight him. Blue should have seen this coming.

"One week of practicing a few self-defense moves

does not make you prepared to handle the kind of situation we could be walking into," he had argued, feeling a lot like a saint when he'd kept his hands to himself. Because his sense of being sucked down into the past wouldn't ease any if he went ahead and christened his childhood bedroom the way he'd always fantasized about doing as a teenager. While his mother was downstairs, for God's sake. "I hope you don't think you can handle yourself because you learned a few things. Because that just makes you a danger to yourself and others. Namely, me."

"I couldn't agree more," she'd said, but since she hadn't physically backed down, he didn't think she was surrendering. And sure enough, she'd kept right on going. "Which is why I don't want to be left here, hoping against hope that these people don't show up again. Hoping that I don't have to try to protect myself and your mother with a few palm strikes. I don't think that would end well."

And that was how Blue Hendricks, former Navy SEAL, current Alaska Force brother, and widely acknowledged badass, found himself driving straight toward potential danger with the woman he was supposed to be protecting riding shotgun.

He figured he'd have ample time to kick his own butt over that decision later. When this was over. When he would have nothing but the towering silence of the Alaskan mountains to distract him from a fearless moral inventory of what a mess he'd made of the Everly Campbell situation.

Later, he growled at himself, and focused on the highway.

His brothers were already on the ground in Chicago.

They were handling the police and the fallout from the firebomb. *As far as we can tell, they climbed a telephone pole and tossed it through the window from there,* Templeton had texted. Blue could have waited for them to make their way out to his stepfather's house, so he could have left Everly in good hands, but he had that gut feeling again.

That drumming, restless sort of feeling in his gut that crap was about to go down. Or already was. That feeling that kicked at him, scraped at him, and wouldn't let go no matter how he tried to reason his way out of it. That feeling that had saved his life more times than he could count. Today it was telling him that he needed to get out to the North Shore, and fast, if he wanted to get on top of this thing.

And certainly if he wanted to end it. And end it well, leaving Everly alive.

Alive and healthy and capable of picking up her life where it had left off just over a month ago. As if none of this had happened.

And if everything in Blue clenched too hard at that notion, he ignored it. Because he might not want to ignore it, but he damn well needed to. The same way he needed to ignore all the rest of the crap she churned up in him. He didn't need to think any harder or deeper about his father and all the ways he could never live up to his legacy. He didn't need to question himself about the possibility he'd been the one to treat his mother or even freaking Ron unfairly. He certainly didn't want to think about *ghosts*.

Just like he didn't want to think about the fact that a little girl on a pink bike he'd wanted to break with his own two hands way back when could have grown up and wrecked him so easily.

He hadn't seen her coming. Even when she'd arrived, spilling out of her car and staggering toward him in the dirt, he hadn't realized his world was already spinning off its axis. How could he? He'd had no intention of helping her, much less coming back to Chicago with her.

And he certainly hadn't planned to lay a single finger on her.

Sleeping with Everly had destroyed him, and Blue still didn't understand how that had happened, only that it had. He'd been caught naked, literally. When that bomb had gone off, he'd woken up with her wrapped up in his arms, and for the first split second, he'd panicked.

That was unacceptable.

Everly wasn't an adrenaline junkie. Blue knew she hadn't slept with him to get a notch on her belt, or even as some sort of shady transactional thing because he was keeping her safe. He knew she wanted him. He knew she trusted him. Hell, he had the uncomfortable feeling that even now she really thought he was a hero.

And his problem was that he cared entirely too much about the things this woman thought.

Like every single thing she'd said to him in the sitting room on the third floor, sinking her untrained hands deep into his chest and cracking it open, as surely as if she'd used a spreader to wrench his ribs apart. Or the fact that she'd witnessed that crappy interchange with his mother, a conversation he'd been avoiding for all this time *on purpose*. Or worse, that Everly had imagined she had some insight into the endless mess that was his family.

He couldn't seem to get his head back into the game,

where it belonged. Blue knew he needed to finish this thing off and get away from here. He wanted the quiet. He wanted the remote splendor of Grizzly Harbor. He wanted the demands on him to be about his skills and expertise, not all this emotional crap he'd never wanted to dig up in the first place.

"Did you find anything?" he asked her now, gunning it as he dodged traffic on I-294, heading north to skirt the city and access the North Shore suburbs.

"I'm looking," Everly replied in a distracted tone. He'd given her his tablet and told her to access her social media accounts to see if there had been any other updates from Rebecca. Or whoever was using Rebecca's account, because Blue didn't think either one of them truly believed Everly's roommate was still alive at this point. "There's nothing anywhere. The last updates were the ones you told me about, but nothing since."

Blue tried to concentrate on the highway. He needed his heart rate to go down. He needed his head to clear. He needed to quit worrying about what Everly was doing— and thinking and feeling, and was he back in high school, for God's sake?—and pay more attention to what he planned to do when they found Rebecca's mother.

Besides interrogate her about her failure to reply to his message, and ask her if she knew anything about the men who had come after them last night, that was.

"That's not good," Everly muttered from beside him.

And he hated the fact that she was still wearing the same T-shirt she'd slept in last night. Because all he could think about was the fact that she wasn't wearing anything beneath it. And how he'd love to get his hands beneath it all over again.

Blue couldn't believe what an asshole he was. He really couldn't.

"What's not good?" he managed to ask.

Everly shrugged. "My boss noticed my absence today, that's all. I need to appear at his desk with an appropriate apology within the next hour, or he says he's letting me go."

"I can send someone to talk to him. Get his head on straight."

He heard Everly take a deep breath, hold it, and then release it. He felt that inside him, like a blow. He'd taught her that, he thought. He'd taught her how to breathe, and now she did it without his having to point out that she'd stopped in the first place.

She'd stood up to him. She'd insisted that he take her with him, and he had.

Everly was going to be just fine when he left. Blue wished he could be as sure about himself.

But there was no point fixating on things like that. Not now. He could feel in his bones that they were closing in on the end of this, and he had no intention of letting it end badly. That meant that everything would be exactly the way it was supposed to be once it was done. He would head back to his cabin in Fool's Cove. He would spend his days plotting out missions and acclimating to civilian life with his Alaska Force brothers. He'd eat at the Water's Edge Café in Grizzly Harbor, the way he always did. He'd drink at the Fairweather. He'd take trail runs on frigid mornings that felt etched out of ice. He'd learn new words for *snow*.

He would not think about Chicago. He would not obsess about his family. He would leave the past where it belonged, and he would live his life exactly the way he wanted to live it.

And he would not think about Everly Campbell or the way she'd wrapped herself around him and cried out her pleasure into his ear, ever again.

"The truth is, I don't care if I get fired," Everly said, snapping him out of what he suspected was a whole host of lies he'd been telling himself.

"I wouldn't walk away from a good job just because you've had a few problems," he replied, his tone short. "I told you we'll talk to your boss."

"What I'm telling you, Blue, is that I don't want you to talk to my boss." She smiled at him. "I can talk to my boss, thank you. I can tell him that I haven't liked my job for some time. When I started, it was creative and fun. Now it's too corporate and, honestly, not that much fun at all. This is as good a time as any to move on."

Blue switched lanes with more aggression than was called for. "Listen to me. What you're living through right now is a crisis. The last thing you want to do is change your life in ways you can't take back in the middle of crisis mode, because everything's going to go back to normal, and then what?"

"I might not live to the end of next week. I might not live through the day, actually."

But Everly didn't sound particularly scared by the possibility. If anything, she sounded matter-of-fact about her prospects. Blue should have liked her levelheadedness. And yet he didn't. He really, really didn't.

She was still talking, shifting around in her seat so she could look at him. "I spent all last week acting the part of the person I used to be. One foot in my old life, with my other foot in the grave. And you know what I discovered? I don't really want this life anymore."

"It's not a great time to go goth and dark, Everly. You might actually have to fight for that life you don't want."

She laughed. "The whole time I was in that rental car, driving all the way to Alaska, I just kept thinking I didn't want to die. And then, once I found you, it was clear to me that whatever else happened, all I wanted was to stay alive. But then last night happened."

He needed to stop her. He needed to cauterize this crap right now.

But he couldn't seem to form a single word.

"That guy showed up at my office. He broke into the apartment. Then they threw a bomb through my window," Everly said quietly. "And in the middle of that, there was you." He assumed she must want something from him, to say it so baldly like that, but if she did, she didn't wait for him to let her down. She kept right on going. "And I understood then. It's not enough to *not die*. It's not even enough to just *be alive*. I want to live, Blue."

There was a tight band of emotion wrapped around his chest, digging in so it hurt, but he refused to acknowledge it. Much less release it.

He didn't want to feel anything.

He didn't want to feel *this*.

"Everly . . ."

"Anyway," she said, and a swift glance told him her attention was on the tablet, not on him. He didn't know if that was better or worse. "The good news is that I don't have to worry about paying rent on an apartment that no longer exists. Who cares if I quit my job?"

"Do not quit your job. Do not do anything you can't take back."

"It's too late for that," she said, and there was a certain finality in her voice. Or some kind of certainty that made all those gut instincts he prided himself on listening to go crazy. "I don't think you can stare down your own death too long without making some changes. Do you?"

Blue didn't want to touch that.

Hard. Freaking. Pass.

"It's not too late," he said again, and even he could hear that he sounded way too invested. A shade too close to desperate for his peace of mind. "The thing about staring at your own death is that, yeah, it can give you some clarity. But it also teaches you to hold on to what you have. *Normal* isn't a bad word. It's what safe looks like when it's not being threatened."

"Drive, Blue," Everly said, sounding . . . self-possessed. Sure of herself.

And Blue didn't know why he wanted to reach over and get his hands and his mouth on her again, almost as much as he wanted to pretend she wasn't getting to him. Indicting him, somehow, with her quiet acceptance of all the changes in her life.

It wasn't like Blue was any stranger to change. He'd transitioned from the SEALs to Alaska Force seamlessly. He'd been sent all over the world on active duty and off. He could situate himself wherever he landed in about three seconds and then get right to work. He was a goddamned poster boy for change.

You can change your surroundings without think-

ing twice about it, a voice inside needled him, sharp and insistent. *But can you change yourself? Have you changed at all from that angry teenager who stormed off to enlist?*

He realized he was rubbing the palm of his hand hard against his chest, right over his heart, and dropped it like he'd given himself a third-degree burn.

"I think you're going to regret losing your job," he bit out. "But it's your life, not mine."

"You keep saving my life," she said in that same obnoxiously calm, certain way that was like more needles deep beneath his skin. Not a sensation he enjoyed. "In some cultures, that would make you responsible for me forever."

"I'll put you on my Christmas card list," he muttered.

And then floored it.

Because whatever was coming would come. And he would handle it, because that was what he did.

And then he needed to get the hell away from Everly, for good, before she ruined him forever.

Winnetka had always been Everly's favorite of Chicago's North Shore suburbs.

Not only was it poised right there on the lakeshore; it was stately and pretty and even featured houses that Everly recognized from the old eighties movies she'd watched as a kid. When she'd been younger and dreaming of a glorious life in and around Chicago, she'd always imagined that someday she'd find herself in an ivy-covered house in Winnetka, with Lake Michigan lapping at the edge of her rolling yard.

Her dreams might have changed, particularly lately, but she still loved the town.

Even if Blue was taking the shine off it with his talk of Annabeth Lambert, Rebecca's mother, and what he called his *gut feeling* about her.

"Maybe she's overwhelmed with emotion and can't return calls," she said, her gaze out the window. It was a pretty summer day, gold and blue filtering through the trees that lined the road and shaded the graceful houses. "Or maybe she's sedated somewhere and hasn't heard the message yet."

"Possible," he said in that very military way of his that she suspected meant he didn't think it was at all *probable*. "Did Rebecca talk a lot about her mother?"

"Never." Everly considered it as they drove through the charming downtown area and kept heading east, toward the lake. "She didn't really talk about her personal life at all."

"Then what did you talk about?"

"We were roommates, Blue. Not buddies. Though we were friendly, sure. We talked about TV shows. Gossipy things, like which pop star was in a feud with which actress. That kind of stuff. Silly things, mostly."

"But not family."

"I probably talked about my family. In the way people do. Holidays and so on, or a lunch date with my mother. That kind of thing. But I don't remember her ever saying anything about hers. Not anything that stuck with me."

"Interesting."

He muttered it in that low, intense way of his, which told her he was thinking it all through, turning the facts around and around to try to get a sense of all the angles.

All while he drove them through Winnetka, right on the edge of too fast. Which only a damaged person would find sexy under the current circumstances, she thought. Which meant she'd sustained some pretty serious blows.

But Everly felt perfectly safe, damaged or not. She had no doubt that Blue could handle the vehicle—and whatever they were driving into—in the same way he'd handled her.

Then she felt shuddery, thinking about *handling*. At a time like this. She shifted in her seat, flushing a bit at the fact that she was so unable to keep her attention where it belonged.

And very, very grateful that Blue had to stop and scowl at some pedestrians, so he missed it.

She'd e-mailed her resignation letter to her boss, right from Blue's tablet. Charles clearly hadn't been expecting it, and Everly had had the strangest revelation that most of her work life—her whole adult life, in fact—had been arranged around threats. That she could be evicted. Or fired. Or simply that people wouldn't like her. Whatever the situation, there was always a looming threat.

Charles had threatened her, never thinking she would call his bluff. Or so his surprised return e-mail had told her. It had also told her that she was an integral part of his team and he'd love to explore options to keep her on board.

All because she'd faced the threat and countered it.

Talk about life lessons in the strangest of circumstances.

She'd received a notification from her landlord to everyone in the building, filled with lots of intense legal language about insurance and police investigations and requests that the tenants wait for the fire department's inquiry to conclude before they tried to get back inside to see what was left.

Everly assumed she'd lost everything. Or if she hadn't, what remained was likely to be a sodden, charred mess. Meanwhile, she hadn't had time to mourn her possessions because she was on the run, and the people who wanted to kill her were still at large.

And yet somehow, she didn't feel as if she had nothing. She didn't feel alone or lost.

On the contrary. Everly felt free.

As if this had all been a dramatic rescue of herself, from a life she hadn't realized wasn't making her happy. She'd been happier in between two attacks last night then she'd ever been. She didn't want to say that out loud because she was sure it would make her sound crazy, but that didn't make it any less true.

Everly had fallen head over heels in love with the man beside her, but it didn't matter that she couldn't tell him that. She knew better than to tell him, because if his reaction to her losing her job was negative, she really didn't want to think about how he'd respond to any declarations about *feelings*. He'd probably spontaneously combust where he sat.

But that was okay. She could keep it to herself.

For now.

"What about you?" she asked.

He threw a dark look her way, then took a turn too quickly. "What about me?"

"What do you want to do with your life?"

"I'm doing it."

"I mean . . . after."

He was already tense, but he suddenly seemed to turn into stone. She stared at his hands, crooked over the steering wheel, and the fact that his knuckles looked whiter by the second.

"After what? This is after."

"After the military, sure. But you can't do Alaska Force forever, can you?"

He cut the wheel, pulling the SUV over to the side of the road, and then stopping abruptly. So abruptly she threw out a hand to catch herself on the dashboard.

"What do you think is happening?" he asked, a kind of midnight in his voice. His gaze, too. But he kept his hands on the wheel, still clenched too tight. "Let me tell you right now, little girl—this isn't some fairy tale where you walk through a deep dark forest and come out the other side a princess."

"That's great news, because I'm not a little girl and I don't actually look good in tiaras."

Blue ignored that. "This is just life, Everly. We're going to fix this, you're going to live your life and apparently start it with some job hunting, and you don't need to worry about what I'm going to do after Alaska Force. That's not your business."

She'd known better than to poke at him, and she'd done it anyway. She had no one to blame if he'd hurt her feelings. Exactly the way she'd known he would. "It was just a question."

"Like hell it was. You think I can't tell the difference between an innocent question and an agenda?"

"I don't know if you can, actually." Everly hadn't been mad at him a second ago, so it was surprising how quickly it ignited inside her. "So far, the evidence seems to suggest you see agendas wherever you look. Your mother can't be happy to see you. I can't ask a question. It's all a big dramatic plot to harm you, headed toward some end only you know."

"The fact that you think you can sit here and talk to me about my mother is everything that's wrong with this situation," Blue said coldly. So coldly it should have frozen her where she sat, despite the summer heat outside. "And it ends now. You don't know a goddamned thing about my childhood. You were across the street living out your perfect little life. You'll go back to pink bikes and fairy tales the minute this crap is over. The end."

"My childhood wasn't perfect. Far from it." She glared at him, and wished she didn't know how to hit things now, because it was all she wanted to do. "You've met my mother. She's driven and exacting when she's on vacation. You have no idea what it's like being her disappointing child who failed to follow in her footsteps."

"Yeah, let me haul out my violin. That sounds terrible."

Somehow, Everly managed to keep her head from exploding. "It's not a competition."

"I should have known better than to touch you," he said, in that same way he'd brought up what had happened between them before. Like a gut punch. And this time, even though she knew it was deliberate, a distancing maneuver he was using to push her away, she found that it worked. It felt like her heart was three times its usual size, bruised, and lodged in her throat. "I knew you couldn't handle it."

"I don't think that I'm the one who can't handle it, Blue." She refused to let him see how much he'd hurt her.

No matter how it cost her to stay calm. "It's pretty clear that I'm not the one freaking out here. Do you want to talk about why *you* can't handle it?"

She knew perfectly well he didn't.

And they were so close, there in the front of that SUV. She could see that fascinating muscle tense in his jaw, and she wanted nothing more than to run her palms over his face again, so she could marvel in the feel of his cheekbones. So she could feel the heat of his skin. And get close to that gorgeous mouth of his, which she really didn't know if she could bear to never kiss again.

But she didn't dare reach out. Not now.

Everly had never seen anyone look more lonely, or more angry and defeated, somehow, than Blue did right now. As if he were carrying an unbearable weight he didn't know how to put down.

She felt tears prick at the backs of her eyes. She felt the ache of wanting to help him moving over her like a kind of flu.

"You don't have to freak out about this," she told him, though she knew better. She really did. But she couldn't seem to make herself stop. "You don't have to worry. I love you."

He let out a sound, not quite a laugh, because it was far too bitter for that.

And he looked at her as if she'd betrayed him.

"Blue . . ."

Everly cast around for something to say. She wanted desperately to take back what she'd said, or modify it so he wouldn't look at her as if she'd attacked him. But on the other hand, she was reluctant to do anything of the kind. Because it was true. And because some suicidal or just plain silly part of her thought that even though he didn't want to hear it, he needed to.

"Blue, you have to know—"

"Stop." His voice was soft. Too soft, and somehow still a stern order. His dark eyes glittered, as if he were holding back a storm by sheer force of will alone. And still, she felt it wash over her—through her—like a hurricane. "We're here."

Nineteen

Annabeth Lambert lived in what could only be termed a mansion. It sat up on a bluff over Lake Michigan, on a stately street lined with other glorious homes made of rambling wings and carriage houses, pools and terraces and acres of manicured lawns. The house itself bore more than a passing resemblance to the one Everly had dreamed about when she was younger, all faded brick and ropes of ivy.

"There's no time to do any decent recon," Blue told her as they walked up the long front path that led them through some landscaping to the imposing front door.

He was all business now. He'd slid those sunglasses over his eyes and cut himself off from her completely. And despite everything churning around inside her, Everly couldn't really complain. She certainly didn't want him distracted.

And if that meant she had to tag along with him on potentially dangerous errands while her heart felt exposed and much too large and hollowed out at the same time, well, that was just the price she had to pay for opening her big mouth in the first place.

"This is a perfectly normal social call," Blue was saying in that same urgent undertone. She couldn't see his eyes, but she could tell by the way he held himself that he was scanning here, scanning there. Looking behind bushes and up toward the house's many eaves for . . . whatever it was he looked for. "You're the roommate. You dropped by to pay your respects in the middle of this troubling time and maybe to see if Rebecca's been in touch. That's all."

"That's it? No good-cop, bad-cop routine?"

But he didn't so much as crack a smile. Not even that tiny curve in the corner of his mouth that she'd managed to eke out of him before.

Before she'd gotten all emotional. Before she'd committed the cardinal sin of falling in love with him and, worse still, telling him about it.

"This isn't a game, Everly." He couldn't have sounded less amused if he'd tried. Though she didn't really want him to try. "Stop acting like it is."

"Once again," she said, as evenly as she could, "the only reason people are trying to kill you is because you're protecting me. I remain the target. And as the target, I assure you, I'm not playing any—"

"Everly."

She stopped talking. And part of her hated that she did, because surely she should . . . do something. Fight. Make demands. *Something.*

What demands would you make? a cynical voice inside her asked. *That he love you? What if he doesn't?*

And there it was, ugly and unvarnished and exposed, right there on Annabeth Lambert's front walk.

Everly's worst fear.

Not that Blue, specifically, didn't or wouldn't love her—but that nobody did. Not really. Her parents were fond of her—she knew that—but they *loved* Jason. They talked about her brother's accomplishments constantly. They didn't always have time to drive an hour into Chicago to see her, but they took vacations out where Jason lived.

She was used to being the disappointing one in her family. No one was ever mean to her. No one ever treated her badly. But Everly had never been as ambitious as her mother and brother, or her father, who had transitioned from academic life to the boards of various charities. And she had always been keenly aware of the differences.

But maybe never so much as she was today, when she'd actually told Blue about her place in her family and he hadn't cared.

He'd been the older boy she'd looked up to all those years ago. Now he was a hero, and more, he'd saved her already again and again. And she had fallen in love with him because who wouldn't? He was beautiful and he was dangerous and aside from all that, she liked him. A lot.

But if he'd taught her anything, it was to attack, not defend. To set the terms of the interaction so an attacker could never take advantage.

"I should never have touched you," she said sadly, because she couldn't palm strike him in his gorgeously unshaved face. "I should have known you couldn't handle it."

His lips thinned, but he didn't say anything. He didn't snap right back at her, which defeated the purpose as far as she was concerned.

And then they were at the front door, and she wondered why she was trying to provoke him when she had no idea what lay on the other side. Maybe she really was the child he kept telling her she was.

Or maybe she was full up on things to take seriously. A polite meeting with her missing roommate's mother was low on her list of fears. It turned out that a Molotov cocktail through the bedroom window really reordered a person's priorities.

"I don't understand why Rebecca was living in an apartment with me if she came from this kind of money," she said under her breath to Blue.

"That's just one of the questions I'm going to need answered," he agreed. "I told you the financials don't make sense for either Rebecca or her mother."

He jutted his chin toward the doorbell, and Everly reached over and rang it.

And then they stood there.

It was a pretty summer afternoon. The humidity had let off and there was a breeze kicking up from the lake, pleasant and faintly sweet. Everly could see the water through the trees, right there where the great houses ended, sparkling blue beneath the sun.

The street they were on was quiet, with tall trees providing shade. There were wind chimes in the distance and the sound of people splashing in pools she couldn't see. It was like a daydream of suburban perfection, and

Everly found it hard to imagine that the kind of scary men who'd been chasing her could have anything to do with a place like this.

"Ring it again," Blue said from beside her.

He'd turned to face the street, standing in that loose, ready stance she recognized from their brief self-defense lessons in her living room.

Those stolen hours after work felt like a lifetime ago.

Everly reached over to hit the bell again. She could hear an echo roll through the house inside, and didn't know why the sound made her tense.

"It's the middle of the day," she pointed out. "She could be at work."

"There's no evidence that Annabeth Lambert has ever held a job."

Blue said that as if there were layers to his statement that she should have recognized instantly, but she didn't. Instead, the longer they stood there, the more she noticed more things about the house that hadn't been apparent to her before. Like the fact that once they'd walked up to the front door, they were hidden from the street. There was a driveway that circled around, but it, too, was hidden by the high hedges.

Meaning anyone could drive up to the front door and park here, and no one on the street would be any the wiser. Anyone could do anything here, in fact. And no one would see. She wasn't sure they'd even hear it, unless the breeze from Lake Michigan was exactly right.

These were things that would never have crossed Everly's mind a month ago.

She felt a weird kind of itchy sensation on the back of her neck and turned toward Blue, opening her mouth to tell him they should leave, but that was when she heard it. A faint sound on the other side of the big, thick door.

Everly rubbed at the back of her neck, but the dancing bundle of nerves deep in her belly kicked into overdrive.

Blue was right there with her, so they would be okay. She was sure of it.

There was the sound of the locks being pulled, and then the great door swung inward.

And Everly actually flinched back in surprise. Because standing before them, rail thin and lightly tanned, wearing a bright orange top and white pants that managed to look both simple and incredibly expensive at the same time, was Rebecca.

Of course, it wasn't really Rebecca, Everly realized in the next second. But the resemblance was overwhelming—and more than a little disconcerting.

The woman standing in the doorway was older than Rebecca, though how much older, Everly couldn't begin to guess. Her forehead was too smooth for it to be at all natural, and there was a suspicious flatness beneath each eye. She had Rebecca's same bright blue eyes and a long, thick mane of expertly blown-out chestnut-colored hair. She had the same narrow nose and the same faintly haughty set to her mouth, though her lips were significantly plumper. She was tall and willowy even without the added height of her glittery platform sandals, and Everly understood that this had to be Rebecca's mother.

It couldn't be anyone else.

"My God," she said without meaning to. "You look just like her."

The woman who was obviously Annabeth Lambert smiled, though it went no further than a strained crook of her overdone lips. "I'm told we could be mistaken for sisters. Perhaps even twins."

And Everly made a mental note to never, ever worry about her relationship with her mother again. Because her own mother might have her issues, but Everly had never worried that she might try to . . . pass herself off as Everly.

She felt Blue's gaze on the side of her face, and remembered herself. And why she was here, talking to a woman she wasn't at all surprised her roommate had never mentioned. Because really, what would she have said?

Come to lunch with my mother and me, but fun fact, she's made herself into my doppelgänger and maybe steals my clothes. Along with my face.

Maybe it was better that she and Rebecca had stuck to the odd revealing conversation about bad dates and, aside from that, shared rants about reality television episodes.

"I'm sorry to show up at your front door with no advance notice," she said, trying to sound whatever normal was under these circumstances. "I know we've never met, but I am—I mean, I was—Rebecca's roommate. And I was—"

"Yes." Annabeth's face didn't change expression. Everly wondered if she was being deliberately flat and unreadable, or if she couldn't actually move her face with all that . . . smoothness. "The roommate who reported my daughter's murder when it appears Rebecca simply ran out on you. Evelyn, was it?"

That was a lot to digest, so Everly concentrated on the part she could actually handle straight off, as it was certainly not the first time she'd been called Evelyn over the course of her life. "Everly, actually."

"What a strange name."

Rebecca's mother didn't smile at that, however woodenly. She didn't laugh to soften it. Instead, she gazed back at Everly as if she were daring Everly to do something about it.

So Everly laughed, as if it had been a joke.

"My parents really love the Everly Brothers," she told this woman, who she was coldly certain didn't care at all. She felt as if she were looking at herself from a distance, standing on Annabeth's pristine front steps in her grubby T-shirt, jeans, and Converse, with her hair such a mess she'd had to decide to simply not care about whatever it was doing. "They named my brother after my mother's favorite uncle, but me they named after their favorite classic band. What can I say? I get to be unusual."

"How is it that I can help you?" Rebecca's mother asked, still not smiling. Or relaxing her stiff posture in any way. Or inviting them in, either.

Everly found herself standing up tall as well, as if mirroring Annabeth would help the situation. "I was just wondering if you've heard from Rebecca?"

"This is some kind of joke, I presume?" Annabeth shifted her attention from Everly to Blue. "Let me guess. You're the one who called me yesterday."

"We're just looking for your daughter, ma'am," Blue said, in his gruffest military voice.

Annabeth appeared immune, which made that odd little itch on the back of Everly's neck start up again.

"You're not going to find her here. Is that why you came?"

"You seem real broken up about the fact she's missing," Blue pointed out, that drawl in his voice was another one of the weapons he used.

But Annabeth didn't seem to notice that, either.

"My daughter is a grown woman who makes her own choices," she said coolly. "In this case, last I heard, she's off somewhere with some new boyfriend." She inclined her head very, very slightly toward Everly. "Despite your theatrics. Now if you'll excuse me."

She went to close the door, and Everly didn't know what came over her. But she threw herself forward, sticking her arm out to keep the big door from shutting on her. She was aware of Blue behind her, and maybe that was why she did it, as if she could muscle this woman's door open if she wanted, when she'd never *muscled* a thing in her life.

"I just want to know what happened to Rebecca. Those social media posts don't sound like her. I don't believe them. I think something's wrong."

I saw them hurt her, she thought, but didn't say.

"Step back," Annabeth said in a frigid sort of fury. "Or I'll be forced to call the authorities to have you removed."

"Come on," Blue said from behind her, and Everly felt his hand at her hip, gripping her like he meant to haul her away if necessary.

But she was holding Rebecca's mother's gaze, and she couldn't bring herself to drop it.

"I was there that night," Everly said quietly. "I saw

what happened. You must know that this act isn't going to change that. *I know.*"

Blue's hand got almost hard enough to hurt, there at her hip, but he didn't yank her back. He didn't step in and stop her, or try to smooth things over.

Everly chose to take that as unspoken support.

"You *know*?" Annabeth stared back at her, seeming to grow another inch as she did it. "What, exactly, do you think you know?"

Everly played a hunch, and smiled. "Everything."

And for a moment, the three of them simply stood there, locked in place.

Annabeth had stepped back into her foyer. Everly was halfway through the open door. And Blue was behind her, a solid wall that for a long, frozen moment was the only thing that reminded her that her feet were actually on the ground.

"You're a little whore, aren't you?" Rebecca's mother murmured, so very politely that it took Everly an extra beat to register what she'd actually said. "You should have died that first night. Instead, you've caused me nothing but trouble."

And everything sped up.

Blue hauled her backward, hard. The door slammed in her face, and as it did, Everly had the confused notion that another fire alarm was blaring—but nothing blew up. There was no fire, no flames.

Blue was beside her, pulling her by the hand and then shoving her ahead of him. She had the faint notion they would run for the street, but he went the other way, breaking ahead of her and then tugging her along with him.

He took a hard right, throwing himself between the garage and the house, headed away from the street and what she would have considered safety. She didn't understand—

But then she heard footsteps behind them and the sounds of men's voices, urgent and loud. She ran faster.

Blue kicked his way through a gate at the side of the house, then hauled her through it.

And then they were running flat out into the back-yard. Everly noticed the perfectly cut grass on a lawn that meandered around a sparkling blue pool. There were several different terraces set here and there, all with stunning views of Lake Michigan as it lapped there at the bottom of the bluff.

That was where Blue headed. Everly had never been much of a runner, but it was amazing what thugs and a firebomb could do. She could never keep up with Blue, but she ran as fast as she could.

She would worry about breathing later—assuming there was a later. And it involved breathing.

"Get down to the beach, then get the hell away from here," Blue growled at her as they ran, but Everly could hear the voices behind them and, worse, the feet pounding into the ground.

There was a loud crack and a whistling sound, and she couldn't tell which was which. But something thudded into the grass near her feet, and Blue swore.

He hooked an arm around her, picked her up, and tossed her farther down the lawn.

The next crack she heard in midair, but she recognized it.

It was a gunshot. They were being shot at—

But then she landed.

Everly hit the ground hard enough to grunt, then skidded on the grass. She scrambled around, trying to figure out where Blue had gone, gasping for breath, because he could have been hit—

But if he was hit, he didn't show it.

He was running. So swift and deadly that it made her feel dizzy. It showed her how much she'd slowed him down.

And he was running *toward* their attackers.

Everly recognized the faces of the two men who charged him. She'd drawn them, ages ago, after that night in the apartment when they'd killed Rebecca.

They'd killed her. She'd been right all along.

Something in her shifted, hard, as if she'd been storing up her grief, holding it like a stone until she knew for sure—

But this wasn't the time.

In the next second, Blue was in the air, launching himself at the bigger of the two men and taking him down with a thud so loud Everly could hear it from halfway down the lawn. The bigger man stayed down, but Blue rolled back up to his feet to face the other man.

Who lunged at him.

And for a few moments, the two men grappled, moving closer and closer to the edge of the pool.

Blue kicked the man away from him, sending him sprawling.

Everly pushed herself up to her feet again.

The bigger man did the same, but he came up with a gun.

Everly started to run, aware that the terrible noise she

heard was her own voice, raw and scared and screaming, but none of that mattered.

She saw the man jerk his arm. She heard the gunshot a split second later.

And she could do nothing but watch as Blue toppled toward the pool, crashed through the glassy surface, then sank like a stone.

Twenty

There was a roaring in her head. As if her throat had done all the screaming it could and had turned it inward instead.

Everly clawed the air, trying to get to that pool. Trying to get to Blue. Her vision blurred, and when she was suddenly stopped, with a hard band around her midsection, she barely registered it.

There was still too much damned noise in her head.

And only a bit of sloshing at the sides of the pool. Just the faintest hint of any disturbance on the top of the water, and less as each second dragged by.

She kept thinking he would surface, but he didn't. She counted off the seconds in her head.

One, one thousand.

Two, one thousand.

Three, one thousand.

But the pool was still and her head was a seesaw, reeling and lurching, and that *noise* was too much to bear and she—

Everly felt the crack against her cheek, then a deep stinging. Her head whipped to the side, and there was the bloom of copper against her tongue.

It was only when she managed to turn her head back, dazed, that she realized the smaller of the two men was standing in front of her. That he'd grabbed her at some point, though she couldn't seem to recall when.

And, more important, that he'd slapped her across the face.

"Keep screaming," the man invited her without any particular inflection, which made her shiver against her will. "I'll hit you in the face until you pass out."

She believed him. And nothing good could possibly come of being unconscious around these people. It was begging for the kind of trouble her mind shied away from fully visualizing.

He grabbed her under one arm and hauled her up from the ground, then began to drag her back toward the house. It was instantly clear to her that he didn't care if he hurt her, and for a moment, she didn't care if he did, either.

The pool stayed still.

And Everly remembered a summer day a long, long time ago, back on the street where she and Blue had grown up. She'd been out playing with the neighborhood kids, but the game had gotten rough. She'd fallen, hard, and had scraped both her knees, her palms, and even her chin.

She remembered the bright streak of the pain. Her face, gritty where it pressed against the concrete sidewalk. The droplets of blood—*her* blood. It was the first time she could remember seeing it.

And then he'd been there. Blue. Her hero.

He'd run off the other children. He'd squatted down and helped her to her feet, eyeing her as she wobbled there before him, with that steady gaze he'd had even back when he'd been a kid himself.

You're okay, he'd told her.

Not as if he was trying to make her feel better. As if he knew. As if there was no doubt that she was perfectly okay, no matter if she was hurt from her fall. She'd wanted to believe him, but she hadn't been able to keep her lower lip from shaking.

You're tough, he'd said. *Believe it.*

He'd waited there, watching her in that same sure, steady way, until she'd stopped crying.

And then he'd walked her home.

The thug was still dragging her, but Everly managed to get her feet beneath her so she could walk. She couldn't do anything about the grip he had on her, or the bruises she knew he was leaving on her skin. She couldn't do anything about Blue. She couldn't change what had happened. She couldn't do anything—

But she could try to live a little longer.

She could try to make it out of here.

She could *try*.

Believe it, a voice said inside her, the way Blue had long ago. *You're tough.*

And that was better than lying down and letting these people kill her the way they'd killed the first and last true hero she'd ever known.

The man dragged her up the stairs and into the house,

and even though she wanted to so badly she could taste it, Everly didn't look back. There would be blood, maybe. Or floating. Or—

She couldn't go there. She couldn't bear it.

This was the end of the road. She understood that with every cell of her body. The stalking, the break-ins, the bomb—that had all been a sick appetizer for this, the main dish.

But Everly was the same woman who had jumped in a car and driven all the way to Alaska to find a boy she'd once known who was supposed to have turned into a warrior. She could stand tall. If she wasn't going to live to see the sun go down, she could do the next best thing.

She could go out the way he would have if he'd had a choice.

Because she'd just discovered that on the other side of terror, when there was no time for grief, there was something else. It was tough and it was hard. It felt impervious to anything and everything—the aches and pains in her body, the anguish sitting heavy on her chest, every step she took with this gorilla wrenching her arm.

She couldn't *quite* feel it. And that was just numb enough.

Everly had a confused sense of big rooms as she was marched through the house, lined in marble with dramatic chandeliers. There were portraits on almost every wall, every single one of them featuring Annabeth in a different pose. At any other time, it might have creeped her out, but she had other things to worry about, like her swiftly approaching death.

She concentrated on the stone inside her, granite and dark and blessedly numbing. She didn't try to move it.

She tried to become it.

The man at her side dragged her into a room on the ground floor. It boasted lovely French doors that opened to a terrace set high above the backyard, but before she could try to see if she could spot Blue in that pool, he shoved her forward.

So hard and abrupt that she tripped over her own feet and landed on her knees.

She caught herself on her hands, thinking it was too much like that memory. Her palms stung. Her knees felt stiff through her jeans, like they were roughed up, too.

"The boyfriend's dead," the man was saying.

"About time."

Everly looked up. Annabeth was lounging on an ornate chair, a pot of pungent tea at her elbow and a small plate with a selection of berries fanned out across it. She was eating the berries with a sharp cocktail fork, one by one.

Blue was in that pool, and this psycho was eating berries.

The unfairness nearly tipped Everly over.

But if he was gone, if he was really and truly gone, Everly couldn't break down now.

He wouldn't want that.

Blue had taught her how to fight, and that's what she would do.

Using whatever weapons she could.

For as long as she could.

"You can stay right there," Annabeth said, her cold blue gaze on Everly. The goon who'd manhandled Everly in from the backyard went to stand beside Annabeth's chair, facing Everly with the sort of blank stare that made her knees feel wobbly.

So it was a good thing she wasn't standing up.

Everly shifted her weight so she could sit back on her heels and look her death in the face.

"Why?"

"Why can you stay where you are?" Annabeth pursed her full lips, then popped another berry between them with that sharp little fork. "Because you're vermin. And I don't like vermin on my furniture. Everything in this house is perfect. And mine."

She sounded completely at her ease. Almost bored, in fact, which made it even scarier that there was a thick-necked man standing beside her, still holding on to his gun.

"You killed your own daughter, didn't you?" Everly asked, and was distantly amazed that she kept her voice so calm. But then, she was nothing but stone inside. It helped. "Why would you do that?"

Annabeth blinked. "Are you trying to make this about you? Don't bother. All you are to me is more collateral damage."

"I don't get it," Everly said, because she had nothing to fight with here but this. *Time.* If she could keep Annabeth talking, maybe something else would come to her. "Is it because she was younger? Prettier? What?"

She didn't know which of those hit the mark, but something did. Annabeth dropped her cocktail fork against her plate with a loud *clink*.

"Rebecca didn't know her place. You don't seem to know yours, either. I despair of your generation."

"Millennials," Everly commiserated. "We're the worst."

Annabeth tilted her head slightly to one side, as if Everly didn't make sense. And as if she was as curious as she might be about a fly that had gotten into the house in the moments before she squashed it.

"I want to know why," Everly said before any squashing could take place. "Don't you think you owe me that?"

"I don't owe you anything, you egregious little bitch," Annabeth said, conversationally and sounding something like merry. And then she smiled. "You were supposed to be working late that night. Didn't you have some presentation or something? You certainly shouldn't have been running through the streets of Chicago, telling stories to nosy policemen." She giggled at that, as if she'd told a joke. Everly supposed it would have been a chilling sound, but she was already chilled straight through. And that was without allowing herself to think too much about the fact that this awful woman knew her schedule. Her whole life. "Rebecca knew better. That's the beginning and the end of it. I raised her here, not that she appreciated it. I sent her to the finest schools. She knew better than to ask for more than what she was given. But she went ahead and did it anyway."

Everly was kneeling there on the cold floor. Annabeth's henchman was standing beside her, his arms crossed but his gun still visible in his hand, as if he were just waiting for the order to shoot. She looked past them, through the French doors someone had pulled wide, out toward the yard.

And the pool she refused to let herself think about too closely.

She could see the summer sky. She could see the branches of the trees, full of green, dancing in the breeze. She could see Lake Michigan, stretching out toward forever.

It was so hard to accept that this was the last time she would see any of those things. Or anything at all.

"Does that answer your question?" Annabeth asked. "Because I have a Pilates instructor coming in an hour. I need to move this along."

Everly reached up to feel her swollen cheek where the gorilla had hit her. Her skin was hot and puffy, like a blush gone wrong. But the burst of pain when she touched it was good. It reminded her not to surrender too easily.

No matter how tired of all this she was, she didn't want to make it *easy*.

"I wouldn't want to interrupt your schedule," she heard herself say. "I don't know why you brought me in here in the first place."

Annabeth's carefully plucked eyebrow rose, or looked as if it might have moved in an upward direction if it hadn't been frozen into that smoothness.

"You said you knew everything. I want to know what that means." She reached over for her teacup and cradled it in her soft hands, her silver-tipped fingernails glinting in the light. "What do you think you know?"

Everly looked away from that empty, evil stare, trying to wrestle together something she could throw out there in place of any actual knowledge. Anything to buy a few more minutes.

Out on the terrace, a man eased into view. One moment she was staring at the tops of potted plants and the sky beyond, and the next, he was there.

Everly assumed she was hallucinating. Seeing exactly what she wanted to see to distract her from the grim reality unfolding in front of her. She blinked. Once, then again.

But he was still there. Sopping wet, no sunglasses, and, better still, no bloodstains on his T-shirt. No gaping wounds. Just what looked like an ugly cut on one arm.

She figured that was what a man like Blue would call *a graze*. And he was a SEAL, after all. She could come up with all kinds of scenarios where he simply . . . held his breath until Annabeth's goons made the mistake of thinking they'd handled him.

But what mattered was that he was alive.

Alive.

His dark eyes met hers. And blazed so hot she could *feel* it, like the touch of his hands. Like his mouth over hers.

Blue was alive.

Everly looked down to conceal her face, because she didn't think she could control the tidal wave of emotion cascading over her. Her heart flipped over inside her, threatening to expose her. She wanted to cry. She was afraid she was already crying. She waited for shouts from the man outside, but when none came, it occurred to her that Blue must have handled that, too.

When she raised her head, his gaze dropped to her cheek. And she knew he saw that it was puffy. She wouldn't be surprised if there was a handprint.

And then she knew there was, because when Blue lifted his eyes to meet hers again, there was nothing in them but murder.

He nodded at her, slow and steady, and she understood.

She didn't know how she understood, only that she did. Only seconds had gone by, but she felt as if she'd aged a decade. She could feel everything she'd shoved aside, and a lot of it hurt, but she didn't care, because he was *alive*.

But it still wasn't over. She had to keep going.

Everly focused her attention back on Rebecca's psychotic mother.

"I knew Rebecca," she made herself say, and she was sure her voice gave it away. That Annabeth and her goon would turn and see Blue and she would have to watch him die all over again, and for good this time. But Annabeth only stared down at Everly, as if she were a very boring experiment. And the man beside her looked like he could stand there like a statue for days. "What did Rebecca do to you?"

Annabeth took a sip of her tea. "Nothing in this house comes free," she said, in that same easy, conversational tone. Everly fought back a shudder. "I live here thanks to the kindness of a certain . . . friend. This friend has no interest in children, of course. He has his own." She shrugged. "He didn't care if I had one as long as I kept it out of his sight and it in no way changed our arrangement."

"Your arrangement," Everly echoed.

Annabeth's gaze turned condescending. "My friend has a very demanding position, a frail and needy wife, and four grown children, who can't seem to stop giving him grandchildren. I'm his escape. When he can get away, this house is his oasis. And the rest of the time, it's mine."

"And Rebecca's," Everly supplied. "Since she lived here, growing up."

Behind them, Blue moved soundlessly. He came in through the French doors like a shadow, his face set and that intent, murderous gaze of his trained on the goon with the gun.

Everly had to force herself to look away from him before she gave the whole thing away.

"Rebecca was an experiment," Annabeth was saying, fiddling with her plate of berries. "But I quickly learned I have no capacity for motherhood. Luckily, that's what boarding schools are for. And I didn't want her to come back, so I gave her access to her trust early."

"There was no sign of a trust. We looked."

Everly said *we*. She ordered herself not to look directly at Blue.

She just had to keep Rebecca's mother talking a few more minutes.

"I cut her off two years ago when I learned she was going behind my back." Annabeth popped a raspberry into her mouth. "Rebecca had maudlin fantasies about reuniting with her long-lost father. She was a regrettably emotional thing. I'm not entirely sure where that came from."

"Didn't her father want to know her?"

"If my friend wanted to know she existed, I would have used her as a bargaining chip a long time ago. He had less interest in her than I did."

Poor Rebecca, Everly thought. Something like grief moved through her, but sharper, as if there was guilt mixed in.

Maybe Rebecca had needed a friend, not just a roommate. How had Everly failed to notice that during all those nights tucked up on the couch watching bad television?

She would never know the answer. And she would have to carry that.

You can live with anything, Blue had told her. *That's the price of surviving.*

Everly hadn't known then how much that price would hurt.

"She should have accepted the truth," Annabeth was saying crossly. "Not everyone gets a family, and there's no point crying over it almost thirty years on. But instead, Rebecca blackmailed him. And that was something I couldn't allow."

"Because you'd lose all this, wouldn't you?" Everly asked quietly, meeting Annabeth's frigid gaze. "You said it was yours, but it's not, is it? Nothing here is yours. All of it can be taken away in a heartbeat, can't it?"

The look on Annabeth's face turned ugly, because there was no amount of *smoothing* that could change the fact that the woman had no soul. Or anything else in there.

"I told him I would handle it. I did." Annabeth bared her teeth at Everly. "And I want you handled, too. You have no idea how much your stupidity has cost me."

"My stupidity?"

"You should have stayed in that apartment and taken what was coming to you. This was a waste of everyone's time," Annabeth complained.

"I'd hate to waste your time," Everly murmured.

Annabeth lifted her fingers, and beside her, her min-ion shifted position. He lifted his gun, seemingly un-aware that there was a pissed-off ex–Navy SEAL only an inch or so behind him.

Blue's dark eyes met Everly's.

And when he surged forward and chopped the gun out of the thug's hand with a blisteringly fast strike, Everly rolled up onto her feet, too.

Only to find herself face-to-face with a squawking Annabeth.

"I told you," the older woman screamed at her, "I have *Pilates*!"

Then she tried to drive her sharp little cocktail fork into Everly's left eye.

So Everly did exactly what she'd been taught.

And used her palm to strike Annabeth directly in the face, taking her down to the floor.

Twenty-one

"I thought you were dead."

Everly's voice was raw. It cracked on the last word and hit a nerve inside Blue.

He'd been sure she was dead. That he'd lost her to these people. That he would have to add her to that sharp-edged list of names he carried in his gut like a stone, forged from guilt and grief.

Blue had been sure that he'd have to find a way to survive her, too.

And he wasn't sure he could.

On the floor at Everly's feet, Rebecca's psycho of a mother let out a loud keening noise. She writhed there on her side, her hands covering her bloody nose, the end table with her crazy tea and lunatic berry plate upended beside her.

Everly was standing over Annabeth, panting, her arm still locked out from the palm strike she'd landed. Expertly.

Blue was sure he'd never seen anything so beautiful. Everly was alive. She was flushed and *alive* and she'd knocked that cackling loon on her butt.

He was so proud of Everly it actually ached.

"I'm not dead," he told her, his voice rough and low because he'd had no idea what he would find in here. He'd floated in that pool until his lungs ached and his head went spinny, thinking his only edge was taking himself out of the bull's-eye without actually dying. Then the bigger goon had made the vast mistake of prodding him with one of the poolside cleaning implements.

When he'd finished teaching the moron the error of his ways, with prejudice, he'd gone to find Everly.

Aware with every agitated kick of his heart that he was probably too late.

He thought he would carry the sight of her in this room to his grave. He expected it to live in his nightmares. She'd been down on her knees but still defiant, staring up at Annabeth as if she could chat all day with a woman who wanted her dead and had already gone to some trouble to make that happen.

And when she'd seen him, everything had changed.

It wasn't the world that had gone quiet; it was him.

Like a key into a lock, smooth and right. A recognition so profound and so simple that it had rocked him. Made him a different man than he'd been a breath before.

And that was before he saw that douchebag's handprint on her face.

He stepped on said douchebag's arm now, happy to share his feelings on that topic as the guy tried to breathe through the brutal takedown Blue had enacted.

With malice.

"I saw them shoot you, Blue. I saw you drown."

Everly looked haunted. But Blue smiled, because she was *alive* and he couldn't seem to help himself.

"I'm a SEAL, baby. SEALs don't drown."

He wanted to go to her. He wanted his hands on her. He wanted things he could hardly articulate, even in his own head.

But it didn't matter what he wanted.

Because that was when the cavalry arrived.

Alaska Force came in like the well-oiled machine they were. Isaac and Jonas entered the room low and hot, weapons at the ready. Blue knew that meant Griffin was on point and Templeton was walking the perimeter.

To say nothing of the guys out in the truck.

"You missed the party," Blue told them, still smiling. "Typical."

"Looks like you had a nice swim," Jonas retorted. "Was it a pool party?"

"We always miss the good stuff," Isaac said, though his gaze never left the woman writhing on the floor.

And that was it, Blue thought, stepping back so Jonas could zip-tie the goon's hands behind his back. He rubbed his hands over his face, and when he dropped them, Everly had moved. She was shakily lowering herself onto the couch behind her, but her gaze was fixed on him while she did it.

Broadcasting things he didn't want to see and certainly didn't want to feel.

"Cheer up, Everly," he said, still smiling like he was having fun.

He ignored the clamoring thing inside him that told

him truths he didn't want to know and refused to articulate, even to himself.

He'd had a job. He'd done it. The end. "It's over."

Much, much later, Blue pulled his SUV back around behind his mother's house. There was no need to hide it anymore, but old habits died hard.

Or you still don't want anyone to see you, a voice inside piped up. *Coward.*

Blue wasn't a fan of that word. But he also didn't park out on the street, where the fact that he was here could be noted by, say, someone in a house across the way.

Alaska Force had descended on the house in Winnetka with their usual devastating might. The local police had come next. It had been hours and hours of giving reports. Clearing up details.

Blue appreciated Isaac's abilities in times like these. The man had contacts and friends everywhere. What might have taken days in other circumstances, thanks to the usual bureaucratic nonsense, Isaac managed to get done in a few intense hours.

Now there was nothing for Blue to do but grab his bag and head back to Alaska, where he belonged.

Blue let himself in his mother's back door, then paused as the screen slapped shut behind him. That same sense of déjà vu that had messed with him last night walloped him again, hard. There were still too many ghosts. It made his mother's kitchen feel crowded, even when there was nobody there but him.

Maybe it was just him. Maybe he was the one who was haunted.

He started across the kitchen floor for the stairs, but then sensed more than saw a figure appear in the entrance to the living room. His mother.

"I'm going to grab a shower," he said. "Then I'll get out of your hair."

"Did . . . whatever you were doing work out?" his mother asked. "Is Everly all right?"

Blue didn't know what to tell her. He hadn't told her why they were here in the first place, so he didn't see the point of laying it all out for her now. What would he say? Everly had been cleared of everything, at last. Annabeth Lambert and her surviving muscle had been rounded up and taken into custody. It was all over.

He couldn't even tell her that the last two weeks had transformed him into a different man, whether he liked it or not—and he didn't like it at all—because he'd made certain his mother didn't know what kind of man he was in the first place.

It was better to say nothing.

Just like it was better to avoid all these entanglements in the first place, Blue thought darkly, because he'd rather get shot than navigate all these . . . *feelings*.

"Everything's fine," he said, and tried to sound slightly more friendly than a drill sergeant. "Everly's fine, too. Like I said, I won't be long. Just a quick shower, then I'm out."

He expected the long sigh his mother let out then. Or he wasn't surprised by it, anyway. But he didn't expect her to stay where she was, hovering there in his peripheral vision like one of those ghosts he wanted to avoid.

"I can't pretend to understand all the hate you carry around in your heart," she said quietly, and he wanted, desperately, for that to make him angry. But it didn't. Because his mother didn't sound as if she was trying to score points—she just sounded sad. And what defense could he have against making his mother sad? "But you've always been too stubborn for your own good. What I'm going to hold on to is the fact that when you needed somewhere to go, you came here. I'll tell myself that means that your heart knows the truth, even if you don't want to."

It was like there was an earthquake inside him, no matter how he tried to hold himself together. No matter how Blue tried to forbid himself to shake, everything crumbled anyway.

He stood there and fought it for longer than he should have, and he still didn't feel solid.

"Mom, I don't—"

But it was too late. When he looked over, his mother was gone.

Blue told himself it was for the best.

He jogged upstairs, threw his bag together, and took that shower. Alaska Force was rolling out tonight. He intended to wake up in his own bed the following morning, so he could get started on forgetting everything that had happened.

Everly was safe now. That was what mattered. He'd done his job.

He got out of the shower, toweled himself off, and finally put on some clean clothes. There was nothing like a fresh T-shirt, a new bandage on his nicked arm, and a nicely battered pair of jeans after a long, drawn-out situation to make a man feel brand-new and something close enough to content. He walked back out into the sitting room, finally feeling like himself again after too many earthquakes to count, to find his stepfather there in the armchair. Waiting for him.

Blue hadn't seen him since last night, when he'd been nothing but a pale face through the screen door.

In his memory, Ron Margate was big. Brawny and mean, red-faced like a bulldog. But the man sitting before him didn't look like a monster. He just looked like an old guy. He was a lot smaller than Blue remembered, for one thing, and whether that was age creeping up on Ron or the unreliable memories of a scrawny seventeen-year-old kid, Blue couldn't tell.

Ron had lost most of his hair. He was wearing glasses, a polo shirt, and khakis—not exactly clothes to inspire fear. And he didn't light into Blue the minute Blue stepped into the room. Instead, he just looked at his stepson.

As if they were both noting all the changes between them. The last time they'd been in this house together, Ron had been bigger. Now Blue could snap the older man like a twig.

The trouble with that was, he knew exactly what he was capable of. And he wasn't about to attack an unarmed man.

"I'm not really in the mood to do this tonight," Blue said shortly. "I have a plane to catch."

Ron didn't snap at Blue to mind his tone. He didn't demand respect. He didn't shout something about *his house*, *his rules* and then shove Blue as punctuation, the way he might have years ago.

"Here's the thing, Blue," Ron said instead, squaring his shoulders as he spoke. "I've had a long time to think about how things went down after I married your mother. Twenty years and then some."

"This will be a short conversation, then. Things were crappy."

The Ron that Blue remembered would have blown up at that. But this Ron only let out a quiet sound, like a sigh. "I don't blame you. You were a little kid, messed up with grief. I was the adult, and I take full responsibility."

That . . . wasn't what Blue had been expecting.

To put it mildly.

Another aftershock slammed through him, and he found himself shifting from one foot to the other. He locked that down, hard. His long-hated stepfather might have just blown his mind, but he didn't need to *show* Ron that.

"I lost my father," he managed to bite out. "I didn't need another one."

"But you see, I wanted a son."

When Blue could do nothing but stare at him, completely unable to make that statement fit with all his memories, it was Ron's turn to shift in his chair. He looked down at his hands, then up at Blue again, as if he were forcing himself to man up. To look Blue straight in the eye.

"I love my daughters. But I wanted a son and was thrilled that Regina came with you in a single package. And I couldn't understand why everything I did to make you that son backfired. Spectacularly."

Blue felt as if something were choking him. He would've preferred it if something really were, because then he could have fought it. As it was, the sensation was almost too much to bear. It pressed down on his throat. It made it hard for him to breathe.

He'd never wanted this man before him to be anything but the villain he'd always been in Blue's head.

He'd never wanted Ron to be complicated. Or conflicted.

Ron was evil. Ron was supposed to be evil, pure and simple.

"I thought I could repair it, in time. But you never came back." Blue was rocked again by how steady the other man's gaze was. "I don't suppose there's an apology I could make to you that would take away how out of hand I let things get between us back when you lived here. I allowed a confused teenager to provoke me, and I'm not proud of it. For what it's worth, I'm sorry."

Blue thought his jaw might shatter—it was clenched so tight.

He still felt like he was being choked. Now there was that tight band of steel around his chest, too, pulling so hard and fierce he thought it might cut him in half.

He didn't understand what the hell was happening.

And Ron wasn't finished. He stood up, letting his hands dangle at his sides, and if anything, his gaze got more direct.

"You're older now than I was when I married your mom," Ron said. It was another unpleasant reality check that Blue didn't know what to do with. "I'd like to think you're not the same grief-stricken kid you were then."

"I'm not."

Ron nodded. "I accept what I did and the fact I could have—should have—handled things better."

"I don't know what you want me to say." He sounded stiff. Formal.

"You don't have to say anything," Ron replied. "I'd

like your forgiveness, but that's your choice, not mine. I understand why you left here and didn't want to come back. But it's not me you hurt. It's your mother."

Blue didn't know, as he absorbed that blow, why he hadn't seen this coming. It was like he'd set foot in Illinois and had lost his crap on every level. No control and no clue where the hell he'd lost it. No idea what was coming and no ability to counter it or, better yet, prevent it.

It was like he was seventeen all over again. He snuck a look at his own arm to make sure it hadn't shriveled away into scrawniness while he hadn't been paying attention.

"Day after day, year after year, you made your mother pay, when the person you were mad at was me," Ron said quietly. It would have been better if he'd yelled the way he used to. It would have been better if he'd lost his temper, thrown things. Made this familiar. Because then Blue could dismiss him. This was like torture. "It's forgivable in a boy. Expected, even. But you're not a little boy any longer, are you?"

"I don't think I need you to tell me how to be a man," Blue managed to say.

He felt as if he and Ron had finally gotten in that fight he'd dreamed of when he was younger, only it was clear that Ron was winning. Because he was still standing tall, while Blue felt battered. Bruised all over.

"If you want to hate me for the rest of your life, go ahead," Ron said in the same quiet way that Blue hated—*hated*—he could feel resonating inside him. "Your father—"

"Careful. Be very careful."

"—was a good man," Ron said, ignoring Blue's interruption. "A great man. Your mother misses him every day, as she should, and the only link she has to him on this earth is you. You, Blue. And you've stayed away for twenty years. All I ask is that you think about that. Think about her."

"She—"

"She loved your father," Ron said softly. "And I know it hurt you that when he was gone, she found a way to love me. But she never, ever, stopped loving you, Blue. Or him. Never. Maybe it's time to stop punishing her. All she did was live."

And Ron didn't wait for Blue to respond to him. He simply walked off down the stairs, leaving Blue to stand there in the wreckage he'd made.

And, worse, to face it.

He didn't want to face anything. He wanted to disappear—but that was what he always did, wasn't it?

It was what he was still doing.

It's what you're good at, he growled at himself.

He hadn't followed his instincts and left Everly to handle her situation on her own, and look what had happened. He was embroiled in twenty-year-old family drama that made him want to shoot himself up with an actual chemical numbing agent so he could stop feeling a damned thing.

Blue made his way back down the stairs, his heart seeming to beat double time, as if he were doing a few rounds of PT instead of calmly leaving a house he hadn't wanted to come back to in the first place.

At the bottom of the stairs, he had a choice. He could hear the television on in the den, and he knew without having to look that his mother and Ron would be in there, sitting together on the couch, a perfect picture of domesticity. He'd hated that when he was younger. More than hated it, he'd seen every instance of the two of them enjoying their life as a personal insult and a betrayal of his father.

He didn't feel that way now. He didn't know what he felt, was the trouble—except mixed-up and battered and something that crept too close to powerless.

All she did was live, Ron had said.

He could go into the den. He could try to act like the son his mother deserved. Or he could do what he wanted to do and GTFO. Now.

Blue hated this. He hated all of this.

And he was mostly afraid that what he really hated was himself.

He wasn't his father. He wasn't that kind of hero. He didn't know how many more times he needed to tell people that before they'd stop holding him up to standards he would never, ever meet.

So he didn't go find his mother. He headed straight through that kitchen and walked out of the house, the way he'd done twenty years ago.

He didn't look back. He flipped the SUV around and headed back down the driveway, where he stopped, because there was another issue glaring at him.

Literally, right there in his face. Or across the street, anyway.

Everly's parents' house was lit up as if they were home, when Blue knew they weren't. They were on their way back from Europe, but they weren't here yet. Which meant the lights on the second floor were Everly's.

After hours in police custody, Everly had been released before Blue. Templeton had driven her out to her parents' house because it was the only place she had to go. The police had told her that there had been some salvageable items in her apartment, but that was a whole project. And tonight wasn't the time to face it.

Blue itched to slam his foot down on the gas pedal and put as much space between him and this street as he could, and fast—

But she'd told him she loved him.

Blue figured the least he could do was tell her good-bye.

He could handle this better than he had with his family. He could let Everly down easy. Maybe even let her hate him if she wanted, so she could get over this crisis crush of hers quicker.

She might have changed him forever. He could feel it, deep inside him, like one more fault line about to crack. But she hadn't changed him enough.

Blue didn't think anything could.

He pulled over across the street and left the SUV there at the curb. Then he jogged around to the back of the house and the door that led straight into the kitchen, because that was how kids had always entered each other's houses back when they were growing up here. It hadn't even occurred to him to use the front door.

As if you have more memories of life here than you want to admit.

He told that voice inside him where it could go, then let himself in through the unlocked back door. Once inside, he stood still.

Because it was much too quiet.

A moment later, Griffin melted out of the shadows

from what Blue assumed was the pantry, lowering his weapon as he stepped into the light.

"I thought Templeton was doing the last watch here."

"He had to jump a plane for Atlanta. Clean up a mess or two on that corporate job from back in April." Griffin smirked. "Am I not pretty enough for you?"

"You're gorgeous." Blue moved farther into the kitchen, hoping he'd managed to school his expression into something appropriately blank. Because Griffin saw entirely too much, like all the rest of his overly trained brothers-in-arms. "Where's the client?"

"At the moment, *the client* is in the shower."

Blue assured himself that he was imagining Griffin's emphasis on those two particular words.

Griffin lifted a finger and pointed it toward the ceiling. It took Blue a minute to understand that they could hear the water in the pipes of the old house, if they listened.

"She's been in there a while. I'm guessing the shock hit her."

"Okay," Blue muttered. "Thanks."

He didn't explain himself any further. Better still, Griffin—possibly the most resolutely glacial of all the men in Alaska Force—didn't ask. Blue walked out of the kitchen and found the stairs, then headed up to the second floor. He followed the sound of the running water down the hallway to his left, and sure enough, Griffin was right. The shock had finally hit her.

He could hear Everly in there, sobbing in time with the pounding water.

It was like someone reached out, plunged a fist into his chest, and mangled whatever was left in there.

Blue knew he should leave her to it. He should go now, and not make this any worse. Let her cry about whatever she needed to cry about and disappear. He could be a part of the memories she had of these awful weeks when her normal life had gotten strange. As time passed, who knew? Maybe he'd fade away entirely.

All he had to do was leave. Now.

But instead he found his hand on the doorknob. Then he was pushing open the door and stepping inside. Steam enveloped him, shrouding him in thick heat. He found his way to the stand-alone shower stall next to the wide tub, and opened the door.

Everly was crouched down in the corner of the shower, pillowing her head in her arms.

He couldn't bear it.

Blue reached in and turned off the water. He grabbed the towel hanging on the hook outside the shower, then leaned in to wrap it around her. Then he lifted her up and into his arms.

She was a sodden mess, and she nestled her face into the crook of his neck. And he couldn't tell the difference anymore between the fault lines inside him and Everly. They were all wrapped in and around him, and now she was, too, and he didn't understand what he was supposed to *do* with this. With her.

With all those things he didn't want to feel, but did.

"I thought you were dead," she said, her mouth against the side of his neck.

"You keep saying that."

"I don't think you get it, Blue. I had to live with it. However long that was, fifteen minutes? Five? You were dead."

That clawed at him.

He followed the light into a bedroom down the hall, figuring it was her childhood bedroom. There were pretty lamps on matching bedside tables. There was a frothy pink comforter stretched across a full bed piled high with unnecessary pillows.

It was exactly the kind of bedroom he would have imagined for her, if he'd imagined it.

But she's not the girl who lived here.

Blue didn't want to have that argument, even if it was only with himself. He didn't want to think about the fact that he'd seen the bedroom she'd put together in her apartment, and while it had been feminine and suited her, it hadn't been pink. It had been comfortable and pretty, sure. It hadn't been a little girl's room.

But that uncomfortable truth wasn't going to help him walk away from her, so he shoved it aside.

He carried her over to the bed and set her down on the edge of the mattress.

"I'm alive," he told her, his voice dark.

It came out sounding a lot like a promise. Worse, a declaration.

"Blue," she whispered. "Blue, I—"

He had come here only to leave her. To say his good-byes and make sure that this thing between them was cut straight through. No ties. No entanglements. That was the way he liked his life. He barely spoke to his own mother, for God's sake. He didn't want or need anyone else out there in the world hoping that he might show up again one day, when he knew that would never happen.

This was supposed to be a good-bye.

So he had no idea why he moved closer to the bed so

he could fit himself between her legs where they dangled over the side of the mattress. And then gently, carefully, fit his hands to her face.

Everly opened her mouth as if she meant to speak.

Blue bent and captured it with his own.

And inside him, a storm raged.

He couldn't make her promises. He couldn't stay. He didn't know how to be the man she saw when she looked at him, and he hated that there was a jagged, yearning part of him that thought he should try anyway.

He thought it would stop at a kiss, a sweet taste of the things he couldn't have and needed to leave here, but Everly had other ideas.

She surged against him. She wrapped her arms around him, gripping his T-shirt in her fists, and then tugged him over her until they both tumbled back onto the mattress.

Blue knew he should stop it. He knew he could have kept her from pulling him anywhere he didn't want to go. He should set boundaries, not break them—he knew that.

But all the things he should have done got lost somewhere in the delirious slickness of her mouth on his. He tugged on her towel, revealing her breasts, tilted and tipped with those rose-colored nipples that tasted better than anyone should. He started there.

He tasted her, he worshipped her, and while he indulged himself, Everly was exploring him. Her mouth was everywhere. Tasting, teasing. It was almost as if they were fighting each other to get to the same fire, rolling this way and that.

Panting, raw.

Perfect.

Until finally, Blue stripped out of his clothes and stretched out beside her, rolling on protection while she settled herself astride him.

And then he lay back, gripped her hips, and let her ride.

He would remember this—her—forever. The way she arched back as she moved against him, breathing hard. Her soft body, freckled and pale and made to fit him like the finest, sweetest glove.

She was burning herself into him. She was making herself a part of him with every delicious roll of her hips.

He had to fight to hold himself back when she started to shudder, that red flush working its way down her whole body. She lit up like a firecracker, bright and hot, and she called out his name when she ignited.

And as she shook and sobbed all around him, Blue flipped her over. He rolled her beneath him and pulled her knees up higher, so he could go deeper. Harder.

So he could make this last even longer.

He tossed her from one peak straight into another climb, and waited for her to break apart all over again.

He loved when she flushed, hot and unmistakable. He loved the way she writhed beneath him, as if every deep thrust might well be the end of her. He loved her, he realized.

He loved her. He was in love with her.

And Blue told her the only way he could.

The only way he'd allow it.

His hands, desperate to touch more of her, all of her. His mouth against her skin.

He threw her into the fire again, then again.

And it wasn't enough. It would never be enough.

But it was the only thing Blue had to give.

And when he finally let himself go, the only word in his mouth was her name.

Everly.

He didn't know how long he lay there with her when it was over. He knew only that he left part of himself behind when he rolled out of the bed and left her there, curled up and fast asleep.

And he wasn't the man he'd been when he'd walked into this house. He wasn't the man he'd always believed he was, period. This place had taken that from him—or, worse, shown him hard truths in a mirror he'd very much like to shatter with his fists.

Blue felt . . . diminished.

Lucky for him, he'd spent years in the navy learning how to suck it up and work with what he had.

He just had to hope it was enough.

It would have to be enough.

Twenty-two

A month later, Everly flew to Alaska.

It took quite a few hours more than when she'd taken the direct Alaska Force jet with Blue, but a lot less time than it had taken to drive. Plus, she'd had a layover in Seattle, which allowed her to drink good coffee while asking herself if she was really, truly doing this.

The answer was yes, she really was.

She landed in Juneau on a crisp evening that felt much further into fall than the date suggested, and stayed the night in a comfortable hotel nearby. In the morning, she looked out on a world that appeared to be half in the clouds, which lingered, puffy and low, over the green hills that flirted with the gleaming water in all directions.

There was time for coffee and a shower to wake herself up, and then she boarded the ferry for Grizzly Harbor.

And for a long time she lost herself in the simplicity of the big boat cutting through the water. Seals and whales made appearances, some close and some in the distance, while glaciers beckoned from afar and islands stretched across the horizon, bulky with mountains and evergreens. She bundled herself up and sat outside, letting the cold, clear Alaskan air and the salt from the sea scrub her clean as the ferry made its way through the many islands of the famed Inside Passage toward Grizzly Harbor.

She stood on the bow as the ferry docked, surprised that the rugged little fishing village looked as good to her now as she remembered it.

Just like the postcard she'd been carrying around in her head.

Because she'd spent a lot of time this past month telling herself that it had all been an exaggeration. That Alaska and Blue and everything in between had all been crisis and panic, fear and terror. She'd tried to convince herself that Blue had been right and she'd had on blinders to get her through her ordeal. That no matter what she might have felt in the thick of it, it had been impossible for her to see things around her as they really were.

She'd tried to believe it. She really had.

When she'd woken up that morning in her parents' house, she'd known Blue was gone. Before she'd come fully awake, she'd known he wasn't there in the pink bedroom her parents used for guests these days.

But she'd still looked for him. Or . . . a note, maybe. A voice mail message she could access through one of her parents' computers, since she didn't have a phone. Even a text.

There was nothing. He was just . . . gone.

She'd walked over to his parents' house and snuck around the side like a crazy person on her way to boil a bunny, but the only thing left to show he'd been there was the marks his tires had made in the grass out back.

Everly didn't need to knock on the door or talk to his mother to know the truth.

Blue was gone. Just as he'd said he would go, way back when.

That time, Everly didn't cry. She'd felt sick. Hurt, she could admit it. But she didn't cry. She'd gotten it all out in the shower, she told herself fiercely. Or all she planned to let out, anyway.

And besides, there was too much to do. Her parents had come back on the next flight from Europe, horrified at what had happened to their daughter and deeply upset that she hadn't told them about it sooner.

"I didn't want you to be disappointed in me," she confessed to her mother the night they'd arrived. They'd all been sitting around the kitchen table together, her parents growing more and more agitated with every part of the story Everly had shared. "I thought I could solve it and you'd never have to know that I'd somehow gotten myself into this situation. . . ."

"I don't know where you get this idea that you're a great disappointment," her mother said fiercely, and then had reached over to grab Everly's hands. "It was as if the minute you decided following in my footsteps wasn't what you wanted, you stopped trying to push yourself to do anything."

"But Jason . . ."

"Your brother knew what he wanted to be since he was three years old," her father had said brusquely, his eyes suspiciously glassy. "That has its own pitfalls, I assure you."

"If I've ever been disappointed in you, Everly, it's not because you didn't live up to some fantasy daughter you imagine I have in my head," her mother had said, holding her gaze so there could be no escape. "I don't need you to be a doctor. I need you to be happy. Whatever that looks like for you, that's what I want."

"And maybe," her father had added gruffly, "no more roommates."

Everly had spent the rest of the month thinking about what happiness was. Real happiness. Not occasional bursts of joy here and there, but the kind of happiness that was sustainable. The kind of happiness that mattered.

First there'd been her apartment to deal with, which was never going to rank at the top of any list of happy activities. It had been a long, depressing week of sorting through the damage and saving what she could. There were memories that were lost forever and a few items of personal significance that could never be replaced. But the truth was that Everly had lost nothing that she couldn't live without.

From her apartment, anyway.

It was an interesting thing to know as a fact instead of a philosophical exercise. Missing something wasn't the same as being wrecked without it. And as much as she still felt violated and still dreamed of flames crackling up the walls, she wasn't wrecked.

The things in her apartment had just been *things*.

Rebecca was the only loss that mattered. She was the only thing that really couldn't be replaced. And the only thing Everly could give the roommate she should have been a better friend to was justice.

She worked with the police. She told them about Annabeth's "friend," and felt vindicated when the father who hadn't wanted to recognize his own daughter while Rebecca was alive found himself embroiled in the scandal of her death.

She was sure that a man like Rebecca's father, a well-known lawyer with local political aspirations, would have sharks for attorneys who would keep him out of the prison Annabeth was going to. But the scandal would hurt him. His "frail and needy" wife announced her intention to file for divorce. His children denounced him.

That wasn't happiness, of course. But it was certainly satisfying.

Once her apartment had been taken care of, she spent a lot of her time explaining herself to all the friends she'd ignored over the past month. And her older brother, Jason, who hadn't been too pleased that she'd stopped answering his calls and resorted to texts with precious few words. She'd lost a lot of things when that bomb had gone off, it was true. And she'd learned that she could live without most of them. The people she loved, on the other hand, she treasured and had treated badly.

There were a lot of tears. A lot of apologies on Everly's part.

And a lot of opportunity to ask herself the same question her friends and family did: Why hadn't she called? Why hadn't she asked for help?

Why did she think she had to go through something like that all alone?

Charles had continued to reach out to her, and some three weeks after she'd quit, Everly walked back to her old office and sat down with her former boss. He'd told her they didn't want to lose her expertise.

And Everly had told him that she had no interest in returning to the office but would be happy to work remotely, doing more of the creative work she enjoyed and less of the things she hated, like the interoffice politics.

To her surprise, Charles had agreed to let her work freelance.

Enthusiastically agreed, in fact.

And she'd had to wonder why it had taken losing everything to make her understand that if she never asked for what she wanted, that was exactly what she'd get.

That was why she'd come back to Grizzly Harbor. And not in panicked desperation this time.

When the ferry docked at the pier, the villagers came out to meet it and help unload supplies. Afterward, she took her time walking up the hill, into the town proper, and finally to the Water's Edge Café. The village was just how she'd left it, except the fog that clung to the mountains and wound through the streets didn't look as if it would burn off today. The mountain up behind Grizzly Harbor was moodier than she remembered. She squinted up at it, solemn and forbidding even shrouded in clouds, and couldn't believe she'd ever pointed a rental car in that direction and then driven over it.

It just went to show that when Everly really wanted something, she found a way to get it.

She was holding on to that.

She pushed her way into the restaurant and had the

strangest sense that she . . . fit. Right there amid the bright walls with the cheerful pictures on them.

And she was unduly excited when Caradine looked up from her place on the stool at the counter and stared at her. Unsmiling.

But not actually scowling.

"Back again," Caradine said. "We still don't have a menu."

Everly grinned, because for some reason, that surly couple of sentences felt like the biggest welcome she'd ever received.

"I want coffee," she said. "And something to eat, whatever sounds good. Oh, and a place to stay, if you know of anything."

Caradine eyed her from across the restaurant floor. There was no one else inside at this hour of the afternoon, not that Everly thought that a crowd would have altered Caradine's behavior in any way.

"Tourist season is over, thank the Lord."

"Good thing I'm not a tourist, then."

"Is this the part where montage music plays?" Caradine asked after a moment. "And we, what? Braid each other's hair and talk about boys? I'm going to pass on that."

Everly grinned wider. "Coffee. Food. Maybe a place to sleep. Braiding hair is optional but actually pretty creepy, if you ask me."

"I don't do friends."

"You know, I'm going to share something with you, Caradine."

"Oh joy."

Everly shrugged out of her coat, then sat down at the

nearest table. "It's not actually a surprise that you 'don't do friends.' It's something about how open you are, maybe. Your sunny personality."

"And also I hate everyone."

"Okay."

"Don't ask for a job. You can't work here."

"I have a job," Everly assured her. "Also, I'd be a terrible waitress. Here, I mean. I waited tables in college one summer and was good at it, but that doesn't really go with your whole . . . thing."

"Are you here for Blue?" Caradine asked in the same mild tone, cutting through the conversation just like that. Skewering it, more like.

"I don't know." Everly settled back in her chair, thought about it, and shrugged. "I honestly don't know."

Because a lot of that would depend on which Blue turned up. The one who couldn't keep his hands off her? Or the one who'd left her without a word?

Caradine smirked. "I'll take that as a yes. And I like it. You can stay in my spare room." She slid off her stool and headed toward the kitchen. "But that doesn't mean we're friends."

"Of course not," Everly agreed.

But she was still smiling.

After she ate yet another perfect meal that she wouldn't have known to ask for but was precisely what she wanted, she asked Caradine for her key. The other woman laughed.

"I pity anyone stupid enough to steal from me," she said. "It's not locked. Just go up the stairs."

Caradine lived above the restaurant, in a cozy apartment with a woodstove and breathtaking views of the harbor from every window. Everly sat there for a long time, not sure if she was relieved or overwhelmed to find that Alaska was even more beautiful than she remembered it.

The kind of beautiful that wedged its way into her soul, making it hard to breathe.

She felt . . . expansive here. Chicago felt too close now, too confined. Even the lovely house she'd grown up in hadn't suited her any longer. It felt like a pair of pants that was just a shade too tight, the button forever digging into her belly, the creases riding up every time she tried to move.

Grizzly Harbor felt wide. High. Endless in all directions.

She spent the rest of the afternoon wandering up and down what passed for streets, the haphazard lanes going this way and that. Funny boardwalks and buildings propped up on stilts, and the happy, defiantly bright colors everywhere, even more magical to her mind when the sky was gray. She poked around in the handful of shops, and even bought herself a couple of local craft items—the first *things* she'd bought since almost everything she'd had incinerated.

There was a bite in the air that suggested the seasons turned quicker here, and might even turn right on top of her. She stopped to untie her wool midlayer shirt from around her waist, then tugged it on. When she pulled her head through, she looked up to find a man standing across from her in the narrow street.

He looked the way she would have imagined an ancient warrior might, if she'd spent her time imagining such things. She wanted to draw him, to see if she could capture his strong cheekbones and the particular brown hue of his skin. His black hair was thick and slightly too long, and looked as if he spent a lot of his time raking his hands through it. He also looked as if he had just come out of the woods, and yet somehow sweat from exertion didn't in any way take away from his considerable, and overwhelming, male beauty.

"Hey, Templeton," Everly said. Very politely, as if the last time she'd seen him hadn't been when he'd transported her from a police station to her parents' house. "It's nice to see you again."

He grinned, but the look in his dark eyes was intent. Focused. "You're a long way from Chicago."

"I am."

"Grizzly Harbor is pretty cute. I guess you didn't have much time to look around the last time you were here."

"You know, I didn't." She smiled. "I heard there were great hot springs, right here in town."

"There sure are." She couldn't tell what accent that was that mellowed out his voice, hinting of time spent in the South. She knew only that he could wield it at will. "Is that why you came back? To enjoy some Alaskan hot springs?"

"Why else?"

Templeton laughed. It was a big, brash laugh that suited a man as . . . *extreme* as he was. It also seemed to echo off the mountain.

"I hoped you were going to put a miserable bastard I know out of his misery, but hot springs are fine. Probably more pleasant, all things considered." He nodded to her, which saved her having to pretend she didn't know what he meant—or having to conceal the twist in her gut at the notion Blue was miserable. Or that she could do anything about it. "Enjoy your time here. There's no other place quite like Grizzly Harbor."

And Everly was all about happiness these days, so that was exactly what she did.

She found her way to the hot springs, which were natural pools carved out of the mountainside that the locals had built structures around. She assumed that meant they used them all winter. There were designated women's hours, which meant that she could go in, take off her clothes, and slip into the smooth, silky water without worrying about a thing.

She sat and let the heat seep into her bones. She tipped her head back, shut her eyes, and listened to the silence all around her. Towering silence.

It made her feel whole.

More women trickled in. They nodded at Everly as they got in, and she nodded back, feeling like a local. Some of the women settled in and shut their eyes, too. Others carried on talking. Everly learned a great deal about a woman named Maria who'd moved here with her boyfriend but left him for a local fisherman sometime over the last winter. In what the ladies in the pools thought was a revenge play, the boyfriend and the fisherman's wife had shacked up. And now both Maria and the fisherman's wife were pregnant, and no one seemed to know whose was whose.

"There are timeline concerns, apparently," one of the women said.

"Last I heard, they were going to build out that cabin and live together," one of her friends said. "All together."

"Can't say I blame them," another woman chimed in,

snorting out a laugh. "I wish I had an extra husband and wife to help with my kids."

And when Everly was overheated and satisfyingly wrinkled, she got out of the pool and dried herself off in the sauna next door. She tried to imagine the two couples she'd just heard about, and all their kids, packed together in one cabin out in a winter here, and couldn't decide if she admired them for their optimism or thought they were fools. The women in the pool hadn't seemed able to decide, either.

But that was true about anything, she thought as she pulled her clothes back on. Grand gestures were romantic when they worked. People only thought you were foolish if you failed.

She made her way outside again, where it was considerably colder. Partly because she'd gotten so warm, but also because the temperature had dropped. The sun was already starting to go down, which made something inside her leap up and spin, as if the sunset were a gift just for her.

Because the last time she'd been here, it hadn't really gotten dark at all.

She liked it here. She could breathe here. Everly liked being on the edge of the world, thousands of miles away from everything, so she could think.

She liked how small it was, how close. So close that if she wanted, she could likely figure out not only who the women in the pools had been but who they were talking about, too. There was no doubt in her mind that if she asked Caradine, she'd get more of the story. That was why people found small towns claustrophobic, she supposed, but she liked it.

Because if something else ever happened to her, if she lived in a place like this, it would be hard for strangers to sneak around. Impossible, even.

She picked up her pace on the narrow trail that wound down from the pools and back into town, not wanting to get stuck in the woods in the dark. She rounded the last curve that took her right above the village, and then stopped short.

Because Blue was there.

He stood as solid as one of the trees, sunset turning him golden. His expression was set and his arms were folded, and her heart flipped over, then kicked. Hard.

"What are you doing here?" he asked.

And it reminded her so much of that day earlier this summer when she'd come careening over the mountain to find him. Her feet were in the dirt again. She was even wearing the same shoes he found so silly. Unserious, impractical shoes, if she remembered it right.

He stood there like a sentry. One who wanted her gone.

And the thing was, Grizzly Harbor fit her. Everly felt as if she'd been searching for this place all her life, without even knowing that there'd been anything missing. She liked everything about it. From grumpy Caradine to the hot springs to the cold, watchful mountain above. She had no trouble seeing herself here.

But the man standing in front of her was home.

He was in her bones.

She could live without him. She had.

What she'd concluded was that she didn't want to.

She opened her mouth to say hello.

"No," he gritted out before she could say anything.

"No greetings, like this is normal. No chitchat. No tourist nonsense up in the pools. You shouldn't be here, Everly. You know you shouldn't be here."

"I don't know that at all."

"Listen," he began. "Little—"

But Everly shook her head at that. She stepped closer to him and lifted her hand as if she was going to slap it over his mouth.

He grabbed it in midair, of course.

She didn't let that stop her.

"Stop," she said with a quiet force she could feel flooding out from somewhere deep inside her, as if she were a part of the vastness all around her. As if it were in her, too. "I'm not a little girl. You don't think I'm a little girl—you just wish you did."

He shook his head as if he wanted to argue. She didn't let him.

"I told you I was in love with you, Blue. I meant it. Did you really think that if you snuck out in the middle of the night, I would forget?"

Twenty-three

Blue dropped her hand like it was on fire, but that did nothing to alleviate the burn. He could feel her touch everywhere, making him hard and hollow and even less happy than he'd been to begin with.

She was here, and clearly had no particular plan to come find him.

She was *here*, for God's sake.

According to Templeton, she'd been sauntering around Grizzly Harbor, unaware that he was tailing her for a good twenty minutes. She'd poked around the shops that stayed open, if only at random hours now that the summer crowds were gone. She'd taken some pictures with her phone. She'd looked, Templeton had been sure to tell him, as if she were just in town to look at the pretty views and then leave, like any other tourist.

"Great," Blue had said, glaring down at his tablet as if he were really that entranced by the latest mission parameters they'd been debating in the lodge. "Then she'll leave like a tourist, too. On the next ferry."

No one had pointed out that today was Monday and the next ferry didn't come until Friday. Everyone knew the freaking ferry schedule. Blue certainly did.

"Jesus Christ," Jonas had muttered darkly. "I can't stand this. You've been running around here like a crazy person for the past month."

"I'm sorry if you can't handle an uptick in intensity, brother," Blue had replied. Through his teeth. "Noted."

Jonas had flipped him the bird. Blue had responded in kind.

But it was Isaac who'd caught up to him when the meeting was over, falling into the same pace beside him as Blue had headed down to the water.

"I don't want to hear it," Blue gritted out.

"You don't know what I'm going to say."

"I can guess."

"If you can guess, then I don't know why you're still here, glaring at the tide."

Blue liked to take the beach route back to his cabin when it was low tide, although not so much today, when he mostly wanted to break things. He and Isaac had stood down by the water's edge for a moment, Fool's Cove deceptively smooth before them. Blue put his hands on his hips and stared out at the water because it was better than sucker punching one of the best men he knew, but it didn't soothe him the way it used to.

The way it had even six weeks back.

The water wasn't doing its job the way it had before.

"You went back home," Isaac said into the silence.

"That gets in your head. It messes you up." He laughed. "Believe me, I know."

"I spent twenty years knowing exactly who I was," Blue heard himself say. And then, having started, he couldn't seem to stop. "I knew what I did and why. I knew exactly what I stood for. There were no mysteries—there were only missions."

Isaac stood next to him, his gaze trained on the water, too. And the fact that he didn't say anything—he didn't jump in to tell Blue what to feel, or argue with him about his own damned life—made it easy to keep going.

To put words to the thing that had been eating him alive since he'd left Chicago.

"She thinks I'm a hero," Blue said, scratchy and low.

"I get why that bothers you," Isaac replied, his voice grave.

Because he did. He knew what it meant when Blue said that. They all knew that *hero* was a word that sounded great to other people and made those other people feel good, too. But every man in Alaska Force knew what it took to earn that title. What they'd done. What they'd lost. What each and every one of them would carry with them, always, thanks to that so-called heroism.

Hero was a weight to carry. It wasn't as simple as civilians wanted it to be.

"She might call you a hero, but you don't upend your life and come all the way to Grizzly Harbor for a fantasy." Isaac shook his head. "That would wear off sometime during the first layover. What she wants is her man."

"That's not me." Blue pushed the words out past that choke hold around his throat. Again. "That's not ever going to be me."

"It's either you or it isn't, but she came a long way to find out." Isaac had turned to look at Blue then, his gaze steady. "You should probably tell her yourself."

And here Blue was. Ready to tell Everly what he should have that night in her parents' house. Which was whatever he needed to tell her to get her to go away and never come back.

To make her hate him.

Or at least make sure she never, ever told him she loved him again.

"You need to go," he told her.

She looked prettier than he remembered, and he remembered every single detail. She'd piled that strawberry blond hair on top of her head, and strands of it were curled up around her face, likely from the heat in the hot springs. She glowed, rosy and warm, and it reminded him of all the many shades of red he could make her turn, which made his body harden. Her eyes were just as green as always, but tonight they were different. It took him a minute to realize it was because there was no lingering fear in them. Because she wasn't on the run tonight. Hell, she was even wearing those dumb shoes of hers—but somehow, this time, he found them cute.

Everly caught him staring at the shoes and smiled, sticking one foot out as if she'd forgotten she was wandering around Alaska in shiny, metallic, *foldable* flats she claimed were practical. "The fire trashed my bedroom but not my closet. Go figure."

Blue ordered himself to get back on track. "You can

tell me you love me a thousand times and it won't make any difference. You don't."

"I do." But she sounded serene, not rattled. And not at all dissuaded.

He couldn't say he'd expected that reaction.

"Everly, listen to me. Intense situations—"

"Do you love me?" she asked him, in that same direct way that was like the slam of a bullet into his chest. When he opened his mouth, she shook her head and moved closer. And then reached up with her hand and placed it over his heart. "Tell me the truth, right now, and I'll believe you. I promise."

He could have taken a punch. Hell, an actual bullet would have been better. He could have handled her angry, her upset. Tears or a temper he could have taken in stride.

But her kindness undid him. Her trust in him destroyed him.

He felt as if he were bloodied and staggering, though he knew he didn't move. It was that earthquake in him, the one he'd been ignoring since that last night in Chicago. The fault lines hadn't gone anywhere.

If anything, they'd gotten worse.

He could feel them give way, right there beneath her hand. He could feel his foundations crumble.

All the walls he'd built. All the lies he'd told himself.

"I want to love you," he told her, the words torn from him, "but I don't know how."

He didn't know what he'd expected, but it wasn't what she did.

Everly moved closer. She slid her other hand on his chest and tilted her head back to look up at him.

"You do know how," she told him, her voice fierce and sure. "Look at what you do. Look at who you are."

But that was the problem.

His own hands came up to push hers away, but instead he found himself holding them there.

"I'm trained to do things that would give people nightmares. But good people don't have nightmares about men like me, Everly. They don't know I exist. That means I'm the one who has those nightmares. I'm the one with blood on my hands." He was too loud, too rough. Too *something*. "And it never goes away."

"You saved my life," she told him.

He shook his head. "You saved your own life."

"I don't mean in that house. I don't mean Annabeth." The expression she wore then was ferocious. "I was sleepwalking all this time. That woman would have killed me and I would have died without knowing that I'd never truly been happy. Without realizing that I had no idea what it was to love someone with every part of me. You set me free, Blue."

She was talking about this summer. But all Blue could see was the past.

"I had to turn something off inside me to do what I did for all those years. I can't turn it back on."

"I don't believe that." She didn't back down when he scowled at her. Instead, she held his gaze as if she were as strong as he was. He believed it. "You became a soldier, an elite one. I'm not going to pretend to understand what that takes. All I can do is admire your commitment and dedication. That alone would make you amazing." She pressed her hands harder against his chest, as if she were trying to brand him with the heat of her palms, and the funny thing was that he thought she was succeeding. "But you didn't turn yourself off then. You know you didn't."

"I had to."

"It wasn't the navy that flipped that switch." Her eyes were so big, so green. It made him . . . restless. "Come on, Blue. Is this really what your father would have wanted for you?"

The last wall he had inside him toppled over then, hitting the ground with a wallop. Hitting him so hard that for a moment, all he could see was the dust. His hands moved of their own volition and gripped her shoulders.

But when the dust cleared, Everly was looking at him as if nothing had changed. As if he were still that man— that hero—he couldn't understand how or why she saw in him.

"You told me he was a man who loved his wife and his son," she said. "Would he have wanted that son to grow up shut off from everybody? Is that who he was?"

Blue thought of his father's smile, quick and ready. The booming laugh that had seemed to light up rooms. The way he'd never met a stranger.

"You've been so mad at so many people for so long," Everly said, relentless in ways he could hardly make sense of. "But ask yourself one question. Are you really mad at your mother because she moved on? Or are you mad that you couldn't? She could go out and find herself a new husband. But you only had one dad."

"Damn you," Blue choked out, and he hardly knew what was happening to him. He was horrified to feel dampness on his face. He felt cracked wide open, exposed—

Alive, something inside him whispered. *At last.*

But when he looked at Everly, he saw that tears were rolling down her cheeks.

Because, he knew without having to ask, she hurt *for* him. She loved him enough to show him the truth about himself, and then stand there and cry with him while it rolled through him, decimating him where he stood.

"Why did you come here?" he demanded again, though he was hoarse and sounded like a stranger. And he didn't let her go. "Why did you bother trying to find me?"

"Here's what I can promise you," she said, smiling through her tears. "I will always find you. Always, Blue."

And he believed her. This was the woman who'd driven over Hard-Ass Pass. She could do anything. She would.

She already had.

"You don't want this," he warned her, gripping her more surely. "You don't know what you're signing up for."

"You have a lot of requirements for women who come to your bed, yes," she said, throwing his words back at him from so long ago, he'd almost forgotten he'd said them. "You like very defined roles. I remember."

"We'll get to that, believe me." Fault lines and storms moved through him, in him. But he kept his eyes on Everly. Like she was light. "I'm not done with Alaska Force. I don't want to live in a city. And I hate peas."

"My job is entirely freelance, and guess what? I like it here."

"You didn't mention the peas."

"I don't have opinions about peas, Blue. I'm not sure peas deserve opinions, to be honest."

"I'm not domesticated. I'm demanding and intense, and I hold grudges for decades." He shook his head when she started to say something. "Don't blow this off, baby. You deserve better than me, believe me. I know it even if you don't. But if you don't walk away from me right now, it's not going to matter. Because I won't let you go."

She sighed and would have melted against him if he weren't holding her the way he was. "I don't want you to let me go."

"Alaska winters are long and hard, and there are times you'll be stranded in a cabin with nothing but me to—"

"The world could end tomorrow, Blue," Everly interrupted, her voice firm. "Here's the only thing I want to know. If you knew that we would die tomorrow, would you want to be with me today?"

"God, yes."

He didn't think. He didn't hedge. He just threw it out there.

And knew two things at once. One, that it was the God's honest truth. And two, that he would do anything to make Everly smile at him like that.

As much and as often as possible.

"Me, too," she whispered. "Peas are negotiable."

And Blue stopped trying to shut off all the things coursing around in him. He picked her up, swinging her around until she wrapped her legs around his waist. Then he held her there while she threaded her arms around his neck and kissed him.

She kissed him like every fairy-tale ending he'd never believed in.

She kissed him until his heart hurt, but this time, because it was swelling. Expanding, whether he liked it or not—and he was pretty sure he liked it.

Or he liked her, anyway, which was the same thing.

She kissed him until they were both laughing, and Blue pulled back so he could look up at her, pretty and perfect and entirely his. Maybe she always had been. Maybe he'd just needed her to find his heart for him and bring it home.

"I love you," she whispered, right there against his mouth.

"I love you, too," he told her, and vowed, there and then, that he would spend the rest of his life showing her exactly how much.

On the first day that could reasonably be called spring, with the sun poking through and the temperature downright mild by Alaskan standards, Blue rolled over in bed and nudged Everly awake.

She woke slowly, the way she always did, especially when he'd already had her awake and beneath him once this morning already. Her green eyes were cloudy and her mouth a little sulky as she stirred, but she smiled when she focused on him.

"Congratulations, baby," Blue murmured. "You made it through an Alaskan winter. Not many people can say that."

"Does that make me an Alaskan?"

"Don't get carried away."

She laughed, and he let her lie there as he went and powered up the generator, then prepared her some coffee with the machine she'd brought when she moved in, because his woman needed her espresso. His cabin sat up the hill a ways, with silence all around and nothing but water and mountains out his windows. The view had always soothed him, and it still did. Snowcapped glory and the endless sea. It made his soul feel light.

But it was the woman in his bed who'd set him free.

She'd brought him back to life.

Everly had talked him into Christmas in Chicago with both their families. He'd caught up with his stepsisters and their lives. He and Ron had gone out for a beer. He couldn't say they were buddies or were likely to end up best friends, but it had been fine.

Good, even. There might be some scar tissue, but the wound was closed. Blue was sure of it.

"I'm glad you came," his mother had said the morning he'd said good-bye. Everly had been in the same room, chatting happily with Ron. He liked knowing she was there. He liked having her close. "I hope we'll see you again soon."

She'd been stiff. Awkward, as if she were waiting for him to hurt her again.

He'd done that, he knew. To his own mother.

"I love you, Mom," he said gruffly. He'd pulled her into his arms and hugged her, tight. "And I'm glad you're happy. I really am."

About thirty years late, but it was something.

More than something, he'd realized, when she started to shake. And had then cried all over him.

Everly had started crying, too, and soon Blue had

been trapped between two weeping females, both clinging to him.

He and Ron had stared at each other in a perfect moment of horrified male communion, and Blue knew that it would all be okay. That he could make it right, those years he'd been off being a bonehead.

All it took was the trying.

Everly had taught him that.

She shuffled out to the porch with her coffee when it was ready, the way she always did. She laughed when she had to pull on only a sweater. No winter layers today. No snow, no arctic winds.

She sat in her favorite chair, and he watched her for a minute while the Alaskan breeze played over her face. Green eyes, red hair, and the freckles he was obsessed with. That smile that lit up his life.

He had no idea how he'd gotten this lucky.

"You asked me what comes after this," he said.

"This what? This coffee?"

"Alaska Force."

She caught his serious tone, and set her coffee mug down on the wide arm of the chair. He waited until he had her full attention. Then he pulled the little box he'd been hiding for weeks from his pocket and went to kneel down in front of her.

And didn't comment on it when she held her breath.

"You, Everly," he told her, very solemnly. "You're what's next. You're my future. I want to watch you smile for the rest of my life. I want your laughter and I want your body and I want you next to me, no matter what. I want to be the man you see when you look at me. I want to make you happy." He cracked open the box while her hands crept up to cover her mouth. "Marry me, baby. Please. I'm nothing without you."

She was crying again, but her eyes were shining.

"You'll never have to find out what you're like without me," she whispered. "Never, ever."

"It's a yes or no question, little girl," he said.

And that got him that big, wide smile that still made him giddy. He understood, from the way his heart lurched at the sight, that it always would.

"Yes," she said. "*Of course*, yes. You jerk."

Blue slid the ring on her finger, and she let out a sound of pure joy, throwing her arms around him. She kissed him, then kissed all around his face, murmuring *I love you*s between each one.

"And I have one more thing for you," he told her, very seriously. "One very important thing."

"How could there be more?" she asked, sounding happy and emotional and all things good and Everly. "This is everything. Blue, you've given me everything."

He had a few ideas about how to express his feelings about that, to this woman who was going to be his wife, but he picked her up out of the chair instead. She flushed at the show of his strength the way she always did, and he loved it more than he could say when she got a little red. Still. Always.

He set her down carefully on the edge of the porch.

"Look over there," he told her. "By the shed."

She looked over and found it immediately. He knew when she clapped her hands over her mouth again.

"You didn't," she said through her hands.

"I did."

"What if I hadn't said yes?" she demanded, pulling

her hands away, the diamond he'd just slid onto her left ring finger glinting in the morning light.

"Then, obviously, I would have ritualistically destroyed it and made you watch," Blue said blandly.

Everly laughed. That deep, wide sound that burrowed into him and made him feel as vast and unconquerable as the Alaskan sky.

So alive he felt electric. That was what she did to him. *For* him.

"I love you so much it hurts, Blue. It actually *hurts*," she told him, and then she was scrambling down the steps and moving over the little patch of hillside he called his yard. It was fairly level here, and she took advantage of it. She jumped on the gift he'd propped up by the shed, still laughing.

He didn't tell her he loved her then, though it moved in him like the sea. That big. That relentless. He'd save it for later, when he planned to celebrate the fact that she'd agreed to marry him in a much more naked and carnal way.

All day, if he had his way.

Here, now, he helped himself to her coffee and sat out on the porch of his cabin in pretty Fool's Cove, glad to be alive at last.

Alive. And so in love, it hurt him, too.

And then he settled in to watch Everly Campbell, the love of his life, ride around and around in circles on a perfect replica of that pink bike from way back when, her pink and white streamers flapping in the breeze.

Keep reading for an excerpt from the next
book in the Alaska Force series

SNIPER'S PRIDE

Available in May 2019

After the second time her husband tried to kill her, Mariah McKenna decided she needed to get out of Atlanta.

The first time could have been an accident. She had gone to yet another strained charity dinner that night, where everyone smiled sweetly, blessed her heart, and made it perfectly, politely clear they wouldn't be taking her side in the divorce. And even though Mariah knew better than to touch shellfish, it was always possible that there could be cross-contamination. Especially in a hotel banquet situation with complicated hors d'oeuvres passed around on self-consciously gleaming silver trays by bored college students.

Mariah knew it was entirely possible that she'd tossed back what she'd thought was a clever little cheese puff pastry when it was really something involving shrimp. She'd been too busy pretending not to notice the speculative, not particularly friendly looks thrown her way to taste a thing.

It could easily have been an unfortunate accident. Or her own fault for not paying attention.

But she thought it was David.

He had gone out of his way to get particularly nasty with her only the day before.

"You can't divorce me," he'd snarled at her, getting much too close to her in the sunny parking lot of the Publix in her new neighborhood. That had been her fault, too, for not paying closer attention to her surroundings. She should have seen David's overly polished Escalade. She shouldn't have imagined for a single second that he'd allow her to go about without permission, having a normal life like a regular person. "*You* can't divorce *me*."

That was why, when her throat had started to close up, the first thing she'd thought about was the way his face had twisted like that, out there in a parking lot in the Atlanta spring sunshine. When David got mad, his accent—what Mariah's mother had always called *high Georgia*—changed. Then there was the red face, the bulging eyes, that vein on his forehead, and the way he bared his teeth. None of that was pleasant, surely.

But for some reason the fact he sounded less Georgia old money and more clipped when he was mad was what got to her the most. Because she'd worked so hard to get the redneck out of her own, decidedly lowbrow Georgia accent and she never, ever let it slip. Never.

Still, accidents happened. That was what the doctors told Mariah when she could breathe again. It was certainly what the hotel hastened to tell her, in the form of half their legal team crammed into her makeshift cubicle in the emergency room.

And despite the leftover hungover feeling that stuck with her every time she flashed back to that ugly parking lot confrontation, Mariah accepted the idea that it was an accident. She wasn't living in a Gothic novel. Her divorce was ugly, but what divorce wasn't? There was no need to make everything worse by imagining that David was *actually* trying to kill her.

But the second time she found herself in the hospital, she stopped kidding herself.

It was while she lay there in another hospital room cordoned off from the rest of the emergency room by a curtain—staring up at the fluorescent lights while she waited for her EpiPen to finish letting her breathe and to see whether she'd have a biphasic second reaction—that she finally understood.

There was no safe space. Not for Mariah.

David shouldn't have been able to get into her apartment, but he had. She was still trying to breathe, feeling like there was a hand wrapped tight around her throat, so she didn't bother telling herself any stories this time. Somehow, David had gotten in or hired someone to do it for him. She figured the latter was more likely, because David was not a man who did a thing when he could hire someone to do it for him. She felt something greasy and sick roll over inside her, then, adding to the panic. It felt a lot like shame.

Or worse, fear.

Because David or some faceless minion had been in her pretty little furnished apartment with its pastel walls and view over Piedmont Park. They had touched her

very few personal things. Riffled through her clothes.
Sat on the furniture she'd started thinking of as hers.
And at some point, done something to her food to make
sure she ended up right back in the emergency room with
a far worse reaction than before.

They'd defiled the one place that had ever been hers,
then she'd put their poison in her own body, and she hadn't
even known it.

Mariah wondered what it meant about her that she
found the violation of it almost harder to take than her
own near death. Again.

"You need to be very careful, Mrs. Lanier," the doctor
said, scowling at her as if she'd thought *to hell with this
potentially lethal allergy* and had treated herself to a big
old lobster dinner.

"I'm always careful," she replied when she could speak.
"And it's Ms. McKenna, not Mrs. Lanier. My name
change hasn't gone through yet."

"Two anaphylaxis episodes in one month isn't being
careful, ma'am."

And what could Mariah say? *My husband would
rather kill me than divorce me, actually. I think he snuck
into my new apartment and doctored my food so this
would happen.* Even if the impatient doctor hadn't already been scowling at her, she wouldn't have risked it.

David's family had a wing named after them in this
hospital. The last thing she wanted to do was find herself
remanded to the psych ward where he could kill her at
his leisure.

"I'll be more careful," she murmured.

But inside she thought there was no longer any choice.
If she wanted to live, she needed to run.

The only question was how to do it.

She had to assume she had no friends or allies in Atlanta. There was no one she'd met here who didn't have ties to David in some way. That meant none of them were safe. And she hadn't been back to her hometown in years, but it stood to reason that she might try to run back there—because people did that in a crisis, she was pretty sure—which meant she couldn't. Especially because she wanted nothing more than to slam through the old screen door into the farmhouse kitchen, let the dogs bark at her, and sit at the table with a slice of her great aunt's sweet potato pie until she felt like herself again.

Whoever *that* was.

Mariah blew out a shaky breath. She could always just . . . go on the run and plan to live that way, she supposed. But that seemed inefficient at best. She would have to take such care in covering her tracks, always knowing that one tiny slip could be the end of her. Every book she'd ever read or movie she'd ever seen about someone going on the run ended the same way, after all. They slipped up and were found or they were caught by whoever was after them or they couldn't handle the isolation and outed themselves.

Whatever the reason, the *life on the run* part never seemed to work all that well.

Panic kicked at her, and for a minute she couldn't tell if it was another episode. Mariah lay her hand against her throat and reminded herself that she was fine. That she was alive and could breathe. She told herself that a few times, then a few more, until her heart slowed down again.

She decided it was nervous energy, and she decided to

deal with it the only way she could. By *doing* something.
She pulled one of her bags from under the bed, settling
for the one she knew she could pick up and run with, if
she had to. And then Mariah took her time packing, letting her mind wander from the task at hand to all those
videos she'd watched online about how to pack a carry-
on bag for a monthlong trip. Or three months. Or an in-
definite amount of time. It had been one more way
she'd tried her best to fit in with the effortlessly languid
set of people with whom David socialized. Women who
seemed to be able to trot off to Europe for a month with
either the contents of their entire house or nothing more
than a handbag, a single black dress, and a few scarves.

David had mocked her, of course, though she'd thought
it was good-natured teasing at the time. She'd told herself that's what she thought it was, anyway.

Maybe you can watch a video on how to make a baby,
he had said once, smiling at her across the bedroom as
if he'd been whispering sweet nothings in her ear.

The cruelty of it took her breath away now, the same
as it had then. This time, however, she didn't have to hide
it. She blinked away the moisture in her eyes, then threw
the shirt she'd been folding to the side because her hand
was shaking.

Had she really tried to tell herself he hadn't meant
that? She knew better now. But she'd spent years excus-
ing everything and anything David did.

Because she'd been the one who was broken.

David had kept up his end of the bargain. He'd swept
Mariah away from that abandoned backwoods town and
he'd showered her with everything his life had to offer.
He'd paid to give her a makeover. To make her teeth

extra shiny. He'd found her a stylist and paid for a voice coach so she could transform herself into the sort of swan who belonged on his arm. Or at the very least didn't embarrass him.

All she'd ever been expected to do was give him a baby.

Looking back, it was easy to see how David's behavior had changed over time with every passing month she didn't get pregnant. Less Prince Charming, more . . . resentful. And increasingly vicious.

When she'd walked in on him and one of the maids, he hadn't even been apologetic.

Why should I bother to give you fidelity when you can't do the one thing you low-class, white-trash trailer-park girls are any good at?

She would hate herself forever, she thought as she packed the last of her little suitcase, for not leaving immediately that first time. For staying in that house and sleeping in that bed. For telling herself that it was a slip, that was all. That they could work through it.

As if she hadn't seen the hateful way David had looked at her.

When she had. Of course she had.

That charming man she'd fallen in love with had never existed. David could pull out the smiles and the manners when he liked. But it only lasted as long as he got his way.

And Mariah had turned thirty. Despite years of trying, they hadn't even had so much as a pregnancy scare. She'd found David with the first maid the following week.

He was never going to bother to pull out his charm for

her again and she'd spent more agonizing months than she cared to recall imagining she could fix something he didn't think was broken.

In the end, after the second time she'd caught him in their bed with another woman, Mariah had been faced with a choice. She could look the other way, the way she knew many wives in their circle did. She could figure out a way to keep what she liked about life as Mrs. David Lanier and ignore the rest.

But it was as if the part of her that had been sleeping for a decade woke up. That scrappy, stubborn McKenna part of her that she'd locked away when she'd left Two Oaks. McKennas had *rough and tumble* stamped into their stubborn, ornery bones. They fought hard, loved harder, and didn't take much notice of anyone else's opinions on how they went about it.

Roll over and play dead long enough, her grandmother used to say, *and pretty soon you won't be playing.*

Mariah had decided she'd played enough. And so she left.

And she would live through this, too, by God.

"I should watch a video on what Mama would do to a man who treated her like this," Mariah muttered to herself, aware as she spoke that *her* accent didn't slip no matter how angry she got.

But the idea of a video made her laugh a little because she already knew what her mother would do in this kind of situation. She'd gone ahead and done it to Mariah's father, back in the day, when she'd thrown his drunk, cheating butt out and had never let him back in.

That was when something clicked.

It wasn't the legend of the way her mother had tossed her naked father out of the house in the middle of the night at gunpoint, then all his belongings after him, though that was one of Mariah's most tender childhood memories. It had something to do with all those videos she'd watched so obsessively over the past years.

And then it came to her. Just the tiniest little memory of one of those late nights she'd sat up, pretending not to wonder where her husband was—or who he might be with—clicking through video after video on her phone, careful to leave all the lights out so she could pretend she was sleeping and David's spies could report back to him accordingly.

Somehow she found herself watching an unhinged conspiracy theorist ranting on about satanic signs he'd found in a children's program. Maybe she'd found a little comfort in the fact that there were people out there a whole lot crazier than a lonely Buckhead housewife whose husband hated her. Openly. She might have been the one staying put in a marriage gone bad, but at least she wasn't ranting out her every paranoid thought to a video camera.

But the man had said something interesting, there at the end of his garbled insistence that the end was nigh. He'd mentioned a group of superhero-like men off in the wilderness somewhere. Like the A-Team, Mariah had thought at the time. But not illegal. Or faked for television.

Mariah cracked open up her laptop and got to work. It took a while for her to find her way back to that odd video. And then another long while to try to figure out whether or not anything in that video was real.

But eventually she found her way to a stark, minimalist website that had nothing but a name. *Alaska Force*. And a choice between a telephone number and an e-mail address.

Mariah didn't overthink it. She typed out an e-mail, short and sweet.

> My husband is trying to kill me. He's already come close twice, and if he gets a third try, he'll succeed. I know he will.
>   Help me.